WRITE, MONKEY

Ged Groves

WRITE, MONKEY

One Monkey,
One laptop,
No Shakespeare:
Write, Monkey...

1

"Honey, the wolf's at the door with a bill."
"Sure it's not a duck with teeth?"
(Mel Cash, *Big Beast*, 1963)

I fell into consciousness on the steps of Leeds Town Hall with my head full of silt and the feeling that waking up wasn't going to clear it. My jaw was frozen into a gargoyle yawn like I was going to belch out some evil expectorant into the world. Coming round, I felt like Lazarus suddenly aware of a world he'd forgotten he'd left.

The early sunlight was rubbing out the last grey of the night over the jumbled rooftops where the chorus birds were ranting their obscene show songs. I was sitting in the shadow of a stone lion that leaned over the steps rising to the studded door of the Town Hall, its gritty eyes staring into the distance. It was one of two sentinels of bureaucracy, their sandstone hides shot-blasted by northern hail, grown over with algae, felt tip pen and the graffiti of snails.

A big old lion it was, with a big cold shadow. Around me, figures in dark coats were straightening their limbs and blowing the night froth from their lips. Sounds like creaking wood broke from their bodies as they slapped their sides to beat life into their hearts and drive out the louse battalions from their fetid recesses. Their faces were the bleached shades of driftwood, long faces sharpened by the wind, scored with the tally of excoriating journeys through a desperate city. Their clothes were parcels of drab patches, wide lapels and garish checks smeared with the scars of the street's lacerations, some lashed with string and antique belts, others held up with braided wire or twisted ties.

Their long coats were heavy as the coats on statues. Their unlaced army boots shifted and scratched as they got hard purchase on the earth. Some rose erect from the dark accumulation and marched away, others scuttled in hunched perambulations down the fuming mouths of alleys. One figure swayed past me and struck up Little Red Rooster on a tin harmonica as he was subsumed into the morning traffic. I sat for a moment till my brains were in working order and my eyes could mould their blurs into edges. Then I stood up. Ezra Monk was returned to the world.

Here I am, I thought, six foot four, huddled on the steps among the flotsam of Leeds. How am I here? Under my tongue, my teeth were carpet tiles and there was a pain in the sides of my head as if my hair had been stapled down with pins pressed through my temples by some maniac hatter. Little lights swam over my sight. In a thousand possible lifetimes, how am I here like this?

Last night the cold had been up and out and laying its death hand on anything it could find, like my face and feet and fingers and pretty much all of me. Through the dark, slobbery breaths and wheezing snorts mingled with the noise of the traffic and the sound of distant feet. Occasional music whined and pounded. I lay alone in the cold shadows as the dark fell, shifting restless and anxious and pulling the collar of my jacket further into my beard. I heard animals burrowing into coats and pockets and hoods as I lay half-awake. There were growls and rummagings and open-mouthed chewing noises. At about two o-clock in the morning the cold had me in a very delicate position. I tried stuffing the corners of my lapels into my ears to lag them against the hooting of the night club animals as they yahooed their way down the Headrow. Cans were footballed through arenas of laughter, styrofoam trays of yellow curry slipped and flopped, flaccid kebabs were unloosed down the walls of shops. Rats hobnailed it down the gutters with greedy eyes, their jaws dancing among the fallen food.

At four o-clock the cries of the lost around me started.

—Off me, demon woman. Off devil!

—Shuttit.

—She's here for me! Off devil, demon devil...

—Shuttit!

—She's at me. She's at it again. Oh, merciful Lord, peel her off me!

—SHUTTIT you feeble wizend!

—She's in me clothing... tug her out, man, tug her... she's at me.

—Will you SShuttit!

But there was no shutting it for the rancid-voiced man wrapped in sleeves of matted wool howling from the bag of his throat to his demon mistress poised above him in the darkness. And soon the whole lot of them began to give it out into the night, shrieks and howls of self-pity and hoarded existential anguish. A right racket. I stuffed the lapels deeper into my ears but I couldn't sleep and so began thinking over the events that had caused me to end up on the streets of the city with my ears suffering assaults of sound usually the province of heavy metal nightmares. And then, hailed by the siren call of the lost, the coppers arrived. In they stamped from the blue beyond, muscling through the coats and the darkness.

—Oi! You lot. Shift. Come on, move. They worked at the words to make them threats, moving outward in a cunning pincer movement. Coats stirred and jostled and one or two of the assembled began to rouse themselves from their torpor and arrange their bodies into a sitting position. Coughs staggered like drunks into the night air and the bodies had begun the long haul to an erect state when up sprang a gangling youth, eyes bouncing in his skull, nattering to himself and rooting about in his coat for something alive.

——You! shouts out one copper, a lad of about nineteen with a sandblasted face mooning over the top of his uniform. Down! Out! Move on, now. But the youth was upon him before his voice had faded, swathing him in hideous whispers with his arms flailing now and his head tossing up and down. The copper slipped on a gutful of spilt curry and the youth writhed him to the ground and pounded him with feet loosely bound in fat brown trainers.

To the tom-tom of these thuds, the others undid themselves from their gleeful transfixion and shambled into the night, a weird dance of desiccated shapes tumbling amongst the folds of darkness. Their laughter followed them clutching its baggy sides. Up sprang the copper, dark-faced and crumpled from the dust. His mate was at his side now, hand on staff. The youth was running, his knees leaping up and down as the yawning trainers slapped the pavement billowing gouts of stale foot-air. Round one of the lions he raced and was heading up the Town Hall steps when the coppers, agile and angry, executed a regulation pincer movement, grabbed him, tucked him under an arm in some mangling armlock and dragged him spluttering into oblivion. Out of the darkness returned the others.

Sometime soon after I almost slept, with the rats tugging at my sleeves.

I had a bedsit two days ago, a snug little box at the bottom of Richmond Avenue. Convenient for all the major routes and a few pubs. It was not much of a room, about ten feet square with a low bed covered in army blankets against the far wall, a Baby Belling propped on a slab of worktop, a sink with an instant hot water geyser and a view of a dusty elm tree whose leaves pressed against the window where the frayed curtains stiffened their pallid flowers. It wasn't home but it was somewhere to hang your washing. If I'd had any washing.

It kept the rain off and if you stuffed newspaper under the door, it kept some of the wind out as well. It was a foul little dwelling but I'd got used to it. What I hadn't got used to was paying the rent. But who can get used to that? Forking out your hard-won cash to some bloated capitalist just for the privilege of keeping the rats out of his precious property. I don't like to be viewed as a wallet on legs, particularly by a landlord. Particularly by Mr Wolffe. In fact, most of my time over the last few weeks had been spent thinking of ways to keep the Wolffe from the door. I'd tried feigning the usual sorts of poverty — late pay packet, lost pay packet, no pay packet — but he persisted with his demands. I tried appealing to his better nature but that was a real provoker. It wasn't that he didn't have a better nature, just that in his case better didn't quite earn the tag human. Last time I heard his rough grasp on the door I was sitting at the table – an interesting specimen, being a thin rectangle of Formica balanced on a frame of tubular alloy legs, about as stable under use as a rodeo saddle – penning some work of enormity in my Rhino spiral. A verse sprang to mind:

I opens the door
And the wolf's smile shows
So I closes the door
On the animal's nose.

Unfortunately, life doesn't rhyme so sweetly. By the time I had gathered the wit to spring to the door and attempt to wedge it shut with a shard of wood that used to be the leg of the spare chair, Wolffe had not only got his nose and his foot but also his shoulder on the room side of the frame and was moving into the picture so fast I saw the air quiver around him like heat haze. He flashed his yellowy fangs at me and seeing my discomfort pressed one of my grey-socked feet under the toe of one of his brogues. I saw greed flicker in the dry pupils of his eyes. I was closer than I wanted to be to someone smelling of mould and Brût. I tried to step back and he grinned at my wincing. Then he grinned again.

—Rent time, Monkey. And very overdue, it is.

—Morning, Mr Wolffe. What was it, now? Rent do you say?

—Dig it out, Fur Boy, dig it out.

—Dig it out?

—The rent, the rent, you slacker. I make it three weeks now, he continued, raising three fingers in turn and waving their lumps in front of my watering eyes. How much Brût can a man use without passing out?

—Three?

—*Three weeks*. And I make that, let me see, three times forty-two pounds sixty is, let me see...

—About ninety eight pounds something?

—About a hundred and twenty seven pounds eighty, shall we say.

—So much?

—Oh, yes.

—Oh, dear.

—So, dig it out, Monkey, dig it out.

But I couldn't dig it out. There was nothing to dig. I strained on my trapped foot. Excuses swam through my head like idiot fish through a vacant globe. He suddenly released my foot and I was sent bowling over to the chest of drawers under the window. It wasn't a long journey. I raked at a drawer whilst trying to massage life back into my flat foot. A hundred and twenty seven pounds and eighty pence. It was unreasonable, so much hard-caught cash for the use of this squalid retreat, even if I'd caught any hard cash at all, which I hadn't. Wolffe folded his arms round his chest and stared at me like a greedy boy. He was an avaricious lad all right, I could tell that just by looking at him staring me out with those mouldy eyes. I opened a drawer, which was all pretence because all it had in it was my spare pair of socks, the one I saved for best. I rummaged around with the socks, looking serious. Glancing across the room I noticed that the bottoms of his trousers were wet and his shoes were dark with damp. He'd been out in the long grass had Mr Wolffe, watching the ladies in the park, no doubt.

—Look, I said in what I hoped was a reasonable voice but which was probably only a whining sort of snivel, could we come to some agreement?

—Oh, yes, he replied, all serious, of course we could. Some sort of agreement involving you paying me the hundred and twenty seven.

—Ah.

—Ah, he mused, thinking suddenly in that slow wolfish way of his, then trying to look smart by talking what he thought was posh. Do I take it that your non-payment and current evasiveness indicate that you lack the necessary wherewithal to meet the required fiscal demand?

—What?

—You're broke, aren't you. I knew it. I was only saying to Mrs Wolffe the other day, I was saying, I've got some right ones in the houses at the moment, all talk and no cash and some of them not even the talk. Youth of today. You could bag 'em and sell 'em as biscuits for all the use they are. Idle. Layabouts. Something for nothings. Good for nothings. I knew it. I was just saying…you're broke, aren't you?

—No. I've just got a sort of…

—A sort of cash flow problem. Heard it before, Monkey, doesn't wash with me. Seen it all before.

—No, not a cash flow thing…a sort of cash loss thing. Hard life, you know.

—You what? Spent it on the booze have we? Been down the The Original Oak have we, supping poor Mr Wolffe's rent money. Or is it drugs? Been snorting up the street talc have we? Bad for your nose, that. And not paying the rent can be bad for the nose and all, if you catch my drift.

I caught it all right, along with a wheeze of instant coffee manoeuvring the room on his breath. I took my hand out of the sock drawer and twitched my nose with two fingers. Wolffe shifted his weight and leaned on the wall. He wormed his shoulder against the architrave and lowered his eyebrows. Then he smirked and looked as if he was enjoying the smirk. I had a go.

—I got mugged, didn't I.

—I don't know, he replies.

—I got mugged by two schoolboys – don't laugh, it's the truth!

—I believe you, Monkey, that's why I'm laughing.

—They had an iron bar. A big bar like made of iron and they were big kids, you know, not the little punky sorts you had when I was at school. They were big. And they were serious, wanted my money or they said they'd do me head in with the bar.

—School kids?

—Yeah, they had the uniforms as well. Said they'd split my head like a paper bag if I didn't give them all the money I had and quick.

—Quick? They said that?

—Yeah. Quick.

—Don't teach them nothing at school these days, do they.

—I don't know. Does it matter? They seemed to know enough about mugging innocent passers-by. An iron bar. Like a piece of scaffolding or something.

He looked at me and pulled himself away from the wall. He heaved a deep sigh and rubbed his hands together. I didn't like the way his eyes were looking at me, sort of serious and cunning and amused all at the same time.

—They don't make scaffolding out of iron.

—They don't? Ah, well, don't know nothing these kids. As you say. But they made off with my money. Well, your money really.

—They did, eh? You gave them the money?

—Course I did. I like my head the way it is.

—Then you'd better have some *more* money, then, hadn't you...?

I noticed it then, he wasn't looking at me, he was looking past me to the chair under the window. I froze. I suddenly knew what he was looking at and of all the things in the room I didn't want him seeing that. Prickly heat was crawling all over me like spiders. He took a step forward. I took a step to the side to try and cover the chair. He took another and more determined step. I looked at the biceps swollen under the sleeves of his suit and decided it was all over. He knew what he had seen. It was his daughter's purse. The black and gold one her mother had bought her. Oh, foolish and forgetful girl. Foolish, foolish Monkey. He lunged at the chair and me with a sudden brute ferocity and the wave of aftershave that lunged with him nearly put me out of things for good. But I dodged. Oh, I dodged with the fluency of a practised dodger and, ducking under the flail of his arm, I got to the door.

As he snatched up the purse and stared at it in shocked disbelief I tore down my jacket from the peg behind the door and swept the notebook from the table which gave a slithering jolt and threw itself onto the floor. That table, that table that I had so hated for the past weeks, saved me. As I twisted through the door Wolffe, with an unholy roar torn from the bucket of his soul, launched himself at me full length across the room. It wasn't a big room and it was a big launch. He hit the table top with the full force of his foot and it shot out from under that foot like a frisbee. Wolffe's legs snapped from under him and he hit the floor with a very nasty crack. I was gone.

2

"I wander through each jolly street
Near where the jellied eels are sold;
And mark in every butcher's, meat,
And in every baker's, rolls."
(Bill Bleak, '*poet*', 1963)

Two days ago I had a bedsit. Now I've the whole street for my habitation and unfortunately through that street prowls an angry man called Wolffe who'd like to redistribute my body parts to the four corners of his squalid little empire.

But, Ginny, you were worth it. Worth every creak in my bones, every bite of the cold. Every glance over my shoulder. I pictured vaguely the two of us wound up in the army blankets after our last togethering. All in all it had been worth it. Life's a bit of a puzzle, really. Each sweet picking brings its baggage, each moment of joy brings in its wake Joy's steaming parent, wanting to unzip you from the chaps to the chops with the stiletto of righteousness. But where would we be without it? I stood up, rubbing life into my cardboard-like body.

The first thing on my mind was food and water so I stumped off up the Headrow in search. I was light-headed with lack of sleep, stumbling through the rarefied ether of consciousness with manic tracelights swirling over the balls of my eyes and the visceral mantra of the street humming in my gut. The city boiled around me, a vast sandpit in which a hundred thousand souls scrabbled out their lives. The Headrow disappeared into a grainy eternity ahead of me where the traffic was already thickening and the dizzy air boiled with diesel fumes. The pavement was uneven and the colour of putty and here and there flagstones were cracked and weeds were elbowing their way towards the sun and litter curled in corners, shaking in the wind. I was walking over a thousand thousand lozenges of spat-up gum: grey badges of diffidence.

I passed crooked flypapers slapped onto windows of dead shops: *Cutters - the Big Place - Coming Soon; Harry Hierophant! Plastic Angels at the Town Hall —Tickets Still Available.* I stumbled into an adshel inviting me to '*The Doorway Foundation: If you're not there, you're not here...*' Whatever. I didn't hang about. Stains swelled in entrances; stenches stank.

Who were we in this city? Some shopping till they're dripping. Some drooping till they're dying. Some just crying. Faint souls muddling through a litter of dreams, poor players coughing our coughs in the shadows of railings, creatures breathing the dust of our own futures, crossing in the street without speaking, following the figures of strangers through crepuscular alleys. Each of us an atom in the body of a snake whose fumed brain's long since forgotten why it's slithering through the looping labyrinth of the streets. Ain't city life the thing? A place where you can ignore everyone without offending anyone.

Later, wiping the cold and the dirt of the night's sleep out of my eyes with a sleeve, I stumbled into an early morning pie shop and swapped a bit of the last of my change for a growler and a can of Tizer. I caught a glimpse of my face in the mirror behind the counter. My eyes were jet black staring back at me, my jet black hair and beard proclaimed prophet or madman. Or slept in the street. Outside I tucked into the pie with a grin. Things would be looking up if I had more than one pound twenty to my name, if my shoes weren't prevented from laughing at me by pieces of string. But let the great grief-guzzler of the universe feast on my despair. At least within the shoes were feet. And it was a good pie. The crust was just moist enough to slide around the gums without the effort of too much mastication, the tender meat a succulent blending of sweet boiled pork surrounded by a generous coating of just-set gelatine. Give me pies like this and I will conquer the world. I snaffled the last of the crust and finished off the Tizer. Above me, the sun was shining.

Like I used to have a bedsit, I used to have a job. I was a storeman at Leeds General, the great gothic Infirmarium. What I had to do was wheel this trolley up and down the wards and such places delivering stuff from the store. Stuff like toiletries, sterile wipes, bandages, general sorts of equipment. I had a brown coat and a trolley that was really good because it had rear wheel steering so you could really get round those corners fast.

I spent a long time whittling tiny ornaments with my penknife out of a bunch of kindling I found behind a filing cabinet under a stained shirt in a box marked 'wood'. Thought I might carve a chess set one day but I never seemed to get beyond the odd knight or two. And they mostly turned out looking like Bernard, my co-worker. Then I lost the job. It happened quite quickly. It went something like this: One day I went in to work and the store manager, Scoby, told me they'd just taken delivery of a wagon load of toilet rolls and if I wasn't doing anything as per usual, then I had to get down to the loading bay and get the things wheeled up to the stock room double quick. They used to call him Long Scoby because he had these long arms that were virtually simian and he used to drag them around the place like they belonged to someone else. Apparently he was mad for stamps but didn't have many because he was allergic to the glue on them. Spent his life looking for a gumless Penny Black. I suppose you could do worse. I mean look at old Ahab. At least a gumless Black wouldn't drag you writhing to the bottom of the briny locked in a sort of penetrative embrace. But these toilet rolls, there were hundreds of them.

Took me all morning. I was on my own because Bernard was

off on the sick after snorkelling too many snifters of scotch no doubt. Took me *all* morning and I mean that's a whole morning's work just humping these damn toilet rolls onto the trolley and wheeling them up to the stockroom. And the last ten yards was a slope of about forty five degrees so you had to get a run up at it and if you did that with a full trolley you just made it to the top before your lungs gave out and the whole thing threatened to bear you back down.

Don't talk to me about Sisyphus, this was the pits. I was wrung out by the time I'd finished. Sweat was sluicing off me and my lungs were like rags. So I hid my trolley behind a pile of boxed bandages and after a couple of minutes I'd managed to make a sort of hollow in the stack of toilet rolls and I crawled into this for a moment, just to get my breath back and let the little lights in front of my eyes drift off and dance somewhere else. It was cool inside the cave of toilet rolls. Crinkly and cool. I closed my eyes and let out my breath.

Then I woke up. I woke with a song on my lips that had dribbled over the collar of my brown coat. I staggered out into the light of the stock room rubbing my stiff knuckles into my eyes. And then, as I sat on the edge of the cart to get my bearings, it struck me. I went cold, not easy in a hot little room full of paper. The door had a Yale on the outside. It was shut. I was locked in. I looked at my watch – seven thirty. Locked in. Could happen to anyone. I banged on the door but I knew it was no good. Storemen were nine to five boys and the stock room was way down by the loading bay, way out of anyone else's ears. I looked at the cracked screen of my Nokia. It looked back at me with its blank grey eye: battery as flat as a constable's footsoles. I went back to the door.

I stopped banging eventually and sat down. Luckily I had some boiled sweets in my pocket, a sachet of tomato ketchup from the canteen and two rich tea biscuits. I wasn't thirsty, so that was all right. I mooched about for a bit. I counted boxes but that was boring. I tried a few wheelies on the cart but that got a bit scary. When I got hungry I tried to open the ketchup. It was one of those nasty little plastic sachets where it says 'tear here' in tiny writing and when you try to tear there it's like trying to pull the head off a tiny flat fish with a very tough head.

After struggling heroically with it for a while I decided to let it have it with the Swiss Army knife I carried habitually in my pocket for small DIY emergencies or getting the tops off beer bottles. There wasn't a custom tool for the business so I ran at it with the bottle opener. That was a bad choice of implement because the sachet burst with relish all over the brown coat. I got a bit of the squeezings onto one of the rich teas but most of it had splurted down my front. All Tarantinoed and nowhere to play. But the biscuit was nice.

To pass the time I carved Bernard's face onto the end of a mop handle. It looked more like a tea cake with holes than a person but I'd always found human beings difficult to carve. Them and chess pieces.

Next morning, my teeth on fire from eating two dozen penny boilers, half-mad with thirst, disorientation and the glee of anticipated freedom, I waited by the door. They all thought I'd sloped off home after emptying the truck, of course so it wasn't until half past nine, when Bernard, now returned and only vaguely inebriated, made his first trip to the store room, that a key clashed in the lock and the door opened.

It should have been funny, Bernard opening the door and me there covered in ketchup jumping up at him with a big sweet grin, but the shock was a lot for his heart and he spent the rest of the morning sitting on a trolley with his hands over his eyes before retiring to his allotment for a month. They blamed me. So did Bernard. He said it wouldn't have been so bad with just the ketchup or the grin but the combination brought back the day his dog had got run down in Meanwood.

They sacked me. There and then. They said it wasn't just the business with the stock room, the toilet rolls and Bernard but it was also the thing about me not turning up on time like a regular worker and the other thing about losing two trolleys — which I thought they'd forgotten about — and, of course, the time the members of my cockroach circus decided to go walkabout. It all added up, they said. They exacted the cost of cleaning the coat from my pitiful wages and bid me adieu. Never trust men in brown coats. That's what I say. That was about six weeks ago, I suppose. I survived for a couple of weeks on the savings I kept sellotaped to the bottom of a drawer but towards the end it was a choice between rent or curry or condoms. So I ate meagrely and loved strenuously. And then found myself on the streets.

I sat on a bench to soak up the sun and let the pie digest. After a while of digesting I pulled my spiral notebook out of my pocket and flicked through a number of scratchings and hatchings to a blank page.

I'd had four or five poems published in the small magazines. Northern Verse, FarSite and La Plume de ma Taunt had all carried samples of the stuff. Now I was working on a sequence of poems about living in Leeds. This would be my second volume. I'd already got together a bundle of stuff titled Monkey's Typewriter and sent it out to some publishers. Dawbert, Pangoon and Rustler and The MacHoolin Press were all significantly underimpressed and had sent back rejection slips to that effect. Dawbert had sent a note of uncommon terseness: *Not for us. Suggest you try a smaller publishing house.* So I'd wrapped it all up again and sent it to Phibre and Phibre. The big guys.

I found my biro and pushed the cap onto the end of the barrel and looked up at the sky beyond the grime and glass of the office buildings and the mock gothic angles of the gargoyled art gallery where cold stone people and piles of arranged machinery mingled with the darkening canvasses of long-dead masters. I wrote on the blank page:

Coming back to my city
I am a wounded man
Entering a hospital
Where I am the doctor,
Nurse and patient
And my diagnosis is being used
As a bookmark
By the sleeping night porter.

I decided to sit and observe things a bit. I folded the book shut and put the cap back on the pen. Two dogs, one grey, one brown, both tattered and collarless strutted past me. Their legs flicked out cockily in step, their devil's noses quivering restlessly for a trace of quarry. Pariah dogs, two of the million that roamed the streets, often in packs, often with the slaver of foam glinting on their black lips. Devil dogs, their fur bryllcreemed into points with streetslime, their muscles toiling under the hardened skin with the energy of primitive mechanics. The brown one turned and nodded at me as it went and then they were off, buried in the horde of legs that seethed over the pavement. I was affronted. It had seemed to know me.

Soon after, someone shuffled up behind me and sneezed voluminously. I jumped up thinking it was Mr Wolffe with his hands out for his money or my throat but it was a tramp in a green dressing gown rolling up a sleeve to get into the bin at my side.

—God, I said, you must be hungry.

—No, he said wetly, it'th me teeth – they've jutht gone in'th bin.

—Ah. Unfortunate man.

—Yes, thir. Thath about the thruth of it.

I slid away from his doubled-up body but when he was straight

22

again, as straight as a tortured man can get, I shuffled over some of my change to him and he curled it into a pocket.

—And wash those teeth before you...

—Of courth, thir, of courth... he said, jumbling away, stuffing the teeth back into his hairy gob as he went.

So it is.

Lines ran around my head. Taxis ran around the street. They elbowed their way over the curbs and pushed along the edge of the crowds. Some had peeling legends taped over their doors. Some had plastic signs pulsating in electrifying spasms. They were gritty and bad-tempered. They were everywhere. Red and black. Blue and red. Black and blue.

There's a story about this taxi guy one night who'd been driving around for hours, for days, doing fares and he'd got his sack stuffed with cash and his meter was melting with the heat of it spinning. And he was dog tired, so tired like his eyes were sealing up with the muscles round them gone like iron with cramp and he'd got one last fare and he takes him out to where he's going and it's a long way out of the city centre, way out in the old sticks of places and they come to this big dark house, a house like a spooky sort of hall with all weeds overgrowing it and he stops and says how much it is to the guy in the back. Only there's no reply.

He asks again and again but there's still no reply. So he gets all angry and the veins are aching in his head and the meter is throbbing like a wound and he shouts and rages but the guy in the back just says nothing. Just stares back at him through the dark like real cool with this pale face. So the taxi guy thinks right, you're not getting off with this, mate so he jumps up out of his seat and gets the back door open and he's swearing and raging like an actual demon. And he gets hold of the guy before he realises something's not right: the guy's dead in the back seat. He's been driving round a dead guy. He'd died in the cab. But the taxi guy's not happy and he's jumping up and down like a bloody whang shouting you're not dead, you're dodging the fare. I'll kill you. And he's trying to open up his pockets while the dead guy just sits there.

So he goes to get on his radio and tell control about the dead guy but he can't get through and when he goes back round to the back seat there's no one there. The cab's empty except for this bag on the floor. The dead guy's gone. And he starts to hear these rustling noises in the bushes. And he looks up and there's a light in one of the windows in the house like an exact square of flickering light. So he spins the cab round and laces it off to the city centre again and he goes right up to the cop shop and he tanks to a halt and starts blowing on his horn till some of the bacon boys come hopping out still eating their burgers.

They think this is a real hoot but the taxi guy's mad with it all and shouting at them to open the bag. They take a while to calm him down and get his head round a bit of reason so finally he says OK, OK, I'm all right. So they open up the bag and it's got nothing in it except a folding bicycle. In working order, oiled up and ready to pedal. It's a true story.

The hairdresser's opposite was all cool glass and shiny bottles. I thought of the red and white pole outside Kerrigan's, the barber of my youth who had cut hair and drunk whisky and cut and drunk and rattled on as he cut and swept and snipped and as we sat there in the stink of the cheap whisky with the black cloth shrouding our school uniforms, hoping to leave with our skin unsliced we'd listen to his babbling tirade of self-loathing and the tolling of feet upstairs up and down. And then sometimes there'd be a creaking and squeaking and strangely-mouthed noises and Kerrigan might break off in mid-snip and disappear and come back sweaty and agitated and grinning apologies. Junior Planxy reckoned he kept a wild animal up there and fed to it any kids he cut like a sort of zoo-time Sweeney Todd. I reckoned it was a mad wife pacing her cage.

When I'd told Ginny the taxi story she'd shaken her head and said that it wasn't a bike they found, it was an axe. This rusty axe. It's a true story, she said.

Later in the afternoon I basked on a bench outside the Corn Exchange, thinking of Ginny. And of Wolffie. He was probably even now raging through the suburbs with a bowie knife between his teeth and his head full of festering revenge. But oh, sweet Ginny, there was a girl. Beautiful, intelligent, funny. And a girl who hung on my every word, hung on my arm through the streets and hung on through the long nights under the dark blankets. She didn't mind that the mattress was like a caved-in animal's ribcage and shot through with broken springs. She didn't mind the traffic noise and the traffic dust and the solitary room. I'm sure she didn't.

I felt a sudden need to see her but I had no idea how I was going to make that happen. She'd always come round to the bedsit – often indignant at the profit her father made from the squalor – or we'd meet in the The Original Oak, which is where we met first, on a night of bitter frost in the final stretch before Christmas last year. There were a few of us in, drawing on pints and making the usual noises of people at drink.

The place was packed with whey-faced office lackeys who felt they'd broken the leash of bureaucracy at least for the season's span and nurses and young managers flushed with the power of merriment and street idlers and the sots and bucketeers who are driven out of the woodwork by the merry tunes of Christmas. Smoke looped and thickened over us, the carpet was groggy with spillage and voices were coagulating in a sort of Christmas hypnosis. I'd gone to the bar and was jiving back with an armful of pints to the strains of The Drogues when this girl in a white tee shirt sprang at me from the blur of bodies to my left, over by the window where a pride of loons were bickering with their beauties. I stopped sudden on the heel of my left foot but the beer leapt from the glasses and spreadeagled itself against her breasts. All time stood still. In that no-time I stood and stared at the magnificence in front of me: the transparent tee shirt, the whole woman of her staring through it. Expletives sprang up in what was left of my mind. I was wild with love, lust and quite possibly terminal obsession. Oh, could I have been that beer, that gush, that huge heroic spillage.

—You *bastard*! she shrieked before disappearing into the Ladies. And she shrieked loud, bringing down on me the twin delights of Maff and Ern, the Christmas bouncers, each visaged like a criminal Buddha but with tiny ears that rested on the tops of their collars. They threw me out and I stood in the street flushed with lust, embarrassment and twisted around in the neck region.

I next met her on Christmas Eve in the Oak and I took a pint over to her table for her. She looked at me for a moment and then twigged who I was and looked for a moment like she was going to douse me in the full pint then she sort of looked at me staring at her and a smile came to her. She had long black hair that framed her face in a luxuriant swath, a Celtic mouth, full and passionate as poetry or the pout of some sex-incensed succubus and eyes in whose unendurable black depths the light of love shone like two tiny monkeys dancing with delight.

And later, when I'd got her face tangled in my fur and my lips tangled in hers, I knew the whole thing was going to get wetter than beer and hotter than havoc.

But we had to be careful. I was gutted when I found out that my rapacious landlord was her father. At first I reckoned she must have been adopted. You just don't get throwbacks like Wolffe siring daughters like goddesses. But Ginny said that she really was his daughter and he wasn't as bad as he seemed. You just didn't cross him. Apparently, the last poor sap he'd caught tip-toeing up to his daughter's bedroom had spent time in a hospital toga in the fallen-down-stairs ward of the General.

Daddy liked Ginny as Virginia. So we never invited the Wolffes round for Bolognese and chips. And some mornings after those nights she had stayed over, a knock on the door would startle her into thinking daddy had come for the rent. A wardrobe to hide in would have been useful but there was only a chest of drawers and, lasciviously bendy as she was, Ginny didn't fold up that small.

With the state of things now between Wolffe and me, I couldn't risk going to the Oak at all. He would probably be patrolling the pubs with a pocketful of brass knuckles. I wandered aimlessly down Boar Lane and made my way to the station to sit on a bench for a while. I was cold despite the sun and a strange rancid smell clogged my nose. Must have been the city smell from the night so low on its streets. When you get down to ground level it must just come along and creep up your nose, creep into the core of your being. If they turned my lungs inside out they'd smell of tar and curry and petrol.

But you can't go on imagining stuff like that. I'd got things to do, if only I could remember what. I sat in the great cavern of the station and tried to forget about my hunger, which wasn't easy because I was hungry. And surrounded by placards exhorting me to eat Big Macs. At the ticket counter ribbons of travellers stared into distances. A guy came past with a dustpan on a stick and a thin-looking brush, swatting at the dropped cigarette packets and shiny overwraps with a practised nonchalance. Eyes nodded in his goblin face like he was just hanging on to consciousness as he wandered over medallions of chewing gum and the grain of diesel-coloured dust that skittered over the tiles of the floor.

There were people standing around up to no good. They seemed part of the same club, all wearing cream chinos and beige blazers. All had earnest expressions and shortened hair with partings like thin cranial scars. I began to wish that I'd stayed and reasoned it out with Mr Wolffe, or at least that I'd disappeared without leaving him writhing on the floor at the mercy of his tubular table, or at the very least that I hadn't called out as I hurtled through the door, 'Property is theft, Wolffie, baby!' Actually, the property-theft thing he could probably have lived with but the thought of me doing the dance of the two-backed monkey with his fairytale Beauty must have sent his old spleen into spasms.

Near the telephones a twentyish guy with yellow hair was poking notes out of a saxophone. He tapped out the rhythm with the tips of his greasy shoes and pointed at people with his chin. A litter of dodgy jazz pecked at the roof struts and fell, scrambling, into my ears. The Blues always made me queasy. Particularly live.

3

"Just get me the money, honey."
(Dane Pool, in *Stabman II*, 1965)

Just don't ask how I found myself at two o-clock in the afternoon behind the Hotel Metropole amongst the algae and other low life, keeping an eye on the back door and hoping that it was the door that led out of the kitchens. Still hungry, you see, but not yet desperate enough to dig in the bins. Someone once told me that hotels throw away masses of good food every day, stuff that people ordered and then didn't like the look of, or stuff they didn't order. Stuff they couldn't eat. Stuff that's gone a bit wrong in the pan. And all this is just dumped out at the back into the bins. So if you can cunningly intercept it before it reaches the bin then you're in for a feast. Providing you're not that fussy. And believe me, when you're hungry, fuss goes out of the window.

I mooched about for a bit, kicking at the loops of rusty iron and faded beer tins. As I kicked about I felt the hairs begin to prickle up on the back of my neck. I had the feeling that someone was watching me and I turned and looked around. There was the entrance to the back of the hotel, a wide gateway in the brick wall that had been painted mottled white. A gnarly yew frowned back at me. Thin privet tangled in the corners of the wall. Silence and stillness. I turned back to the tall walls of the hotel whose terracotta blushed at my predicament. But I still felt I was being watched. I held my breath and then twisted round really quickly and caught a sliver of shadow slide slickly back behind the wall. I shuddered. I strolled over to the gateway and peered round the corner. The road was empty apart from a yellow dog stalking a parked Polo. I shrugged and dismissed it from my mind, which, as it turned out was a big mistake, and went back to the business in hand.

There were two main bins, big blue things with grey sloping lids. One was full and the lid was propped on the bulging rubbish. The other had the lid shut tight. A sick smell hung in the air like someone had thrown up candyfloss and pepper. There were some magazines and things lying around and I had a shifty in case there was anything of interest or possible stimulation. I nosed my toe amongst the curling pages.

And that's when I found it. I turned it over with a toe. It looked clean, like it hadn't been there long so I picked it up. It was heavy, a small black leather-bound book, something like one of those Filofax things crappy busy people wave around so they look important. It had a clasp with a lock on it.

I looked over my shoulder; the shadow of the tree faltered in the breeze. I shivered again and turned back to the book. I weighed it in my hand and smoothed it with my palm. I had a look the catch and but it was locked. Some of the flashing had come off the metal where a key had been scraped. I started to reach into my pocket for my penknife but then paused. Maybe it was valuable. Greed overcame curiosity. At least temporarily. I told myself I could split it open later if I wanted and, thinking of its potential, I was clutching it in a sort of muted hysteria when the door opened and a man wearing a blue apron appeared in the frame. I pushed the book into the poacher's pocket in my jacket. The man was holding a plastic tray. From the distance I was – about five yards – it looked to contain all manner of tasty delicacies and the old saliva glands began to remember what they were about. Involuntarily, I took a step forward which brought me out of the cover of the bins. The man had taken a step down the stairs and when he saw me he stopped. He twitched his nose which caused his little moustache to writhe revoltingly. His hands re-gripped the plastic tray and we faced each other like dogs over a bone.

—Oi! Get out of here. Go on. Get.

—What?

—You heard. Get out. This yard's private property. You're trespassing.

—All right.

—What'yer doing here, anyway?

I slipped on my real loser face, the one with the pathetic eyes. I looked at him. I could see he was going to give me the whole tray of goodies.

—Nothing, really, I just . . . And I stared at the tray and made like real hungry eyes. Something moved in his face.

—Hey, it's Monkey, isn't it?

—It's what?

—It's you, isn't it - Monkey.

—It might be . . . And then I realised. My eyes, fixed on the tray, had failed to notice that the man holding the tray was familiar to me. It was Dirk or Dale or Derbert or something, some friend of Angus Roneo who held forth on the virtues of drink and delight at The Skyrack and knew everyone. He used to sell digital watches and rolling tobacco out of his many pockets. Good for buying you a drink. What was his name? Digby? It was on the tip of my tongue.

—Not seen you for a while. He came down the low stone stairs and propped the tray on the end of the iron railing. He'd grown a moustache since I saw him last. It looked awful, like a piece of orange carpet coming down his nose.

—No. How're you doing...? I fumbled for the name.

—John....Where've *you* been hiding? he said.

—John...?

—John Smith, remember? Smug. Everybody calls me Smug.

—Sorry to hear that, I said, searching for an appropriate reply.

—No, no they don't think I'm smug, they just call me Smug.

31

With a big S. Get it? He grinned at me, stretching out the ginger moustache like a row of orange socks on a washing line.

—Smug? But why do they call you that if you're not? Not that I'm saying you are…

—Don't make such an issue of it, Monkey. It's like when you call W H Smith's, Smug's. Like that. Anyway, you must owe me about a dozen pints you must, he said, thankfully changing the subject. Where've you been? Remember Angus? Angus Roneo? Nearly died, you know. He was choking on this chicken bone in The Skyrack from his chicken meal with chips and this big guy, this rugby type, starts to do the Hi…Hi…*Hein*rich manoeuvre on him and almost breaks him in half. You know how skinny Roneo is. Anyway, he's selling insurance now with some company door to door. Nearly had two of him. Two halves, anyway. He laughed.

—I've been around…I said, thinking that at least the Roneo person had had a chicken. I couldn't help my eyes from gazing adoringly at the array of broken crusts and oddments of ham, trifle and a whole Danish pastry with only one bite missing. They knew how to spoil their beggars, all right.

—You hungry or something, Monkey?

—It's sort of a long story but hunger's a part of it, yes.

— Tell you what, he says, just let me dump this crud and then if you're quiet about it you can come in the hallway there and I'll chuck some food at you.

I waited for him in the hallway which smelt mainly of roast lamb fat. There was a loud hiss and a crash from the kitchen and someone swore venomously. Then more hisses like fat snakes were at each other in anger and then a woomph of flame trailed by sizzles and swishes. I imagined that upstairs in the dining room the well-off were licking their lips and stroking their cutlery in anticipation of their trough. The white paint of the hallway was beaded with yellow fat, globules of which stippled the wallpaper and clung to the tips of the carpet pile. After a while Smug clumped up the outside stairs and flung down the plastic tray in the hall. He sighed wearily and ran a hand through his hair.

—Wait there a minute, can you?

—I'll wait.

—I'm not supposed to do this, you know. More than me job's worth, you know. So just keep yourself real quiet. And if anyone asks what you're doing, tell them…tell them…

—I could tell them I was just waiting for you for a pint.

—Don't be daft. They'd have me for that, they would. For a pint!

—I could just run for it.

—You could do that. Or you could just pretend to be foreign or something. That's it, pretend to be…

—I don't think so, John.

—Oh. Oh, I see. Well…

As he hesitated and I thought why doesn't the witless git just go and get the grub, a large man in a white, stained coat and battered white hat came out of the kitchen and stared at him for a second and then said something all muddled up on his lips in a slur of fricatives. I strained to hear. Then he spoke louder. So loud it flat-handed my ears.

—You've not been finished with that sinkful yet, have you?

—Nearly, replied John, keenly, looking past him into the kitchen from where another clatter jolted my stinging ears.

—And you, the white-hatted one continued at a bellow, swatting at the bowl of his stomach with his floury hands, and staring at me like I was a bad bit of meat. You, why's you not at your sink you skiving bugger? His eyes bulged at me, gauzed with an alcoholic's explosion of traumatised veins and blackened with the hatred that years of cooking for his betters had exposed in his soul.

—What? was about as much as I could manage, but John, seizing the situation a little more swiftly than me, grabbed my arm and wrestled me through the door into the steam of the kitchen, pushed me in front of a large sink swimming with filthy washing-up water and festooned with grease-clagged plates and mottled pans, threw a blue apron at me and told me to put it on and get scouring. Around me the kitchen clashed and bellowed like some spitting, poisonous inferno. I shuddered. I scoured. And later I ate.

4

"A little room, a little bed,
A little place to rest my head."
(Trad. Rhyme, Yorkshire)

And so I had a job, washing up in the pit of the Metropole. John's previous co-washer and slop man never re-appeared. Lateness had apparently been his practice and now he'd perfected it. I also had somewhere to stay. There was a little room behind the kitchen store room where the night duty pastry chef used to sleep when the hotel was owned by Sir George Baltimore who had the habit of craving pastry dainties at all hours of the night, especially when he was entertaining the ladies. According to John.

So there was a little creaky bed and a little chair and a little cupboard to put your things in if you had any things. There was a bijou shower with the usual little hotel smellies in there for your enjoyment, even a shower cap if you had the hair for it, and a white square of hotel towel, fraying at the edge, embossed with *Metropole Hotel Brighton*.

It was a veritable home from home. Smug wondered if anyone would mind, in that sort of jobsworth way of his, tweaking at his orange moustache like he was going to sneeze or something. I said I didn't care, really. I didn't mind if they minded, I just minded if they threw me out again onto the street. They wouldn't do that, John, would they? You wouldn't let them do that? He looked at me as he might look at a dog and looked out of the window like it was raining. He shook his head. No-one'll know, he assured me, unconvincingly.

Later that night, as I sat on the little bed and creaked up and down sipping a small whisky that I'd poured from a little bottle I'd found in the little cupboard, I thought of Ginny. I'd send her a postcard just as soon as I got up tomorrow. I tried to do some more work on the poem but I was too tired and distracted. I managed:

The nutter in the gutter was giving me a stare
As I stumbled through his kingdom completely unaware
Of the ...

Of what? Who knows? What about bit of ballad? After a while that went better...

A crow and a beggar sat in the street
Both as black as the crow's black feet;
And one to the other begins to say
Where shall we two dine today?
Shall we dine on the city wind?
Shall we dine from a wheelie bin?

Come I will show you a sweeter sight,
A hotel yard and a right light bite;
The fat yet on the plates is hot,
The meat half-chewed but the pastry not.
And no one knows that it lies there
But a chef and a lad with ginger hair.

The chef is to the bottle gone,
His belly sways as he wanders home;
The slop boy sits with a pint in the pub
So we can feast on th'abandoned grub.
Our meal is sure, our eating's free
So come and dine tonight with me.

You can sit where the bins are sat,
I will chew on the cold pork fat;
You shall gorge on the pasta quills,
I will suck up the coffee spills.
The crusts that from the tables fell
Will serve to make our bellies swell.

As I fell asleep I remembered the book and made a shuffling sort of gesture towards my jacket which was sprawled over the floor. It was out of reach and I gave up, falling into the sort of sleep you sleep when you're in a strange place. Nervous dreams hiccupped round my head and I woke twitching to the noise from the kitchen. Someone was yelling and bellows shoulder-charged the walls. Pans clashed and danced like the devil's kitchen was getting ready for some feast of the damned. A falsetto rendition of some forgettable Beatles' number went through my ears like a kebab skewer.

I'd had no idea hotels were that noisy at ground level. I looked at my watch. It said five thirty. I went back to sleep and was woken by what sounded like a pan bouncing off the wall. I looked at my watch again. It said five thirty and a bit.

Life went all right for a while. The money was poor but so was I. There was a public bar with an entrance at the side of the hotel. It was frequented by loners in weird grey macs and couples wanting to sit in silence somewhere other than their front rooms. I took to drinking there. After a couple of days I sent the postcard to Ginny and arranged to meet her in the bar two days hence at ten in the evening. That should do, I thought.

I took a shower in the en-suite that night at about nine thirty. It was so bijou I had to keep my elbows tucked in and avoid any sudden movements. I pampered myself with the available mini-products, working up a big furry lather and sluicing with the Metropole's best water till my beard dripped like a gargoyle's chin. Pipes hammered and whined and I was afraid that someone would come and shovel me naked into the street. No one did. I emerged cleaner, wrapped a small white towel round my waist and set to washing my clothes in the sink with a tiny bar of soap that smelt of plastic flowers. Not my choice but there you go. I was hanging the shirt, boxers, socks and jeans over the warm radiator when I heard a sort of scuffling out in the corridor.

I patted the clothes happily and saw a minute fragment of steam rise into the air. The sound of a heel clicked on the lino outside my room. I listened. Silence. So I listened again. Could I hear breath or was it the hissing of my shirt on the radiator? I tightened the tiny towel round my waist and opened the door. I peered out into the corridor. It was cold and empty. I closed the door and padded across the room towards the bed. Clothes would be dry tomorrow, I was thinking, and I would be raring to go, you old sweet-smelling monkey. There was a tap on the door. I checked my towel and went to the door and opened it a crack, expecting to see some hotel person or security guy with a shaven head sort of attitude.

—Good evening, Mr Monk, purred the sexiest voice I'd heard all day.

—What? I looked out a bit more sharply and standing in front of the door was the most stunning woman I'd seen. All year. Ever. Her big eyes gazed at me. She was adding me up like an abacus. She was wearing a long red coat and carrying a bottle of champagne. I goggled at her stupidly for a second or two before my brain caught up with my goggling and started to ask itself questions. Like would she spend the night and should I have combed my body before opening the door?

—Well, Mr Monk, she said, like she was licking up cream. How well you look, how svelte, how slim… how so *you*.

—How…how…who… do I…have we met?

38

—Met? Don't be silly, Mr Monk, of course we've met. How could you forget?

As she spoke these last words she moved towards me and I backed into the room. She followed, stroking the champagne bottle like a whore in a hurry. How could I forget? Silly question. I could never forget her as long as there was breath in the old Monkey body. So why didn't I remember her? And did I care? She advanced on me licking her lips. She put down the champagne bottle on the bedside table and slowly unbuttoned the front of her coat, never taking her eyes off me. I was transfixed.

—I've been watching you, she said.

—Of course you have, I joked in return, watching her very closely.

—You and I need to have a little talk. Would you like that, Mr Monk? I need your co-operation.

—Sit down, please...can I get you a...look, stop calling me that. Everyone calls me M...monkey. Co-operation sounds fine. Co-operation sounds good.

—Are you going to pour the champagne, or do I have to do everything around here myself?

As she said these last words she undid the last button and her coat swayed open a teasing little. Was I fantasising or was she stark stunning naked under there? She sat demurely on the edge of the bed. It squeaked helplessly. I picked up my whisky glass and a chipped yellow cup and with a strangely shaky hand tried to wipe them on the towel round my waist. It was a delicate operation and I feared for a moment that my movements might betray my feelings. In seconds I had two greasy vessels on the bedside table and with huge self-control had managed to pop only the champagne. I passed her the glass.

The whole night lay before us. I watched, in my mind's eye, her crimson lips pouting good morning and felt, in my mind's loins, the squeeze of her fingers conjuring a night's lascivious acrobatics. I raised the cup and looked at her again as she sat on the bed, her legs crossed, revealing a splendid arc of tanned thigh, an exquisite knee and a glossy shin descending to a red high heel.

In my mind I was already crawling over to her, pushing aside the coat and whispering sweet nothings to her hot little breasts; I was already pushing her back onto the bed, sloughing off my towel and taking her till she fainted in a frenzy of ecstasy. The coat, encouraged by a little twist of her shoulders, fell open a bit more and I glimpsed...

There was a noise again outside the door and by the time I'd looked up there was a knocking on the wood. Ah. So near and yet so.... I put down the cup and went over and opened the door. It was John Smith. He was wearing a black shirt and jeans and an inane smile. Am I missing some sort of fashion statement here, I was thinking, amongst other things.

—Yes? I barked.

—Oh, didn't know you had company, he answered, looking past me into the room. He looked back to me, nodded, raised his eyebrows and mouthed, 'wow'.

—Yes, I have company. What was it you wanted?

—I was going... he was interrupted by the woman who pushed past us into the corridor, turned and said —Well, Mr Monkey, we shall be meeting again so don't worry that head of yours. And we shall - her eyes smouldered like the fires in the bedroom of Passion Castle - get to know each other...really well.

John Smith's jaw was bouncing up and down like a zombie on a bungee rope. My lips were set so tightly in what I hoped was an encouraging smile of agreement that the tension was shooting over my skull like I was wearing a hat called pain. She sashayed down the corridor and round the corner leaving the air so suffused with the scent of seduction the spiders were tumbling out of their webs and a passing roach rested its head on the wall, gasping. When she'd gone John Smith turned to me with his eyebrows dancing.

—Who was *that*? he said.

—I have absolutely no idea.

—Like you expect me to believe that.

—It's true. I have no idea who she is or what she wanted.

—I'd have thought, Monkey, that last bit was pretty obvious. Pretty obvious indeed.

—What?

—Now what have you two been up to?

—Nothing. I mean it.

—The same sort of nothing John Duane used to get up to with the wives of his mates. And the mothers of the wives of his mates. And even with the daughters of the wives of his mates so long as they were past puberty. That sort of...

—You mean Don Juan?

—Who?

—Don Juan, the famous lover.

—Don't know what you're talking about sometimes, Monkey. I was talking about my mate John Duane, the Headingley Humper himself. Or should I say ex-mate. Since that business with Sheryl.

—Who?

—Sheryl, the girl I was going to marry. Come on Monkey, do you live with your head in a bag? Come on. Sheryl.

—Ah, yes, I said, having no idea what he was talking about but, finding the scalp tension had reduced to a level at which brain function was returning, thinking at that moment of stoving his stupid head in with the champagne bottle. We went into the room. I felt suddenly vulnerable standing there in my towel with Smug so I picked my combat jacket off the floor and put it on.

—What're you doing here? Why now? John, John, look what you've done.

—Ah. See your point. Do you think she went because of me?

—Are you extracting the Michelangelo? Of course she went because of you.

—Ah. And that's not good.

—That is very much not good. What're doing here?

—Well don't take the hump, Monkey...

—That's exactly what I'm not taking – now.

—Don't get your nuts in a knot. I came to see whether you could see fit to buy us a pint in the bar. Many are owed, Monkey. Many are owed.

—A pint in the bar? Are you mad? Why didn't you say something today at work?

—I didn't think, did I? All that washing up seems to take things out of your mind.

—Well it might take things out of your mind, mate, I said.

—Do I take it from your tone the answer's no?

—I don't know.

—Well don't put yourself out or anything, he said, pretending to be offended.

—She was so close... so close.

—Come on, now, Monkey, it's not healthy for a man, dwelling on the likes of her. She's a bit posh for you. A bit sophisticated, if you know what I mean.

—What? She's not. She's...

—About thirty, for pity's sake.

—That's not old. And anyway, I don't care. Thirty's mature. I like mature women.

—I bet you do.

—Do I see the green tinge of envy clouding your eye, SMUG?

—What? Me? You must be joking. But I'm sure I've seen her before.

—You have? Where? You've got to tell me where. Recently? Do you think if I followed I could catch up with her? If I ran? If I ran fast?

—You're not ever going to catch up with the likes of her,

Monkey. I reckon you've lost your chance there.

—Well thanks a bloody lot, mate. You might have helped me look on the bright side.

—Nah, optimism's for wimps.

—But she brought champagne!

—Now you're talking, Monkey. Let's have a sup, then.

—You can have a sup if you tell me where you've seen her.

—Course I'll tell you. When I remember.

—When you... you've got to remember. How can you forget someone like her?

—I haven't forgotten her. Just forgotten where I saw her. And when, actually. But a drink might loosen your memory. Come on, Monkey, give us a drink. To be honest I've not a coin to me name tonight. I've blown the lot of me wages on the gee gees. Honest, he added, noticing the reaction of my eyebrows.

—It's the way you pick them.

—It's the way they run. I mean, take that nag today, I reckon it was double jointed. I reckon it was a mutant of some sort, the way it moved – like its legs were bending in all the wrong places. Shouldn't let a horse like that on the turf, they shouldn't. Nag it was. And it had looked so bloody all superior.

—Is that why you backed it, then?

—Well how was I to know what it was like till I saw it waltzing down the turf like the biggest bloody spotty dog in the world? It had a good name.

—What was it called? Nay, Mrs Smith?

—What are you talking about?

—Nemesis? Oh, forget it, John.

—That's right, take the piss, Monkey, why don't you?

—What was it called?

—Do I get a drink, then?

—Oh, for god's sake, all right. Just one, mind, I need something to help me sleep tonight after what I've just missed.

—Cheers, you're a mate. Just one. I'll get the bottle.

He was over to the glass and that was emptied and then he was at the bottle, refilling the cup with the aplomb of an alcoholic wine waiter serving himself freebies. I picked up the cup and drank it off. It was like fizzy wine with a sort of petrol aftertaste.

—Quicksilver Service, said Smug in a slurred sort of voice, that's what it was called. What a nag.

5

"How do you get to act so stupid?"
"I practise stupid."
(Bill Benny, Ross Dalton, in *Fool's Gold*, 1989)

I woke up in a shop doorway. The light was dim and it was freezing cold. I was lying under a heap of newspapers. I seemed to be wearing some sort of plastic skirt. I felt blue with the cold and my nostrils were stuffed with the stench of the newspapers, of rancid fish and chips and dog hair and those murderous smells you get under the insoles of dead trainers. The arms of my combat jacket were twisted round my neck so it fell over my back like a cape. My head was on a carousel singing déjà vu.

My head hurt. In fact everything from the neck upwards was in serious pain, including my hair. I ran my tongue round my mouth and my teeth winced. I sat up with difficulty and peered into the dimness. I couldn't work out what time it was or what I was doing wherever I was. What was the light like when I last had my eyes open? I couldn't think. Thought seemed to be a novel idea to my brain.

A car went past. Then another. A bus blurted into view, stopped a little way down the street and let some blurry shapes get off. Something was heroically trying to make sense of all this in my head but was failing fast.

Something hit me limply on the arm. Startled, I turned round and saw Smug sprawled in the doorway beside me, rising from a sea of garbage. His mad, blinking eyes tried to focus on me. His other arm was lodged inside a witch's hat and he was wearing a small red plastic bag on top of his head. Down the street the blurry ones turned away from us and hurried in the opposite direction. A wise move. I felt mad as a band of hatters.

—Oh god, Smug slurred, this isn't happening.

—I agree, I slurred back. This isn't really happening.

—Can't be.

—Where am I?

—You? Smug answered, you're parked in a doorway dressed in a bin liner. I'm dreaming, aren't I?

—I'm dreaming, too.

—You're not dreaming. You're in the black bag all right. You're in the street.

—Rubbish, I said. I'm the one who's dreaming.

—Don't talk to me any more.

—I don't think I can. I don't think I'll ever talk again.

—Good.

—But if you're dreaming why can't I be dreaming this too?

—Don't be absurd, man. We can't both be dreaming we're here, can we? he said.

—My head hurts. I've had enough.

—Shut up. If you'd shut up I could waken up.

He closed his eyes and fell backwards. I stood up unsteadily and pressed my forehead against a cold drainpipe. Then it came back to me. The champagne. Kick like a bloody mule on acid. I looked down at myself. I was wearing a black bin liner. It came down to mid thigh and my legs poked out of the bottom. I wanted to lie down. But not there. I kicked Smug and he coughed himself awake and staggered up. He breathed a bit. He shook his head.

—I was having this bloody nightmare, he began. Then he stopped, staring at me, and his jaw dropped and swung there like a swing. Oh God, he said.

It was not much fun getting back to the hotel, sneaking in the back door and shuffling round the corridors until we got to the little room. I was suffering from flashbacks, ghostly memories of running down the Headrow at some unearthly hour of the morning drunk as a bitch. Life could be embarrassing, it really could. Smug could hardly walk, such was the weight of his pain. I crackled along like a giant bag of crisps, my bare feet tender from the tarmac.

The room was sort of as I had begun to remember it apart from the spilt cup and the knocked-over glass. All the things in the room looked in their usual places relative to each other but something was odd, as if everything had been moved an inch to the left. The bottle was empty and there were the carcasses of a dozen bottles of Whittaker's Export as well. I tried to work out what had inspired me to spend my money on such beer. Smug sat miserably on the bed and held his head.

—You've been done over, mate he said, looking round the room with a practised eye. By a woman.

—I wish I had.

—No, I mean the room, you've been...

—I know what you mean. But why?

—Dodgy things, rooms.

I looked at my watch on the bedside table. It said six fifteen. I picked up the champagne bottle and sniffed at it.

—Not your regular booze, eh? I said.

—A dodgy bottle, Monkey, a dodgy bottle.

An hour later we had recovered enough to start work at the giant sinks like two dough boys and well aware of it. My clothes were still damp from the radiator and filigree whispers of steam rose from under my apron. Chef was blathering and bellowing and the kitchen was full of the clashing of pans and big spoons. Knives sliced and scored at great speed; oil bubbled and graters rendered. Huge orange flames leaped and bounced.

Chef boiled and ranted. I was amazed that the man could cook anything other than seriously destroyed meat but every day queues of delicate dishes wound their way out of his kitchen and made their way to the slavering masses above. We made it through to the lunch break. Half an hour of quiet. We went outside and Smug lit up a Regal. He offered the packet to me but I declined with a grave shake of the head.

—Got to start someday, Monkey.

—Not today.

—Way I see it is: a smoker's mate's always going to turn out a smoker, isn't he. He snorked up a lungful of smoke and blew it down his nose. No wonder his moustache was orange. There was probably enough nicotine in there to keep him going for days. The smoker's equivalent of a camel's hump. I was going to take issue with the term 'mate' or the spuriousness of his argument but settled for silence. He put the packet back in his pocket.

—All you have to do is ask. Fancy another drop of that Whittakers while we're kicking about? There's still a bottle somewhere.

—Look, Smug, if I want to pickle myself I could sleep in vinegar. OK.

—I've just thought of something. His brow wrinkled up like a pig's.

—What?

—Don't be like that. You can be really aggressive, y'know.

—OK. What have you thought of?

—I've seen that girl before. The one last night? The one you fancy.

—But where? Smug, the cruciality of it is *where*.

He walked around a bit breathing out smoke and flexing his crinkled brow. Then he scratched his head and came back over to me and said in a quiet voice:

—Here.

I looked round.

—No, not here, here at the hotel. It's all coming back to me now.

—I'm glad something is.

—I've seen her up at the front. She was in the lobby. I was talking to Eugene at the desk and she comes in and asks for a room, but it's got to be a particular room, see, it's got to be room…eh…room 613, that's it. It was room 613. She had to have that room.

—Why that room?

—Well I don't know, do I?

—And did she get the room?

—I can't remember, can I?

—Oh, that's great. You can't remember.

—No need to be so bitter, Monkey. I'm doing of me best, you know.

—Yeah, yeah… sorry Smug. It's that woman. I've got to have that woman.

—What about Ginny?

—Ah, sweet Ginny.

—Yeah, sweet Ginny. What about her then, Monkey?

—Bit of a problem there with her father, you see. Old Wolffe and I don't get on at the moment.

—Something you've done.

—Some things I've not done, really. I've not paid him any rent for weeks and I've not managed to keep my hands off his daughter. The said sweet Virginia. Now only sweet.

—I see. So you've been a bad Monkey, then.

—Oh, shut it, Smug. Look, Ginny and me, we were OK.

—Past tense, now, is it?

—What? I don't know. Look, we're OK. But she's not to know, is she?

Well, how was she to know? I had to have her. Her glorious smooth body, those thighs. Ah, when she parted the folds of her coat I could have slid inside and made the world a better place. Those eyes. Her eyes were scary now I came to think about it. Seductive and yet scary. Which of course made her all the more enticing. Smug would help me to get her, I felt sure of that. Big chemicals moving through my brain made it obvious that the world was a meaningless ash heap of unendurable bitterness without her. Something else concerned me too but I couldn't put my finger on it. I was confused by the sudden changes to the normal flow of things. I'd put the book under my pillow, thinking that it might provide me some bedtime amusement and distract me from staring at the mould on the walls and constructing fleshy fantasies about the woman. As if. I was going to have another go at the lock, subtly, of course, with the penknife or a paperclip if I could find one. I was feeling lucky.

We went back to work. I knew that I was going to see her again. Then the postcard came back to mind. I'd always been brought up to say what I meant and mean what I said and as I'd said I would meet her, so I would. Besides, Ginny wasn't bad. She didn't have that smouldering suck you in and set you alight seductiveness of the woman but we'd been good for each other. And she'd never know. And what you don't know, you don't know's hurting you. Or something like that.

The old Monkey brain pondered its fate. Monkey was smiling. Twenty three years ago I was born and because conception seems to be very much in vogue at the moment, let's begin nine months or so before my bewildered entry into this world. Imagine. There's a bedroom with mauve floral wallpaper, a bed and a turned-off lamp. Two figures are engaged in a complicated ritual involving pyjamas. There is a disagreement over buttons. A second or two pass.

—God, slow down, Zeke, my mother is exclaiming, not without some petulance. And then, Did you remember to turn the TV off at the mains? And moments later, my father, Ezekiel Monk, clipper of bus tickets on the great journey of life, lies back and closes his eyes. He has a vision at that instant of a small child swinging through the trees towards him like Tarzan, calling Daddy! Daddy! and goes to sleep grinning like an ape in the prescient knowledge that the Monk dynasty is not yet at the end of the road. Later, my mother dreams of waking up and sensing there's a third person in the room with them. I had become.

Odd figures haunted my childhood. I remember Aunt Greenwich, timelessly fragrant, busty and blonde, with lips like glacé cherries, who entertained me with her stories of hitching around in Tibet and of her encounter with the Yeti who would have carried her off to his icy lair in the heights had not she had the presence of mind to sing *Jerusalem* in so high a key that the great beast became frozen in a sort of simian ecstasy, giving her the opportunity to slip away to the lower slopes of the Gongkala Shan and safety in the arms of long-armed ski instructor Karl Clench.

Clench later fell in with a bad crowd and made it into the movies, where he achieved small-time fame playing gorilla villains in endless Tarzan remakes. It's a small world. And she once showed me a lock of hair she claimed was from the Sasquatch, that elusive hairy Canadian. She got around, Aunt Greenwich. She told me they'd met quite by chance when she was out riding one November afternoon and that she'd taken him back to her log cabin for a week of energetic love until the poor beast had escaped with most of its fur intact leaving behind a little clipping and a lifetime of hot memories.

I remember asking why she had rejected the Yeti and yet embraced the hairy man. In answer she asked who could take a creature nicknamed Abominable seriously. When I asked about Bigfoot she just coughed politely and cut another slice of cake. That a woman had been so enamoured of the hairy man gave me much comfort in later years when I grew a pelt a beast would have been proud of.

Other characters wandered through my life. There was Dave Spiggot, the Backgammon champion of Harehills who led his life by the roll of the dice, throwing a pair of antique ivories at moments of decision and acting out his life according to their fall.

This eventually won him the pools, fame, fortune and the reasoning power of a baboon.

He was killed at the age of forty six, when, having broken down on the A64 he ended up chasing a rogue die into the fast lane where he was sliced down by Sam 'Snake Eyes' Samuels who had been distracted by the furry dice dangling in his windscreen momentarily showing a double six. It was one of life's little tragic ironies I never forgot and I resolved from that day on to make decisions in my life through the subjugation of the will to the power of reason. It seemed a good idea at the time, though by then I had not yet been ambushed by the distracting energies that come free with the hormonal purchase of adolescence.

I also remember Mr Planxy who used to go drinking with my father down at the Fox at the weekends. He had a big face and red hair that stuck straight up off his scalp. His eyes were a limp shade of washed-out blue and his fingers were jointed like broken biros and stained yellow from years of pincering tight little roll-ups. He would offer me smokes when he came round to the house, stooping down to my level and looking at me seriously. I always refused politely, being only about eight at the time, and then he would tuck one behind my ear and tell me to have it later. I've always taken it that my loathing of cigarettes came from the fact that Mr Planxy, though jovial and probably a worthy swilling partner for my father, smelt like kippers and sweat and would often blow his nose into a brown handkerchief.

His son was called Junior Planxy and he was dragged round to our house sometimes to play with me at Monopoly or Cleudo or poker. He was a tiny green-tinged child with mean eyes who used to catch spiders and put them in large matchboxes to take home for his mother who apparently was studying the effects of magnetism on them. I asked him what she actually did with them and he said he wasn't sure but it seemed to involve his father screaming a lot. But what did he know? He'd been wrong about

Kerrigan the hairdresser and the wild animal. It had been his wife upstairs, though she wasn't either mad or imprisoned. She was a keen amateur hiker and used to practice in the bedroom going up and down in her boots. And walking brought on her passion…and then Kerrigan had to go to her.

Eventually it was all too much for the tonsorial tippler and he keeled over clipping a fringe one spring morning. She'd sucked the sap clean out of him and what they buried was but the husk of a hairdresser. Junior grew into a tiny yellowish man and got a job with Toy World. Something to do with putting things into boxes. I stopped buying toys, which could have had something to do with Junior but was probably because I was seventeen years old by then.

When my father retired from the bus lane and my mother took to drawing a cartoon strip for the local rag about a talking tortoise poet called Shelly (this was her call to fame and she would talk to anyone for hours about the death of the novel and how Steve Bell and Fred Bassett were the now voice of the people and that the future of literature lay in what she termed Stripture) I left home to seek my fortune in the big world of the city. When I next came home, some two weeks later, a little disoriented from the whirl of city life and stiff as a board from sleeping on my mate Dave Pillet's floor in a strangely rigid sleeping bag, I found that my room had been re-decorated in brothel kitch and rented out to Vaughan and Eileen, a couple from Brighton.

My parents were kind and helpful but I still had to sleep on the sofa and ask permission from Vaughan and Eileen in their yellow and black diamond jumpers to retrieve my moneybox from under the loose floorboard in the corner next to where my wardrobe used to be. It was the one thing of mine left but I found it was empty apart from a lead soldier, a marble and a grubby pack of marked cards.

I seemed to remember it being loaded with Victorian coinage, a silver lion-head ring and a cut-out of Raquel Welch in a leather bikini. One Million Years BC. That's my kind of era. The original 1940 B feature was billed as 'Man and his Mate' but the one to see is still the Hammer hit and that's not because the animated dinos are so superior to those sleazy magnified lizards but because it has Racquel Welch in the Carole Landis role. What a girl. I was disappointed it wasn't still there. Maybe I'd swapped it for something at some time or just worn it out. Memory can be a frail friend at times.

And it was because of my frail friend that I forgot about Ginny the following night. That was until she arrived as arranged at the hotel bar, wearing big black shades and dressed in a khaki jacket and jeans. And that really put me on the stage without a script.

You see, Smug had been asking around by then, talking to Eugene who was that week beginning to work in the bar as well as doing his usual shifts on reception. Eugene reckoned that the woman had moved that day into room 68 as it had been vacated by the Australian couple with the large mini bar bill and the loud jokes. *And* he reckoned that he knew why she had wanted that particular room. It had been in the papers, he said. Didn't I read the papers, or what?

—What?

—The papers. Well, the Argus to be exact. It was in there last week according to Eugene. This guy, see, he's gone missing.

—Lots of people go missing, Smug.

—I know that, but no, look…this guy was some kind of writer. Like he'd written books. He was like a real writer, so to speak. And he went missing.

—Look, Smug this may or may not be of any interest but what has it to do with the woman? Remember the woman?

—You can be right sarky sometimes, y'know that?

—So what was his name, then, this important writer?

—Well he might not have actually been an important writer.

Eugene just said he was a writer.

—So what was his name?

—It was … something or other. Sounds like that bloke off the tele. Y'know.

—He was that big you'd never heard of him.

—I've heard of the bloke off the tele. He's good, he is, you know the one I mean? Does that show with the goldfish.

—Now you're taking the piss, Smug.

—No, serious.

—Sounds serious.

—Oh, come on, Monkey. This could be important if you want to find the woman. Not that I think you should. Leave well alone, I would.

—Just tell me what all this has to do with her.

—Well…

He put down his coffee cup and stared moodily into the distance. We were in Bloaters, a risky little diner tucked under the blackened storeys of the historic mill shops down on the south edge of the cut. The area was under redevelopment and the chances were that Bloaters would soon be reincarnated as some pastry café themed in faux historical navigation chic. Which would be a shame as the place was one of the last bastions of unpretentiousness left in a city where to be considered classy you had to wear a micro fibre suit and nibble wedges of tofu eased down with sips of decaffeinated tea brewed in art outré pots and served by a whey-faced clone in the manner of a machine.

Bloaters was a real eating house where you could get bacon butties and baked beans and eggs fried in lard and chips made from potatoes and instant coffee. A place where they left the ketchup bottle on the table and were proud of it. But now there was Smug teasing me along with his innuendo and half-suggestions so I was just about ready to brain him with the salt cellar.

—Smug, if you don't hurry up with this lot of rubbish I swear

I'm going to kill you with this, I said, brandishing the crusted cruet and sprinkling him with clots of damp salt.

—That's just seriously unpleasant, even for you, Monkey. You've right put me off my cherry gateau.

—Is that what it is? I thought it was a door wedge with acne.

—You git, how do you expect me to eat after that?

—Gone off your food, have you, Smug. Pass it over then.

—You are kidding, right? I paid for this. You stick to your coffee. I'll manage to get this down. But look, this writer guy, the one who disappeared, remember?

—I'm trying – seems so long ago he was mentioned.

—Shut up. Listen. He stayed at the Metropole. Eugene said. There was like his picture in the paper and Eugene, well he remembered his face.

—Eugene? Are we talking here about Eugene with the zero-sighted eyes? Like, Eugene, that was a ten pound note I gave you' – 'Oh, was it I couldn't be seeing it so good in this light'?

—Nothing wrong with his eyesight, Monkey. I've seen him seeing things. And he said that you couldn't mistake this guy. Said he had an unforgettable face.

—He had a... oh, come on, that sounds like the cue for a song. He had a what?

—He was quite definite about it. Said he had boring eyes.

—So what? Couldn't be more boring than this.

—No, Monkey. Try to follow, will you? *Boring*. As in boring holes.

—Ah. And that's what Eugene remembered?

—Well, yes. But he did keep the article. WRITER GOES MISSING, that was the headline.

—If he was a writer why wasn't his name in the headline?

—Well, it might have been only I can't remember it, can I. Or he might have not been any good. Like a little guy. But listen, he were in room ...

—Let me guess. He was in room 68.

—Absolutely, Monkey. Absolutely.

—Well, how about that? So what's the connection?

—The connection, Monkey, is that the woman is obviously looking for the writer man. That makes sense, doesn't it? That's why she wanted to have the room he'd been in…

—Like he might still be there, sort of hiding behind the pot plant?

—Fool. Like she were looking for clues.

—You've got it all worked out, haven't you? The most seductive creature in the known universe spends her leisure hours trawling through dumb hotels in search of missing hacks. Come on, Smug.

—Then why has she appeared right now. And why does she want that room?

—Co-incidence. And she probably wants that particular room because her great aunt Enid once stayed there or because she remembers lying on that particular bed in the arms of some supple lover. Or because 68's her lucky number.

—Monkey, you don't half have a weird mind. Nobody has a lucky number 68.

—Why not? My lucky number's 69 - that's close. Anyway, it's no weirder than your theory.

—So why was she in your room? She was looking for answers. She must think you know something about this missing bloke. She must think that you hold the answer to the whole riddle. You might not know you do. But you do. Like in the film. That whatsitsname?

—I sort of hoped she was there because she fancied me.

—Monkey. Be serious.

—Thanks for that little note of encouragement, Smug.

—But listen… that's the champagne, isn't it. She were going to get you drunk and then do terrible things to you…like…

—And then you clumped in and spoilt it all.

—Don't sound so bitter. I might have saved you from a fate

worse than death.

—Or, Smug, you could have saved me from the attentions of the most fabulous creature this end of the Milky Way. I mean, did you see her, did you really see her? I bet there's not a creature in the known universe — humanoid or whatever — who's anywhere near her. Even the unknown universe.

—You wouldn't know that, though, would you.

—What?

—You wouldn't know if there was a better bint in the unknown universe because it's unknown, isn't it? he said, smirking.

—Whatever. She's the one.

—Better than Sheryl?

—Who?

—My bird Sheryl. Who was my bird.

—Absolutely.

—OK. Better than Raquel?

—Raquel Welch?

—Her.

—Yes, Smug. Better than. And she's 3D. And she wanted me. I could see that in her eyes.

—Are you sure it was her eyes you were looking at?

—Smug, I was looking at the whole woman.

Later, in the sweating steam of the kitchen, with chef bawling and the massed ranks of the filthy plates and cutlery and pans and lids swaying around us, Smug had elaborated his theory about the woman and the writer. He reckoned that the disappeared writer, the writer bloke, had left something, maybe a manuscript or a book or something in the room or at least in the hotel but it was hidden or something and the writer was probably dead or at least would never be seen again, disappeared for good he was, Smug reckoned. And the woman was after the whatever it was that was missing and that's why she was in my room, because she reckoned I knew something about it all. Or something. There were a lot of somethings in the theory. But why should I know anything? I protested. You might not, he said, but she must think that you do. But why must she think that? I reasoned. She just did. Women were like that. They called it female ignition.

So there I was in the bar with a pint of Bass mulling all this over when in walked sweet Ginny. She looked a knockout in those shades. She saw me straight away and came over to the table and I asked her if she wanted a drink, all cool-like, which was not bad considering I'd completely forgotten about her and was at the time indulging in a little Mature Woman fantasy. She sat down and I went to the bar to get her a cider, dry, with ice and no pickled onion. As Eugene was pouring it shakily into the glass I turned to the room and Ginny smiled at me and shrugged up her shoulders in conspiratorial glee. I raised my eyebrows and smiled seductively back, looking forward to a little romantic screwing tonight.

As Eugene rattled the bottle into the big brown bin on wheels, the door to the bar swung open behind me. Something passed a chill hand over my spine and I found myself gripping the change in my hand with a ferocity usually associated with riding the big dipper. I knew it had to be Wolffe. I couldn't turn round, my spine had stiffened into a stick and the muscles of my shoulders were curling up into the foetal position all by themselves. Eugene's bland face swam into my field of vision and smiled at me like a white carp gawping out of a pool.

—You having another, are you now, Mr M? he asked. I couldn't speak. I just nodded with an vigour I hoped he would correctly interpret as meaning not only yes but also make it a double pint and a couple of whiskies because they could be the last things the poor old Monkey drinks on this earth.

He nodded along with me for a moment and, as we were locked in a bizarre session of synchronised nodding, I felt someone stop very close behind me and a whisper of warm breath slide over my neck. Sweet breath. The breath in me stopped. As I turned to my left and Eugene waddled over to me slopping the edges of the pint onto the lino, she slid up to the bar beside me and slipped her hand down the brass rail towards me.

—Well, hello there, Mr Monk. We meet again.

Quaking with lust, I turned towards her and offered what must have looked like a horrified grin. How could this be happening? To me. Now. I had to say something to her. I had to. Why did the words stick in my throat? Her delicate hand was still creeping over the rail towards me. Why did I hesitate? Her fingernails had found the hairs on my forearm. It was at this moment of contact that I saw the scene from Ginny's perspective: hunched Monkey over the edge of the bar, Eugene hovering in front of him with his balloon face gaping and some woman poised on his left teasing poor Monkey to a state of sexual hysteria with her hand sliding even now like a serpent over his arm under the front of his shirt and over the quivering fur of his chest.

I saw it all with her eyes and I felt it all in her breast and when her jaw clenched like a nut cracker and murder lanced through her mind I felt that too. At least sort of felt it, being at the time distracted beyond reason by the hand at me.

My eyes ran all over Eugene's face and scampered over the bar top pleading for help. Of all the bars in all the towns, why was I in this one? The woman's exploring hand paused over my right nipple and began a teasing journey downwards. I pulled free, reluctantly, and, moving away from the bar staggered off in the direction of the door mumbling, 'Goin' to the…back soon.' I must have been wrong about Ginny, she didn't look at all concerned. She made drinking motions with her hand and raised both of her eyebrows simultaneously. I loped through the door and made off down the corridor without looking back. I turned into the toilet and collapsed against the peeling wallpaper resting my head on something cold and only moving when I realised it was the Durex machine. Ah, I thought, but what prophylactic could have prevented this little situation? I used the urinal as slowly as physically possible. Which was not actually a good idea, as my stippled shoes showed.

I made my way back to the bar in the vain hope that one of the two of them might have disappeared. The door leading into the bar was open and I advanced on it with my head close to the wall to get the advantage of being able to see through into the bar for a fraction of a second before those waiting in anticipation of my return could see me. As I got close my cheek brushed against the imitation Victorian wallpaper. I lingered by that wall for a moment before I trusted my snout to protrude round the corner and my eyes to scan the bar for the two women who had me stretched on the rack of desire.

For a moment I couldn't see anything and then I saw Ginny sitting with her drink wearing an expression of cold withdrawal and tucking a wisp of her silky hair behind her ear as it fell and fell again over her cheek. Leave it alone, woman, I thought. It was endearing but it was also bloody infuriating. She to my left. The bar to my right. I peered over to see the other woman. From this safe distance my eyes played over the brass rail of the bar. There was Eugene slopping beer into a glass for a figure hunched over the bar towels. It wasn't her.

My eyes swivelled and gaped. Then I stared hard at Ginny, trying to get her to look at me so I could beckon her out of the bar, bundle her off home with a sweet promise and a shilling for the bus and then get back to the delights that the woman was so keen to thrust upon me.

Suddenly she looked up at me with a start and I beckoned furiously. She hesitated and then rose to her feet and pouted at me. She bent and took another sip of her cider. She began to walk towards me. I was just settling the breath of relief in me when I was seized from behind by the arm and a voice said, 'There you are. Now come with me, we have so much to talk about.' And before I could gather what was left of my wits about me the woman had me in a sort of lover's armlock and was propelling me through the door into the bar.

So there I was, dangling like a monkey in the grasp of a surprisingly powerful woman like some sort of plaything with Ginny advancing on me wearing an increasingly hostile expression. Her face toyed with configurations of puzzlement, amusement and wrath in turn and with an intensity I thought must break the skin of her cheeks. The air seemed to close around me like glass and the carpet had developed an attraction for my feet.

What was I going to do?

There were about thirty feet between us and Ginny was craning her neck and straining as if to see more clearly the sight before her. I wanted to say something but the words were just not there. For the first time in my life there were just no words at all in my head. I didn't choose to not say anything to the woman who was bundling me along, there was nothing I could say without any words. A big pain grew up from my arm and began to cover the sheets of muscle surrounding the palpitations of my heart. And then I realised that I was speaking.

Words were torrenting out of my mouth like there was no tomorrow for words. God knows what I was babbling but it made no difference to the wrestling woman. And then all time stood still. A door had opened at the back of the room – it was the door through to the kitchens – and a figure had come into the bar and collided with an ear-piercing shriek into one of the tables, sending a geyser of cheap beer and wine into the air from the flying glasses.

The couple sitting at the table leapt, despite their elderly years, like gazelles. There was a panic of arms and lunging legs and red-veined eyeballs. There was a flash of orange moustache and another shriek.

I broke free of the woman's grip and shot forward, seizing Ginny by the arm and leading her swiftly over to her table where I almost pushed her into the chair and thrust her half of cider into her hand, cried in an uncharacteristically high-pitched voice, 'Got to get me pint!' and lurched to the bar.

I don't know what was going on with the logic circuits in the old monkey brain, my imperative was simply to keep the two of them separate. I succeeded. For about eight seconds. I don't know how she did it but the woman was at the bar when I reached it. The air was still full of outraged cries and elderly voices threatening violent retribution and I could hear Smug mumbling apologies and righting the furniture he had wronged.

—Listen, I said to the woman, listen, can I see you later. I mean now is just not a good time. I'll get rid of her only I don't want a scene. Hardly know her really, see what I mean?

What was I saying? Words frothed at my lips. I slavered words. Just keep them apart, I was thinking. One at a time, one at a time. Not this both together that will end with none at all.

—Mr Monk, I've just got to get you alone. You don't know how important this is to me.

—Yes, yes, alone. Good. Good. But... and I was about to say something else about the problematical situation when she moved up close very fast and I sat down abruptly on one of the bar stools. Her beautiful oval face looked down on me from above.

—We have just got to talk...privately, Mr Monk. I think you have something that I very much want.

—I think you might be right there, I replied. I think you might...you and I might...

At this point we were interrupted by Smug shouting, 'Well, I'm *sorry*. You should have seen me coming...I'm big enough, aren't I?' and Ginny who appeared with the suddenness of a harpy over the shoulder of the beautiful one. Her eyes had the horrified look of someone confronting something both repulsive and vulnerable, like a cheating man. Oh, shit.

—Who is this? She was saying, pointing with the glass in her hand. Slops of cider spilled over the edges and fell onto the carpet by her feet.

—This is…I began and then realised that I had no way out. This is…

—Yes?

—I think, said the woman, turning to Ginny and turning on her those pitch dark eyes in which the pupils disappeared like black holes. I think that you'd better go home, dear, Mr Monk and I have some grown up business to attend to.

—Mr…began Ginny with a look of frightening amusement, Mr *what*? Now you listen to me, you…you slutty slapper, Monkey and I are an item so clear out of here before I prise your eyes out and serve them as bar snacks.

—Listen dearie, said the woman, placing her hands on her hips, if I were you I'd go home right now while I could still flutter my eyelashes.

—What? shouted Ginny. Her eyelashes tensed. Eugene's brain began a slow dialogue with itself as he fiddled with the lopsided tie that ended somewhere about his right nipple. He looked as if he were going to say something, his mouth opened, his tongue prepared. He looked at me and shut up before he got started. People stopped talking where they sat. I heard the big second hand of the bar clock clunk out a dull second and pause…

A dust ball wafted across the lino of the bar. I felt like letting them slash away at each other till the victor rose from the dust to claim me. I looked from one to the other and for a moment was convinced that Ginny was going to throw the first punch. The glass trembled in her hand. The floor was getting wetter. The woman turned to me and I could see that she was not pleased. Then I thought, seeing the expression in her eyes and the ghastly slash of red where her mouth should be, that she was going to be the one to start the lashing. It was all getting brutal. Time to take a back seat for a while, I thought. But how?

There was an explosion of ice cold liquid in my trousers. Ginny stood there, the empty cider glass in her hand like a dagger.

—Lap that up, love, she drawled to the woman and then she turned to me and said, My, my, what a pair, eh? Monkey meets Vampira. And she turned briskly on a heel and strode out of the bar. My eyes, following her caught sight of Smug at the other end of the room biting the rim of his glass to stop the laughter shuddering over his face. I realised with a twinge that I was holding the woman's hand. She had my fingers in quite a grip. I looked down. Her fingernails were square and shiny.

—Now, Mr Monk, she murmured, I have you all to myself.

My trousers squelched.

6

"Love is but a springe of delight,
Who struggles more, more feels its bite."
(John Selby, *The Oldest Game*, 1726)

I had wanted to go back to my little room but it was the inflection she put on 'squalid' that gave me the idea more might be achieved if I followed her to wherever her penthouse was. As I'd left the bar I bumped into Smug who was trying to get across the room without being interrupted by the furniture and said thanks for the attempt to save me from the situation. He looked at me in irritation, the pint poised in his paw.

—What are you saying, Monkey? I just tripped, all right. Why won't people just leave it alone? It's bad enough with the crusties complaining to the bloomin' suits about me without you trying to implicate me in your bloody love life. OK?

The fresh air caught me and the two of us walked to her car, a black job shaped like a bullet. Some sort of Ford, I think. Bloody pretentious, I thought. She drove like a maniac, darting through the streets with her left hand whipping away at the gears and her eyes hard with glee. I was doing my best to dry out.

Her flat was somewhere in Shadwell, about four miles from the hotel, and by the time we got there I was wondering why she wasn't speaking to me. I knew why I'd stopped speaking, I was high as a kite on adrenaline. Where did you learn to drive, I'd asked her, Alton Towers? She looked at me. Then she didn't say anything. Must be that confrontation with Ginny, I reasoned. They'd both gone off in a huff.

—Whisky? she asked soothingly as we stepped into the dark

room. I went across the carpet and stood by the window. The long red coat slid from her shoulders. She caught it before it reached the floor and draped it over the armchair. I remembered the champagne. Had to keep sober for this.

—Just a small one, please.

—Neat?

—It is, isn't it, very compact, I agreed, looking round the flat.

—The whisky, she said.

—Ah, the whisky; please.

She turned on the candle lamps and lit up the place with glowing spikes. There was a chaise longue in scarlet with a couple of silky pink cushions propped on it and there was a black dining table and chairs and there was a small gilt candle-cluster on the table. There was also a Dracula teapot with a fixed white grin and glazed blood drips. It was all a bit gothic for my taste. She brought the glass over from the tray on the sideboard and went back to pour herself a gin. She looked anxious with anticipation. I sidled up to her, feeling I had to make the most of this now there was no one to burst in on us. She moved to one side and walked over to the window.

—Look out there, Mr Monk. Isn't it magnificent?

—Eh, yes, I answered, joining her and staring out into the darkening evening.

—The night sky. There's something about the night sky that is so...magnificent.

—Yeah, magnificent.

—But enough of that.

—OK... then...

—I'll get to the point straight away, Mr Monk.

—OK.

—You have something that I want.

—Oh, good.

—Something that I need.

—Oh yes!

—Give it to me, Mr Monk!

—Now?

—Now!

I scrambled some more whisky down my throat and spluttered. It seemed to have got very dark outside and very hot inside. Out of the corner of my eye I saw two glazed lovers framed by the window caught in impromptu in a silhouette of passion. She held out a hand. I took it in mine. With a whimper of disgust she snatched her hand away and stared at me with a look of incredulous horror. At that moment I realised that everything was not all right. She knocked back a mouthful of gin and laughed a little brittle laugh.

—Oh, I'm sorry, Mr Monk, she whispered in a false voice, I thought you had something for me. She finished the gin and put down the glass. Have another drink. Have two. I'm sure we can...would you like to get out of those wet things?

—Good idea. Where?

—Did I show you the bedroom? She asked with remarkable suddenness.

—Did you... no, no, you didn't do that.

—Have another drink and I'll show you.

—OK. But just a small one. I was still remembering the champagne.

—I'm sure that will be most apt.

—What?

She poured another drink for me and passed it over at arm's length. This was most strange, I thought. I stood there with a glass of whisky in each hand in a strange flat with a strange woman. I'd lost Ginny and was beginning to think that maybe that wasn't a good idea. And the woman was behaving so oddly. One minute she was pushing the champagne, the next she was all for fighting to the death with Ginny for ownership of my body and then she was pulling faces like I'd suddenly developed the look of a maggot. It was just strange. And now she was talking about the bedroom and yet keeping her hands the safe distance of a barge pole away.

What did she want? And maybe more to the point, what did I want? Why was I here? Stupid question. I was going to spend the night with the woman. We were going to screw till sunrise like slaves to the great goddess Sex.

She moved away from me and sat on the edge of the chaise longue. She put down her drink on a low table whose glass top seemed supported by braided serpents of solder. Very modern. She looked ill at ease and smoulderingly seductive at the same time, which is no mean feat. There was something she wanted and I was getting the idea that it wasn't me.

—Do you think, Mr Monk...? she asked, sipping at her gin. I waited for her to finish.

—Do you think, Mr Monk? she repeated sharply.

—Sorry? Do I think what?

—Do you think at all? She flashed me a black look.

—Yes, I think. I'm quite good at it really. I do a lot of it, had a lot of practice, you know, lot of practice. Been doing it for a long time, really since I was very young...

—Please don't babble.

—Stop? Oh, I see. Babbling. Yes... I'll...

—Do you ever think, she said - I moved closer, lifting the glass in my hand towards my lips and sipping warily - do you ever think what this life is all about, Mr Monk? Do you ever think what life could offer you? Do you ever think what delights the world has to offer you? What rewards could be there for the right man at the right time? She paused and then asked, are you an ambitious man, Mr Monk?

—Look, can you stop calling me Mr Monk. Nobody calls me that. I've been called a lot of things in my time but no one calls me Mr... you know, by my name. Everyone calls me Monkey.

—And would you like me to call you that? she asked with an expression of slight but noticeable distaste. Her hands moved with sensuous delight over her hips and stroked down over her thighs where the red dress swooned so close to her skin it hurt, reaching to its hem where her fingers played fiddle-with-me. I found both whisky glasses at my lips. I was sucking away at the stuff.

—Well, I said, it would be more friendly.

—It would, wouldn't it.

—And what, what could I call you? I feel I hardly know you but here we are as if we knew each other quite well. And talking of bedrooms and things. I mean, I'm all for the comfort of strangers and all that. But I don't even know your name. Do I? I mean, I'm sorry, have you told me and I've forgotten?

—What was it that stupid girl called me?

—Who?

—Vampira. That was it. What a bitch she was.

—That's not really your name, is it?

—Don't be ridiculous. I'm Stella. She paused and then asked, Are you my friend Mr Monk? The way she made those *M*s melted the marrow in me.

—Stella? Like the stars?

—What d'you think? My parents were big lager drinkers? She stood up and came close and began to help me off with my combat jacket, not easy with me holding the two glasses.

Ten minutes later I was sitting on the bed, wishing I'd drunk more of the whisky. A lot more. There was something predatory about the woman that was exciting in a scary lustful way. She paced about in front of me fiddling with the buttons on her dress. After a while of me staring stupidly at her and her doing the pacing, she sat down impatiently on the edge of the bed and licked her lips, giving the scarlet lipstick a mirror gloss. Her eyes narrowed at me.

—Where is it, Mr Monk?

—Where's what?

70

—You know exactly what I'm talking about.

—I'm all here, just take what you want, I said, going back on an elbow. She leaned forward, bending over me like a praying mantis. I was going to get the night of my life. Right here; right now. Oh, yes. Our eyes met. Our breath entwined. I offered up my lips to her soft waiting lips. She pushed me back onto the bed with an impatient dismissal and disappeared through the door.

—Hang on a minute, she called over her shoulder.

I hung on. I looked round at the furniture in dubious shades of mock birch wood and the candles in iron candelabra with their whiskers of wicks curled like question marks. She'd drawn the curtains. The room was dim. I could make out the smudged outline of faces in picture frames but none of the detail. When I looked up I saw, in the mirror on the ceiling, the image of a hairy man at rest. Oh, lucky Monkey.

I stretched out and basked in the bliss of the moment, watching my *Iron Rhino* tee shirt tighten. Couplets were swimming through my mind like hyperactive fish. What a piece of work is Monkey, how noble, how admirable; what a handsome brute, the paragon of animals. And how like an angel is she? A beauty of beauties. What delight there is in her. What delight there'd be in us ensnared together.

All I had to do was work my Monkey charm on her, which should be a breeze as she was obviously besotted with me. All that odd stuff back there was clearly a signal that she wanted me but didn't want it to come across as too obvious. It was a strange ritual and I'd have to play it cool but knowing the form gave me some advantage. I tucked my hands behind my head and waited, watching the smile settle into my face in the mirror above. What I was imagining is none of your business.

I'd started to unbuckle my belt with the intention of removing the wet trousers when a sudden explosive expletive sprang in from the other room. I sat up abruptly. Peering round the door frame I saw Stella kneeling on the floor in front of my jacket. She was holding an enormous pair of scissors and the jacket was in ribbons. She looked up and her mouth ran into a bitter smile.

—You can't do that! I shouted at her.

—Where is it?

—Listen, lady, that jacket was expensive.

—Expensive? Don't be ridiculous.

—Me? Ridiculous? I'm not the one playing slash the jacket.

—Don't play games with me, Mr Monk. I don't like games. The only games I play are the ones where I hold all the cards.

—What, like Patience, you mean?

—Patience is exactly what I am running out of, Mr Monk. Now, tell me where it is. It's not here. Where have you hidden it?

—What?

But she had stopped in mid-sentence and was now twisting the tatters of my jacket in her hands and staring into the distance. It wasn't a big flat and the distance wasn't far. She'd got the hump all right. But not in the way I'd been…oh, I'd been here before all right. There was a taste in my mouth. Tasted strange that whisky. It must have been one of those single malt jobs I'd never been able to afford. I licked my lips and waited for her to carry on. She looked at me and then pouted sulkily and stared into the distance again. She looked so damned sexy when she did that I began to think up ways to make her sulk. I could offer her something like…like…. And then it dawned on me and I looked at her knowingly. Why had I been so slow?

For a moment – quite a long moment – greed swam around my head. I kept coming back to one thought: if I gave her what she wanted, was there a possibility that she might give me what I wanted? Set against this beautiful thought was another thought: maybe this thing was valuable. But then what more could I want than the seductive charms of Stella? I turned to look down on her. She looked up at me with a devilish smile in the corners of her mouth. But her eyes were difficult to make out.

—You want the book, don't you? I asked.

—Of course I do. Then her eyes mellowed a little and she forced an apologetic look into her face, stretching it over her cheek bones, trying it on for size. She leaned back against the dining table and adjusted her dress so her legs were less of a temptation.

—You've made a right mess of that jacket, you know.

—I just wish you'd still been wearing it, she muttered to herself.

—Charming. You really can be quite charming. Worth a lot is it, this thing, this what do you call it?

—The Doorway is the truly profitable way of life.

—Oh, give me a break.

—You have it, don't you? I saw it in your hand. At the back of the hotel. You picked up the book and put it in your coat. You put it in some big sort of pocket.

—OK. I did. So what?

—If only you knew what you were saying. The book must be returned.

—Who to?

—Me, of course. She was getting tetchy.

—So, it's your book, then?

—Not exactly. But I've got to return it to who it belongs to.

—So if it's so precious, how come it's on the loose? I said, all smart. It was a reasonable question.

She took a breath and paused with it and looked at me as if assessing what she should tell me.

—Mick Dyker. That's how. You must have heard of him. He's a writer. Wrote that book, you know: '*Dreams and Realities*'. I read it. He was researching another book and it was when he was looking into the things people do to improve their lives - mind improvement, meditation, you know the kind of thing - that he got interested in The Foundation. The Doorway Foundation. Mr Damon – he runs everything - wasn't keen to have someone like Dyker around. He's so careful about what people can say about The Foundation, is Mr Damon. Because The Foundation does really help people, it does make them successful and clever. It's a wonderful thing.

—Whatever. Never heard of it.

—Of course you'd never heard of it. You're not in touch with your profitable mind, are you?

—My what? I don't expect so, seeing as I'm not in touch with anything much these days, apparently. But Mick thingy had obviously heard of you.

—Dyker was a real smooth talker. I can see that now. I was really taken in by him. He flattered me. He took me out. He told me I was the best thing that had ever happened to him...

—Good god, woman, clichés like that went out two by two.

—Well, he didn't say it like that; he was a writer, he used all big words.

—Go on, what did he say? What did he actually say?

—I can't remember.

—He said that, didn't he? What you just said, best thing that had ever happened to him.

—All right. Yes. That's what he said.

—What a prat.

—All right. Don't rub it in.

—If only I could...

—Mr Monk! Stop it. It was awful. I trusted him. I trusted him and he betrayed me. She smudged a hand over her eyes. He disappeared with the book. I was working on files in Mr Damon's room and Dyker was there. That's when... I think that was when he came over all smooth to distract me. The book was on the desk. It was awful. Mr Damon called me into his office that evening and asked me about where the book was. He worked out that it must have been Dyker. It didn't take him long; it wasn't difficult, was it? Mr Damon told me I had to get it back and quickly. He said I was finished at the Foundation if I

74

failed. He got really angry. And he'd always been so polite. He went all hard and I thought he was going to shout at me.

—I know exactly how he feels.

—What? Shut up, Mr Monk and listen for once. I knew I'd let Mr Damon down and I had to find the book Anyway, I traced Dyker to the Metropole but he disappeared again and whilst I was looking around for clues like where he had gone to I saw you pick up the book. I'd thought I was going to have to go through the bins. At least you saved me from that. But I was so sick I really was sick when I saw you with the book. Out in the alley. If only I'd got there first. Horrible man. He was a creepy little man. What could I ever have seen in him? Look, Mr Monk, I want you to help me put right the wrong he committed. I want you to help me.

She stood up and advanced towards me. She had a lop-sided smile on her face and little twinkles were playing in her eyes. Her big eyes. Her eyes were melting the sinew in me. I looked down at the scissors in her hand. She dropped them onto the table and sat down on the settee.

—I searched your room. I brought you here and searched your clothes.

—Don't tell me. You were going to seduce me and dash back to my room as I slept and turn it over again. Smug said it was a woman, didn't he? Neat job, ladyo, but not neat enough.

—Seduce you? Don't be ridiculous. You look like an animal.

I must have shown some offence at this because she scored her fingers through her hair, lowered her face and looked up at me past raised eyebrows.

—I'm sorry, I didn't mean... I meant you know, you're an *animal*, if you see what I mean. She shuddered but whether with passion or revulsion it was difficult to tell. I'm just a little emotional about it all. You see, I really need your help. And we could be so good together. Look – she put her head in her hands and gazed up at me with a lost expression on her face - I've got to have that book. I've just got to.

—Unbelievable.

—Just help me get the book back, she pleaded.

—So, what's in the book? I asked.

—It's The Book, she said, capitalising it for me.

—And...I prompted.

—It's the book that Eeve told Mr Damon to write in. She told him what to write. Eeve. She's the Chosen One who chose Mr Damon to tell the secrets to.

—What secrets? Who's Eeve?

—The secrets of the universe. And all about The Portal which is the way we can all understand our profitable selves and get to be happy. Mr Damon had to write it all down in the book because it was him who met Eeve. No-one else has.

—Why doesn't that surprise me?

—I don't know, she said, simply.

—So let me get this straight. Damon – your boss – says he met this Eeve who told him some stuff and he wrote it down in a book...

—In *the* book, she said. And a lot of it's in Eeve's language that only Mr Damon can read. But don't you see? The book is, like, holy.

—It's wholly something. I can tell you.

—He met her on Ilkley Moor.

—Really? I've been there.

—Really? she said breathlessly.

—Oh, yes. Didn't see an Eeve.

—You're not chosen. Only Mr Damon's chosen. And he's a Chooser as well, like Eeve. So if we follow Mr Damon, he might choose us and we can open our Portals and everything will become clear. And...

—OK. Just forget Eeve for a moment. I take it the book's worth something to Mr D? I said, glad I hadn't had a go at it with my knife.

—It's priceless.

—Priceless, eh.

—Oh, yes. Mr Damon's got to have it back. He said it was the only one of its kind in the world. It was a revelation.

—Well, I said. Now I know what's in the book, the question is, what's in it for me?

—If you help me, the knowledge that you've kept a fellow human being from the dogs? And probably saved the human race.

—Ah. And what about us?

—Us?

—You know...*us.*

—Oh, I see. Well, who knows how grateful I might be if I get the book back?

—Well...

—Oh please, Mr Monkey.

She'd changed, hadn't she? Still that seductive appeal smouldered under it all but she was turning on the emotional stuff now like there was no tomorrow. It was kind of cute in a way. I ran my eyes over those legs again. She purred *please.* I heard the please and I heard the purr.

My mind went back to the moment I had found the book. There I'd been on the edge of things with the deep notes of hunger sounding in my belly when the book had found itself in my hand. Smug had appeared at that moment not only with a tray of grub but also with employment and accommodation. That find had changed my life. Then I looked at her. She curled her legs under her on the sofa and the slashed skirt showed a flash of thigh. Here was a woman I would walk over hot coals to be with.

—I'll see what I can do, I said.

7

"I've swept your floor so where's yer bin?"
"I've been out in t' yard."
(David Harrison, Mark Pentel, in *Woodchips*, 1967)

I got back to the hotel at about three in the morning. The taxi dropped me at the door and I was stopped by a couple of policemen. They wanted to know who I was and I told them. A long-headed sergeant wrote it all down in a notebook and let me pass. I knew they'd check with the hotel management and find out that I didn't really exist as far as their records were concerned. Time to move on. But why all the men in blue? I scuttled round the back and let myself in.

When I got to my room I found it had been trashed. Smug was standing in the middle of the chaos looking around blearily.

—Smug, what have you done? I shouted.

—Not me, not me, he squealed. I wouldn't do this, Monkey.

—You're right, of course you wouldn't. Would you? The bloody bacon men, then.

—Who?

—The police, man, the police.

—No, Monkey. Ginny.

—What? Ginny did this? How could she do this?

I looked around at the mess. I didn't have much but what there was had been strewn and piled and smashed. The cup and the glass were broken. The chair was upended in the corner and the bed was leaning up against the wall by the window. She had some muscle, that girl, when she was angry. She'd put the mattress in the shower. It was wet through and stank of biscuits.

The sheet was in the sink and the pillow thrown down the corridor. The duvet she had spared. What a girl!

Two things puzzled me. Firstly, how did she know where I'd been living? Secondly, where was The Doorway book? I seemed to remember putting it under my pillow. First things first, though.

—Smug, I said to him who was now trying to pull the mattress out of the shower cubicle. His hands were slipping on the damp surface and the mattress, bent in two like a sumo wrestler, was resisting his efforts. Sweat was bubbling over his pink forehead.

—Smug, how did Ginny know where I was living?

—Search me, Monkey. He stopped the struggle and looked out of the window, fumbling in a pocket for a fag.

—Don't tempt me, Smug. I'm not in the mood for frivolity. Right now I could search your brain with a corkscrew.

—Monkey, he said with mock hurt, there's that unpleasant side coming out again.

—Smug? How did she know?

—Maybe you wrote your address on the postcard you sent her? He sparked up and tried to hide his head in the smoke.

—No, I didn't do that. Nor did I put out a bloody flag or beam the address to her telepathically; nor did I announce it over the radio, nor employ legions of street children to search her out and tattoo it on her arse.

—OK. OK, steady on, mate. There you go again. Give us a hand with this mattress, will you? He fumed away and tucked the fag into a corner of his mouth.

—How did she know? I asked, steadily. He put down the mattress again and turned to face me. His eyes looked guilty as hell. He shuffled his hands together damply.

—OK. I told her.

—Go on.

—Well, it was after the do in the bar. You know with the

79

shrieking and me falling over the table - I've still got this massive bruise on me leg if you want to see…well, OK fair enough - and well, to cut a long story short, which is always the best way if you ask me, after you'd gone off with that woman - and I didn't like it, you know, I've warned you about her before - after you'd gone Ginny came back into the bar and were looking round. She looked like she'd calmed down a bit so I went and introduced myself to her. First she thought I was trying to chat her up and she got all prickly and so I said I wasn't trying to chat her up. Then she looked all hurt for some reason so I told her I knew you and she asked where you was staying these days. Before I could stop myself - sorry - I'd told her about the little room. She seemed to think for a minute and then she were off like a shot. Then I thought for a minute and I was off quick as well because it suddenly occurred to me that you and the woman might be back here and I had to get there and warn you or something. I went the back way which was a mistake…

—Another one.

—Because I got caught by Chef who was coming up the stairs in some kind of tweed underwear. He was absolutely stoned. Blasted. Never seen him so bad. He was going on about Molly someoneorother, whoever she is. Molly this and Molly that and how he loved her or wanted to go home or something - I couldn't hear the detail of it all because his words were coming out drunk. Then he wedged me against the wall with his belly and wouldn't let me past until I listened to him sing about bells with hands on. He was really gone. Couldn't remember the words. I got drunk just on his breath. By the time I got down here I found all this. I felt really bad.

—Good.

—Sorry, Monkey.

That little tale answered both my questions in one. And then I thought of another. Why was he still standing there at three in the morning?

—Oh, I'd been back in the bar talking to Eugene and drinking free beer until the police arrived and I came down here to see if you was all right, you having disappeared and all that.

—And what are the police doing here?

—Haven't a clue.

Smug went away and I slept rolled up in the duvet on the floor. The next day Eugene told me all about the grim discovery. Chef had drunk until about two in the morning when, exhausted from singing, he had felt the need for fresh air so out he went to the back of the hotel to take in some of the stuff. The night air hit him hard and the whisky rose in his stomach like a snake trying to get out of a sack. He'd staggered to one of the big bins and flung back the lid to throw up and found as he stared down into the depths, lit by the security lights, a face staring back at him. A sickening experience indeed. Yes, it was Mick Dyker, dead. He was wedged in the bottom of the bin like a starfish.

I got the room back in order which was good because one of the hotel suits came prowling round the next day. His plastic name badge, repaired with sellotape and pinned to his breast pocket, said *Sly Storrit*. He said he'd talked to Chef who'd done his best to explain what was going on but was really only good for cooking. Sly stared round the room without much interest, pursing his lips and nodding. He didn't seem much concerned about me. I was still ostensibly the previous slop man. He shrugged his shoulders and said he'd check with Mr Magnum – whoever he was – how much rent I should be paying. So it all turned out all right. Apart from the loss of the book. I had to find Ginny and get it back which wouldn't be easy the way things were between her father and me. But I was so relieved not to have found the thing nailed to the wall that I was quite optimistic when I set out that day.

I had to wait until after work. Then I set off with my pay in my

81

pocket for the pubs where I was sure I would meet Ginny. There was also a better chance of me evading the attentions of Mr Wolffe in a crowded environment. So I reasoned. The coolness of the evening reminded me that I had to get a new jacket before the real cold weather was upon us. I made a mental note to get down to the Oxfam shop that weekend. I had, at that point in time, no idea how I was going to get the book back from Ginny. I was just optimistic.

I wandered through the streets in the general direction of the bus stop but then, as it was a fresh evening, I decided to walk all the way to The Skyrack. The streetlights were just flickering into life by the time I got to the KFC in Hyde Park and I stopped off for a bucket of bits. I smeared the grease from my fingers over a napkin or two and poured out a cup of coke.

I got out my notebook and opened it up at a blank page and stared out of the window and watched for a while the mooching people cluttering up the street. A taxi slid up like a fish and hung around at the kerb listlessly.

I wrote something I couldn't even read when I looked over it and immediately forgot the sense of it anyway. Times were hard. That was my excuse for not writing anything any good. Still, when Phibre and Phibre wrote back to accept Monkey's Typewriter things would really change. How could they turn me down? There were some cracking lines in that book. I should know, I wrote them. It would help, I thought if I had a real address. Must do something about that. They might be trying to find me even as I think about them.

I went on to The Skyrack, got a pint and had a look around. Since they opened the place up into one large-size drinking emporium the place has lost a lot of its charm. One or two red-nosed spivs in greasy raincoats leant against the bar. The air was sluggish with cigarette smoke. The back of the bar was lagged with students drinking their brains away. I felt sneaky and furtive looking around like this. But there was no Ginny. And no Mr Wolffe. Good and bad together.

I sat down at a round table and stuck my feet on its cast iron chassis. I got out the spiral bound and did a bit in it with my biro:

In the hotel bar three drunks
Are arguing
About poetry,
Whatever that is.

I'm standing myself another whisky
Waiting for you to arrive
So I can lay you on the bartop
And show you a good rhyme.

Later, I propped myself against the bar and started to muse on what exactly I was going to say to the girl when I eventually encountered her. The night passed slowly as I made my lonely way around the pubs. I'd begun to see ads for The Doorway Foundation around the place. Maybe they were new or maybe I'd just not noticed them before. There was a billboard opposite The Hyde Park, a blonde with an arctic smile and eyes like two images of earth. It said: 'My World is My World'.

Days passed. Nights passed. How long can a man continue washing up without losing sense of the world? I thought this as I scoured particular stains from the inside of an obscenely large saucepan. I had froth all over the place and the wire pad was going at it wildly but I might as well have been rubbing away at the barnacles on a boat with a tissue. Jeb and Dozy, two of the waiters who looked like refugees from some cheap slapstick, came in and stacked the pile of dirties to cartoon heights. Where do we go from here? Was this how I was to spend the days of my life? If that book was worth something maybe I could sell it. Or ransom it.

I hadn't seen Stella for a while now. And what about Mick Dyker. I read about him, the story was in the Argus the following week. Dead from natural causes, apparently. Heart attack. They reckoned he must have climbed into the bin for reason or reasons unknown. He'd had a history of getting into small spaces, according to the article. They'd dragged up a number of squealers from his youth to attest to his squeezing into school lockers, small wardrobes and pedal bins.

Comfort zones, they suggested but I reckoned he was mad as a snake or hiding from Stella or one of her ilk though he picked a rubbish sort of hiding place if you ask me. He must have dropped the book as he climbed into the bin. Not a good way to go, really.

The paper didn't make much of his death beyond the oddity of its circumstance. He'd been a bit of a hack, really. Earning a crust from the unusual business of other people's lives. Drag-netting the flotsam and jetsam of Leeds, trawling through the varied detritus like some sort of deranged fisherman labouring to net the sick and the broken and the sad. It was what city folk liked to read best, tales of the failure of lives, stories of the sleazy world you found if you tipped back the foundations and looked close enough. I thought of my own state at the back of the hotel and wondered where I might have ended up if it hadn't been for that chance encounter with Smug. I'd probably have been king of the road by now.

I suppose it was inevitable that I got another visit from the suits upstairs. This time it was, according to his little shiny badge, Mr David Arnoldo, assistant to Mr Magnum's assistant. Basically, he told me to get out. Vacate the premises. Take myself elsewhere. Mr Magnum was cutting back. And I had to go because I was always late, wasn't I? I started to explain that I wasn't the one who was always late, that had been the previous employee but he said that according to the records I'd been taken on as extra – there was no previous employee. So I had to go.

I assured him that wherever I went I would be sure to take myself with me. And when would he like this to happen. He said that he would like it to happen with immediate effect. I said would tomorrow do as I had to have a lie down to get over the shock of the news. He said I had to be gone by the end of the day. He was sorry but that's the way it was. And if I didn't disappear he'd escort me off the premises himself. He looked as if he might enjoy this. He smirked complacently and flexed his pigeon chest. He was about half my height but the wrists that protruded from his sleeves were as thick as Popeye's.

I went back to my sink where I was later accosted by Chef. His belly preceded him through the kitchen like a wheelbarrow full of sausages. Sweat was running amok all over his face and his teeth were littered with pastry crumbs. For the first time since I had started work in the kitchen I noticed that he didn't smell of whisky.

Meeting the face of Mick Dyker at the bottom end of a bin might have unhinged the best of us and driven us into the arms of Sweet Mother Alcohol. But chef suffered a reversal of this and found himself sober for the first time he could remember. And now he didn't recognise me. Where was his dear little slop boy? He pressed me back against the sink with his belly and lowered his glistening face to mine. Who *was* I? I began to tell him that I was researching for my book on repetitive strain injuries of the mind but he just looked blank. So I told him that though I wasn't who he thought I was I was pretty mean at washing up and I needed the work to support my aunt Greenwich's polar expeditions.

He frowned and really seemed on the point of thinking about it when he looked up at the tottering tower of dirty crockery and then down at the pan in my hand. Not only had soapy water drained itself over his shoes but the thing was still, despite my efforts, caked in brown stuff baked to the consistency of armadillo plating. He questioned my competence, demanded to know my qualifications and made hurtful allusions to my birth and death. I was out of work again. Smug stood to one side and raised his shoulders in a shrug of defeat. It was all over.

8

"Darling, who was that guy I saw you with last night?"
"That wasn't Guy, that was Garth."
(B. K Thomas, ed. *More Southern Wit*, 1987)

There's a stone lion in Hyde Park. It's about four feet high and it has a stone snake wrapped around it so that the two of them look to be writhing in mortal combat. Or weird sex. And they change colour on a regular basis. I was sitting on a park bench staring at them vacantly. The lion was lime green and the snake was silver with dark gold diamonds. I've no idea who paints them but it does liven up the grassland.

I was mixed up with feeling happy at having escaped the trouble of washing up without having had to coward out of it like a kid and feeling anxious at the thought of finding somewhere to hang my hat. If I'd had a hat. Smug had not been happy to see me go. He'd wanted to argue with the suited ones but I'd asked him what was the point. I was a slop man. Ten a penny. Besides, I said, putting on the brave face, I was fed up with working in the devil's kitchen scraping plates for my sins. The world is a big old place waiting for me with open arms. I'd find something else.

I grinned at him the famous Monkey grin and he shook his head at me and called me a strange odd bastard. I left telling him I'd see him for a drink at the Oak or something sometime. He nodded mournfully. He said I could stay at his place till I found somewhere for myself. But I waved at him from a small distance and shouted that I was for the world and the world would provide a shelter for a wandering man. He shook his head again.

So I was sitting watching this lion humming to myself 'Hello blue and hello sky, I got the girl and the girl got I,' when someone came and sat down next to me. I ignored them and carried on with the watching. I heard the clearing of a throat as if a football pump was sucking up jelly. I turned a little and looked at the figure out of the corner of my eye. He was thin and gristly, dressed in killer tweeds and had a ratty leather briefcase under his left arm. He was staring at the lion but when he saw I had turned he twisted his face round to face mine and showed me his washed-up eyes.

Then he looked away again as if bored. The sun glowed behind the steel clouds and the sky was stretched to breaking point between the horizons. The man shuffled his legs and I caught a glimpse of brown shoes past their sell by date, beyond the hope of polish or the luxury of waxed laces, shoes with dust in the seams and the tooling of the brogue. Here was a man, I thought, in education.

A couple of slender hippy types sloped by on the path, their bowing heads muttering some nonsense, their pixie shirts fluttering in the breeze over their jaded jeans. We both watched their passing. Their hips swayed together, their hands trapped in each other's back pockets. He, being of some indeterminately ancient age and significantly dismantled, watched their retreating forms with unarticulated sighs for the lost freedom of youth.

—That lion's an odd beast, he suddenly remarked for no particular reason. His voice sounded like a ratchet, each word a notch. For a moment there was a silence as if I recognised that there was no particular reason why I should reply, then I said,

—It's better for the paint.

—Couldn't agree with you more.

—Especially as it keeps changing, you know, getting a fresh coat. Keeps it bright. Keeps it interesting. Green suits it.

—No doubt about it. The mysterious adoption of the lion by an artist unknown is one of the most interesting aspects of Hyde Park. There are those, he said, turning slightly to face me again, who would have a shade of bronze or a stone colour or white, for pity's sake. I've heard people talk of the lion in terms of its lack of tradition, in terms of it being not what it is if it's a colour other than the colour of its materials.

—Ah, I see.

—By that argument, books would not exist except as white paper, paintings would be stretched canvasses or framed virgin whiteness, music would be silence for with instruments the original state of the air in their tubes or the first condition of their strings is stillness. Look at that lion. It is a canvas upon which is represented the mind of the artist who created it. Green, for instance, is the colour of rebellion, and the selection of 'lime green' from the paradigm 'green' represents the selection of the exotic over the mundane. Also, of course, the connotations of corrosiveness from its resonance with quicklime and the implication of health and vitality from the association with citrus may be readily inferred. Further...

He paused for a breath and did the jelly thing with the membranes again and then placed the briefcase down on the bench as if he meant to stay, though I did note that it was placed between us like the bulwark of a teacher's desk. He looked over at me mournfully and nodded at the lion. I was patient and sat on.

—further, of course, the silver of the serpent here, locked in its eternal embrace around the lion's body, fixes it as a thing of value, presenting it as artefact, as a thing cast like a thing cast in metal. And the two colours are combined into a syntagm of extraordinary tension, like an oxymoron of uncommon profundity. So we find by means of our circuitous approach that what is represented here is that energy of man's generative compulsion, which our culture so likes to associate with the lowness of the serpent, forever with its stranglehold on the majesty of the lion. You see? The lion, sovereign like reason is sovereign, is perpetually entangled within the coils of sexual urgency.

—It's wonderful what an education can do, I replied in some confusion. Through his speech he had been rocking nervously backwards and forwards on the edge of the bench, clasping and unclasping his hands in great agitation. When he asked his final question he was looking at the lion as if addressing his linguistic contortions to the thing itself.

—You look to be a man of sense.

—Are you a teacher, or something?

—Ah, he replied in a mournful voice, what was it gave it away? The briefcase, maybe?

—The shoes, really.

—Oh.

He sounded surprised and looked down at them and frowned as trying to puzzle out what I was talking about, which was fair enough because I hadn't got much of a clue what he was talking about. Then he reached into the leather of the briefcase and pulled out a litre bottle of scotch clumsily wrapped in a Morrisons carrier bag. When he saw I was looking at it he fumbled the plastic bag round it more tightly and then unscrewed the top and flung the contents at his mouth. Having done a mouthful he replaced the top and then the bottle, hesitated as if he were going to go for another hit, changed his mind and quickly fastened the clasp of the case.

—I'm beginning to see what you mean, he said after a pause. Always start with the shoes, isn't that what they say? As an actor, always start with the shoes. So what do these shoes say about the role I am playing in this brief drama that is life? Maybe the brown of them signifies…

—So what you're saying, I interrupted before he could begin another skirmish with the English language, is that the sculpture of the lion and the snake is only a canvas for the work of art that's the paint?

—In a manner of speaking I might be saying that. As the

canvas or the paper or the instrument are a part of the painting or the story written or the sound of music, so is the sculpture a committed part of the painted sculpture you see before you.

—Ah, I see. So where do you teach, then?

—Teach? he muttered viciously.

He had another go at the whisky till it shone on his lips. He mopped at himself and jammed the bottle back into its leather holster.

—You think they still let me teach? All this — he waved his skinny arms expansively round his head to indicate the whole of Hyde Park or maybe all of Leeds, or maybe it was some global gesture meaning to take in the whole of everything and the feelings that go with it all — all this is for what? I'll tell you what. All this is to reduce you to a smudge of dirt on the smallest cog in their diabolical machinery. All this is for nothing.

—Whose machinery was that?

—Whose…isn't it obvious? Do you think I'm just some raving paranoiac gabbling on a park bench, rolling in the clutches of drink, held together by the bitter glue of bile? Is that what you think? Look at me. Am I not a man? A man like others? And are we not forced by the nature of the institutions for which we work to chase the endless paper and work the endless chase. Are we not driven by the fire of ambition to climb the slippery pole, to insinuate ourselves ever more into the corporate entity. I was ambitious once, you know. You know, I had a friend once was a policeman and he said to me, he said, do you know the number of forms I've to fill out just for nicking some minor low life? He said, this job's got more forms than a school. And I said to him, I said, what do you know about forms? What do you know about college work? My god, man, the paperwork hits my desk sobbing every morning. I've to stare at classes over the summit of it. Don't give me paperwork, I said. I've got enough of that. Where do I teach? As if I haven't better things to do with my time.

Out came the bottle again. By the time it went away his eyes were moist with it and the fume of it hung over the bench like petrol.

—So that was the problem, then, was it? All the paperwork?

—That wasn't a problem, oh, no, that wasn't just a problem, that was an evil perpetrated on us by the spawn of Satan. But that was just the beginning. And don't think I'm making this up... when I started lecturing I had classes of sixteen, I had time to mark the essays I set, I had time for research so I had something to teach. I kept up with the times. I kept up with it all, theory, modern stuff at that, latest ideas. I was fresh. I was *keen*. It didn't last. Education's all gone to shit. Do you know how big my classes were when I finished? Do you know that?

—Bigger, I expect. About thirty, maybe?

—Thirty? *Thirty*! We used to dream about classes of *thirty*. Thirty, he says! When I was...when I left I had classes of eighty four...no, eighty seven. *Eighty* seven. Sea of faces. Couldn't move for the marking, I'll tell you. To the ceiling, it was. Filled the bloody room. Bloody seas of faces. Couldn't move for them. And the bloody paperwork. The managers loved it. They could cosy up to their computers and fiddle with the figures all day. No more for them the cut and thrust of the classroom, no more the real business of education. They hadn't a clue what was going on. All they had was the paper, so paper became a sort of specious proof that things were happening and the whole thing became self-justifying. A wish-fulfilment prophesy on a grand scale. But they were happy in their little offices away from it all.

Glib little acronyms became attached to everything we did. All targets had to be...had to be Traceable, Well-understood, Agreed and Time-constrained. So we were tripping over TWATs all the time. Spawn of the devil. Really was. Everything had to written down. Forms for everything, you know. We had forms to fill in about the bloody forms we were filling out. They all had these names. Like SPAM: Standard Projected Annual Markers, where you had to predict student attainment in a year's time based on the GCSE results of other students in the previous year. Does that make sense? I think not. It's all right looking at the big picture that way but you can't look at individuals like that, it just doesn't work. Fit them into little boxes of expectation. Wish bloody fulfilment. Bureaucrats have taken over education. Men in little offices with computers and statistics and pie charts and bar graphs. Residuals with positive or negative significance ... are you listening?

—Sure.

—Initiatives. That's what they said they were. Initiatives. Week after week, new schemes, revised practices, course content all made up by bloody bureaucrats! - and then classroom practice determined by civil servants – bloody list on bloody list and none of them could see it was only a trend. This week's fad, next week's fad. They had no idea about educational debate. None. Had about as much vision as a blinkered ass in a rut in a one-way field. Central control. We became monkeys dancing on the end of a string to the hurdy-gurdy of absurdity.

Target setting became talked about in tones of holy awe. All targets had to be met. All targets were met, institutionally, nationally. They had to be. Inclusivity, you see. Everything had to be proved to be working to show that everything worked. More people on courses, more people passing exams. And the devil's acolytes and all their little imps in the corridors of power and the power-carpeted offices of the glorious hypocritical sipped on statistics and feasted on pie charts. Then one day I was talking of SOWs and Ellis Herringbone - he was head of something or other, big car, new suit, never in a classroom unless he was sitting at the back with a clipboard and a shopping list of 'good educational practice', about which he knew damn all which was why he was at the back of the room and I was at the front — he looked at me like he'd trodden in me and said, 'Schemes of Work, now that does not make sense, really, does it? They are Schemes for Teaching now. I looked at him as if he'd grown two heads and neither of them knew what the other was doing. And each was barking. Spawn of the whatdyoucallit.

I could tell you stories that would make your hair curl - he looked over and I noticed the cascading ragbag of curls that festooned my head - make your blood curl. I was once there in the class room with the lot of them. Stacked like sardines in a sauce of their own sweat, they were. I had three on each window ledge. And they were bloody small windows. The rest were arraigned around me shoulder to bloody shoulder. Had to write their notes with paper perched on their knees - no room for more than eighteen desks, you see - had to write with little squiggling motions of their wrists. Everybody's handwriting looked the same because of it, like the graphical expectorations of moles. Every last one of them. And I had to write on one of those whiteboards – no chalk and talk any more, you see, all marker and barking now. And some of them were so far away from the board. I remember one girl shouting out, "I can't read it, Sir, it's just like grains of sand in my eyes". I told them to bring opera glasses, and I wasn't joking. Though it was more Oprah than opera by then. Shakespeare and social work. You couldn't make it up.

All the students' faces had the same look of anguished concentration. Apart from the hordes at the back crammed into class for their own good who spent the time texting each other and snortling on sexual giggles. I couldn't bear it. But I couldn't get out. I kept looking for the door but it was like looking down the wrong end of a telescope.

He ground a finger into his left ear and grubbed away at it for a minute. When he pulled it out he rubbed it over his tweed sleeve and then rubbed at the ear with the flat of his hand. He refuelled from the briefcased bottle and sighed.

—So did it do them all in? All the teachers, I mean.

—All of them? No, some adapted and took on the manner of domesticated animals. I descended into a hell of criminal bureaucracy. I should have just told them to go and piss on their eyes. It's the McDonaldisation of education. Homogeneity. Every lesson standardised, scripted and sanitised so it doesn't matter who delivers the package as long as they all do it in the same way. They could train monkeys to do it. Probably do.

—A bit of a traditionalist, eh? Good for you.

—The real principles of education are not difficult to grasp.

—It's a people thing.

—Nail on the head there, my boy. You sound like an educated man. College? University?

—Don't start me on about school. Somewhere between Gothic torment and a bloody laugh. Yeh, then uni, here in Leeds, for my sins. Didn't quite make it right through, though I could have done. You know how it is…the girls, the drink. We had a laugh.

—A shame, he said.

—Life goes on, I said.

He rummaged round in his hair for a while and I let the breeze play through mine.

—Knew I was getting past it, he said, when I couldn't take the drink any more. Had to sip it, you know. Knew I was getting old. Sipping the bloody stuff. Grew hairs in my ears. Bloody hairs in my ears. I said to my class one day, I said, you know you're getting on a bit when you've got to shave your bloody ears. Must offer some sort of evolutionary advantage, I suppose. Maybe if I grew it long it would stop out all the bloody nonsense. They did for me in the end. I wouldn't be scripted by some oaf with a clipboard. I taught what I had to teach. So they did for me. Out on my ear. My bloody hairy ear.

He ran his fingers through his hair and it all stood up thin on the top of his skull. The sun carried on as if nothing was happening, lighting his forehead, casting inky shadows in the ragged furrows. He turned his eyes back to me and grimaced. I was just about to get up and go when he opened his mouth again and the words were tripping over each other to get out. I resigned myself to it for the moment.

—And another thing, you know, before I forget, here's a word of advice for you. Never believe a man in an off-the-peg suit can tell you anything of importance. Now me, I've never found a way to stop them…

Through my glazed vision I was watching two figures approaching over the grass. There was something familiar about the way the one on the left moved. A little laughter skimmed over on the air. They jostled each other affectionately, stopped, embraced and then came on towards us. About twenty yards away they suddenly veered off to the right and cut across to the path. I sat up straight. It was Ginny. It was Ginny with someone else. A man, for pity's sake. Spiders of alarm scrambled through my hair. The teacher creature looked at me in mid-sentence and then looked to where I was looking. He didn't seem concerned that Ginny was with someone else walking through Hyde Park. And laughing.

—Nice talking to you. Really, I said, already off the bench and down the grassland with speed coiling in my heels.

—Just remember, he shouted after me, just … Oi! Listen! Just 'cause I'm bitter doesn't mean I'm not right. Ten thousand vacant teaching posts must mean something. You think about it.

His words were tiny things in my ears as I was by this time hurtling down the grass in chase of the girl and her ludicrous paramour. Well, I say hurtling. I'm not as fast as I used to be. Actually, I was never fast. I've got this funny way of running, you see, as someone once said, like a chimpanzee with its arse on fire. Well, I might not be fast or elegant but I can still cover the ground.

I raced after them but they were ahead of me and got out of the park and onto the road before I could catch them up. They were making their way up towards the bus stop. I took a short cut over the edge of the park, heading them off and burst out of the hedge just as they were passing some flash car parked rakishly by the kerb. My lungs were grabbing at the air like a drowning man clutching at clouds. I wiped at the strings of saliva around my lips and gasped to a halt in front of them. They looked startled. Then Ginny gave a pained smile.

—Hello, *Monk*ey.

I carried on gasping and the man on her arm looked down his nose at me. And that was a long look.

—This is Danby Houghton, Monkey.

I looked Danby Houghton over. He was smug inside a beige jacket, buttoned at the front by the middle button. His shirt was topped with a fawn tie and his chinos looked fresh on that minute. His face looked like it had been Mr Sheened and both his eyes seemed to be made of plastic. He put an arm in a gesture of stiff protection around Ginny. There were big cheesy cufflinks hanging from his cuffs and he had on one of those square watches you see advertised on the front pages of newspapers. He looked about forty, an old git wanting a bit of delight like Ginny to drape over his arm and show off to the other wrinklies at the nineteenth hole or the decrepits' reunion ball.

She squeezed up against him with a delighted shrug of her shoulder. It was sickening. I was really sickened. It was life in the embrace of death. It was Beauty and Ken, a hell of a lot more disturbing than Barbie and the Beast might have been. He was turning her to go when I got enough breath to address her in the wheezing language of the terminally romantic.

—What do you mean…?

—What?

—What do you mean, this is Danby Houghton?

—You know what I mean. This is Danby and I'm *with* him. He's the present and you're the past. I don't know how you dare show your face after that scene in the bar. I don't know who that revolting woman was with her hands all over you but I've never been so insulted in my life. Inviting me over and then turning up with vamp of the year hanging off your arm. I didn't know where to put myself, I really didn't.

—It wasn't like that, Ginny, honest it wasn't.

—It never is, is it? I suppose you'd never seen her before in your life.

—Well, not exactly. But it wasn't what you think.

—Did you ever know what I think? Well, it doesn't matter now, does it? You're history. I should have chucked you years ago.

—But we've only known each other six months.

—Well it seems like years.

—Come on, baby, said Danby in strangulated falsetto. She was going with him. It didn't make sense. I knew one thing, though, that without the book I had neither of them. I was on my own without it, that was for sure. I had to have it. Then, when I'd sorted things out with the Stella I could sort things out with Ginny. Or something like that. It wasn't too clear in my mind beyond the book.

—Ginny, I began, but Danby had moved to the side of the flash wheels and was reaching into the lock with a key. It was a bright yellow BMW, showroom shiny. Bastard. He had the car as well. She paused as he opened the door for her and looked over at me in one long last pitying gaze of goodbye.

—Ginny, said Danby.

—Ginny! shouted Monkey. Forget the room, it doesn't matter. I was going to trash it myself anyway. To punish myself. I understand why you did it. But I lost everything because of it. The room, the job. I've nothing left. There's just one thing that matters to me, Ginny, and that's you. But...

—But? she repeated, lifting an eyebrow, one leg already inside the car. Danby Houghton had walked round to the driver's door and let himself in. He leaned over the passenger seat and called out to her to hurry up. Bastard. He got to fiddling with the key in the ignition and the engine peffed into life and purred. I went closer to Ginny so Houghton couldn't hear.

—But there was a sort of book in the room. A black book with a leather cover. Like one of those Filofaxes. And I need it. See it doesn't belong to me and the person it does belong to is getting a bit heavy, if you know what I mean.

—I think I get the picture, Monkey: top heavy, eh, is she? Bit of a tart? So the book's not yours, then. Disappointing. I wondered where you'd got the money for one of those things.

—Ah.

—Very expensive. I thought…well, no matter what I thought.

—Good. Good. I knew you'd understand.

—And you want me to tell you where it is, do you?

—You know where it is? Oh, good, that's such a relief. I knew you'd know. I said to Smug that you'd know. Good old Ginny, I said, she'll know where the book is.

—You want me to tell you where it is?

—Yes. Oh, yes, please.

—If you really cared about me, if you really cared about my feelings, if you were really sorry for what you'd done, you'd forget about the book.

—Yes, yes. I see what you mean. I do care. I really care. OK. But…

—It's that 'but' again, Monkey.

—Please, Ginny. For the good old times, eh?

—God forbid, Monkey. You just don't listen, do you? You're gone. Ditched. You're last month's flavour, past your sell by date. You're bad memories. I want to forget you so hard it hurts. But because I hate to see an animal in pain I'll tell you this. That book you're so keen to get your nasty little hands on is at my father's. I don't live there anymore, she smirked, I've moved in with Danby. Goodbye, Monkey.

—Your father's? Ginny, you don't mean at your *father's*. Why did you do that? Why did you take in the first place? Wasn't trashing the room enough?

——I thought it was all your poems and stuff. But I couldn't even open it. So you might as well have it back. If you've got the guts to get it, that is. So, goodbye, Monkey. And I mean...Good*bye*.

After the car had purred into the street and slid away I let the news roll round in my head for a while. It looked bad. It looked very bad. I mean, I didn't know where her father lived and even if I knew where he lived, how was I going to get into fortress Wolffe and retrieve the book? It looked very, very bad. And then I thought of a plan. A plan so simple and yet so ingenious a child could have thought of it. A very bright child, that is.

9

"One can get attached to a dog in a number of ways."
(H P Lovejoy, *Large Dogs and How to Enjoy Them*, 1967)

Smug was looking at me with an expression of bewilderment, amusement and horror. His moustache seemed longer and more orange. His eyes were hunched into their sockets. He was sitting on the edge of a chair and staring over at me. I was sitting on the floor with my back resting against a bookcase and a can of beer in my hand. The beer was tinny. The bookcase was full of more cans. No books, just cans.

He'd just questioned the wisdom of my plan. Actually, he'd called me a mad, sad loony bastard and refused to have anything to do with it. Which was a shame because it was a cracker of a plan and he was the lynchpin of the whole thing. Without Smug, Plan A was a goner. And there was no Plan B. I asked him if he had a charger. He looked at me with a mixture of bemusement and blankness.

—A charger. For my phone. A Nokia charger? Don't look at me like that, I'm not asking for some sort of war horse or anything.

—I know what you mean.

—You just looked weird.

—I was thinking.

—And do you think…

—I've got an old Motorola.

—That must be nice. No charger, though, that might do mine? You know, a Nokia one?

—No, Monkey. Sorry, mate. Got no horse either. Sorry. Is that Plan B, then, a horse?

101

—There's no Plan B, Smug, I said. Have another beer.

—Now *that's* a good plan.

He tore the tab of another tin and sucked at the rim. He'd smoked about a pack of cigarettes since I'd arrived. The butts were stashed in the overflowing retro onyx ashtray balanced on the chair arm. I kept him at the drinking for a while and then went and got some chips and curry sauce. He fed himself the pale chips dipped in sauce between gulps at the beer cans.

When he was nicely glazed over I fed him the plan again and this time he said it was much more reasonable. He said I could borrow his Moro*tola* if I could find the cranking handle. I smiled and he smiled back a soft-headed smile. Operation Two Little Pigs was on. I raised my solitary can in a toast to our conspiracy and Smug waved his wildly back at me. The ash tray fell off the arm of the chair.

We had to wait until the weekend before we could put the plan into action. I had to show Ginny that Danby Houghton wasn't for her. Which should be a doddle. I mean, you only had to look at the man. He made cardboard look interesting. But I also wanted to keep Stella from the dogs. Ho, hum.

The other problem was Smug's accommodation. When I'd gone back and told him that the world was not yet ready for me it had been good of him to put me up and all that but it was hardly ideal. He had a living room and a bedroom and a kitchen and a bathroom. But they were all midget sized, as if they'd been designed for tiny people. And Smug was neither tiny nor tidy. He hoarded things. There were piles of yellow Reader's Digests and dog-eared copies of the Beano and empty cigarette boxes and till receipts all just shucked around in loose piles and overrun by DVDs - none in their boxes - and beer cans, out of date TV guides, a hamster cage by the bread bin and a dart board, with two darts in it, nailed to the back of the door.

There was a vinegary smell of blocked-up sinks and the corner where the cat slept was suspiciously damp. The wallpaper was a cheerful yellow where it hadn't faded and the carpet tufts were a nondescript mongrel colour. There wasn't much room. It was all dark and airless.

Smug didn't seem to mind this as he spent most of his conscious time in his armchair watching television. But for me it was like living in a sock. Someone else's sock. And at night, as I lay on the sofa cushions on the floor covered in a rather dubious sleeping bag, I had to keep one eye open for the cat. All night. I don't like cats. I keep my distance and I think that they should keep their distance too. Bony little Napoleons. All spine and joints. And claws walking all over you. And this one, Smug's cat, was an appalling specimen. It had tatty ginger fur and one eye, having lost the other in a dispute with a Rottweiler round by the dustbins in death alley. And it liked to sleep on my face. I knew if I wasn't careful I'd wake up from erotic dreams to find myself choking on fur.

It happened once, on the first night. And it wasn't easy to get the beast off. I'd get one paw free from my hair or beard, shift to the next and Wham! the first was back. When I finally managed to get it unpeeled it came off like velcro. I bowled it into the corner of the room where it sprang to its feet on tip-toe. I thought it was going to go for me and looked round quickly for the ashtray to crack it with but it just looked at me in a superior way for a moment and then leapt onto the sofa and curled up happy as a bastard. I didn't get much more sleep that night. Nor the next two. The cat's smirk unnerved me.

When Saturday came I was pleased to see the weather was better and though the sky was the colour of tin, it was at least a dry day. After I'd done the usual ablutionary things I tried to rouse Smug with a cup of coffee. He was having none of it. Saturday morning was for sleeping. He reckoned that he could get by with any small number of hours sleep through the week as long as he could recoup them on Saturday.

This last week being no exception to his nocturnal drinking bouts, he wasn't impressed by my sense of urgency. He snored on, despite the tempting aroma of the fresh instant coffee. I wanted to get on with things. I was anticipating the need for further persuasion, knowing that once he was roused he would have changed his mind about the plan.

I'd picked up a new jacket from *Save the Rodent* a couple of days before so I put it on and went out into the morning, thinking that I'd give the weary wuss a few minutes to waken before I pitched him out of bed on the point of his garden spade. Don't know why he had a spade. He didn't have a garden or anything. But he had all sorts of things that didn't make much sense. Like a miner's helmet, an empty parrot cage, odd pieces of linoleum, a car wheel, that sort of thing. There was a push bike with green Wildgrip tyres, though I'd never seen him ride it. And two panels of a Bosch triptych on top of the fridge where he stuck notes to himself with drawing pins. There was one there at the moment that just said, 'Find the hamstr'. I put on the new jacket which was OK though I was still pissed about the old one. This one was like an up-market donkey jacket. It had a button missing. I wasn't complaining, I just would have preferred the one I had before. I got some fresh milk at the corner shop and went back. Smug was still dead to the world. I went for the spade.

Two hours later I was in Meanwood. How did I know where to go? How had I found out where Mr Wolffe lived? How do you think? Simplest way possible. I looked him up in the phone book at the post office on the Friday. There were quite a few of them. There were Wollfs and Wolffs and Wollfes and Wolfs. Now this was a bit confusing as I didn't remember which sort of a Wolf was my Mr Wolffe. And I had no idea what his first name was. Bart would suit him, I thought, or Derek or Des or some other name like Lou, as in Lupus, or a fanciful monika like Bandit or

Nob. I started phoning them up. There were only about half a dozen but it took ages. Some people let their phones ring for an unacceptably long time before they answer. They can't all be in the bath at three o-clock in the afternoon or up ladders with the white gloss or bedding the wife or the mistress or milkman. Not at that time. Not all of them. And one or two didn't answer at all. Which was unreasonable of them but not, as it turned out, a problem as I eventually heard the dulcet tones of Mr Wolffe trying to be polite to what he must have hoped was a potential tenant. I garbled some nonsense about needing short term accommodation at a moment's notice and was he in the business of having at his disposal a flat or a room or a bolt-hole I could avail myself of. I thought I handled it well. There was a moment's silence and then he said —Monkey! in a growl of triumph.

—Who?

—Now then, Fur Boy, he continued with menace, I'm after wanting to see you, aren't I?

—Who is this? I questioned him in a chirrup of alarm.

—I can hear, you, Monkey. This is your worst nightmare, this is. I'm going to find you. Or have you called – oh, wait a minute – have you called to arrange the hand-over of a certain amount of money, namely the sum of, what was it? Two hundred and twenty seven pounds eighty. I never forget a debt. Is that it, now? Have you called for that. And have you called to tell me of your self-immolation after your horrible work with my fair daughter? Is that it?

—Listen, I said, without knowing why. I really do need a room.

—You need a...I don't believe I'm hearing this. Listen, you little sod, you're going to need a box by the time I've finished with you. A very small box.

It went on in this vein for a while and until I cut him off. So far, so good. I had an address. And now I was standing at the end of Castle Grove Avenue in Meanwood and it had started to drizzle.

—Look, I'd said to Smug for the fourth time that morning, after his late emergence, it's simple.

—It's simple, all right. And so are you if you think I'm going to do any of this.

—Look, I can't do it without you and I really have to have that book.

—Do you now?

—Look, Smug, maybe I'd better give Goldfish a call.

—Goldfish?

—Well, if you're not up to it...

—What do you mean, not up to it?

—Look, I know Wolffie's a scary bastard and all that but...

—Are you saying I'm scared, Monkey, because if you are...

—Not at all, Smug. I understand.

—I'm not scared, all right.

—Right.

—Goldfish would forget what to do.

—He'd be all right. It's simple. And Goldfish is a bit hard. He'd handle it.

There was a pause.

—Monkey, it's a stupid plan and it's not going to work. So don't blame me if it goes wrong or anything.

—Good man.

We went our separate and scheming ways. As I went I versified thus:

So lover you've left me
But I can't let you go
Like something falling to nowhere
Like water running from snow

I want you here before me
I want you with me now
Something can come from nothing
We've just got to work out how

I sweat my love for you baby
You left me nothing but sweat
And the horns of the cuckolded lover
Is as horny now as I get

I know you'll come back baby
I'll have you here again
You're hurting now without me
And you can't stand the pain

I kneel before your picture
As you knelt down to me
Kneel before me baby
So you can set me free

Wolffie's place was a largish, ugly semi with weeds poking through the bars of the gate. Over the hedge I could see the gables and a Sky dish. I pushed the gate open a little, and looked at the brass furniture of the door at the top of the concrete drive. The woodwork had recently been painted black and the light gleamed weakly on its panels. Even from that distance, the knocker was clearly a wolf's head. Very droll.

There were things writhing in the hedges, noises like sparrows with claws. Hedgehogs moving slowly through the crackling leaves, chewing on bacon rind. Behind me I heard a door slam down the street and I turned and saw a fierce little figure speeding up the pavement clutching a rag shopping bag. A rat-faced dog surfed after him on the end of a leash. Two youths came round the corner and went into one of the gardens opposite, picked up a large garden gnome and disappeared into the house laughing. Good morning, Meanwood.

Fifteen minutes earlier I had been waiting on the street corner trying not to catch the eye of any passing motorist and peering round the stonework every few seconds. I'd been there for about ten minutes when Wolffe came out of his house, climbed into his Rover and snorted away into the distance. I waited another five minutes. So far, so good. I just hoped that Smug could manage his end of things. My bedsit was still empty. I knew this because I'd passed it a couple of times on automatic pilot and peered in. I think Wolffe was waiting for me to return. Maybe he thought that I would try to sneak back and get in with my key so I could retrieve my best pair of socks just when he happened to be hoovering up the lucre from the other tenants. Or maybe he'd just not found anyone suitable yet to replace me.

So I'd got Smug to phone him up and ask about the place, to say he'd heard it was vacant and that he was in need of somewhere quickly. He arranged to meet Wolffe there at twelve thirty. His instructions were to keep him there as long as possible and not to hand over any money.

—But Monkey, he'd whined, how long is it going to take him to show me round? It's one room. It's not big. There's hardly anything in it. How could I keep him talking for more than a minute?

—Smug, I'd replied, mate, you're good at talking. Ask him about the rent. Ask him about the facilities. Ask to see the shared bathroom. Ask him about hot water or door frames or having parties in the place or if the bed's upgradeable. I don't know, just keep him talking for as long as you can.

—It's easy for you to say.

—Just do your best.

—You'll owe me big-time for this.

—I owe you big-time already, John.

His part in the plan was the easy one. All he had to do was pretend that he wanted my old flat. My part was more difficult. And as I stood there in front of the house I began to wonder whether the bright child who thought of the plan in the first place was really all that bright. But of course he was. It was all going to work like a dream. Wasn't it? Oh, yes.

I was going to appeal to Mrs Wolffe's better nature. I felt sure that though her husband was made of some inflexible and dog-like substance, his wife was relatively human. Ginny had said she was cool. I was going to throw myself on the mercy of this good woman, sure that she would listen to my sorry tale of the lost book of poetry with compassion. I visualised her kindly face crinkling into a sympathetic smile and then her kindly hands passing me the book as I waited in the hallway looking at the family photos.

Everything was going to be all right. In the light of Mr Wolffe's feeling about me I decided to present myself as just a good friend of Ginny's and if Monkey was mentioned, to feign contempt for the wretched creature who had so treated her daughter. I went up the gravel path. The sun disappeared over the top of the house. I was feeling miserable from the drizzle, which was to my advantage, making me look forlorn and maybe even a little pathetic. There was a thick glaze to the fresh black paint on the door. The knocker wasn't actually a wolf; it was a lion. A pretty ordinary looking lion. It was disappointing but I used it anyway. It was a noisy one. I rapped with it again. The knocking echoed deep in the heart of Wolffe Castle. I waited.

I suppose it took me some time to realise that there was no one in. I was a bit anxious by then as I knew that time was not something I had a lot of. I shifted around on the door step. The youths came out of the house opposite without the gnome. There was a third person with them carrying a fishing rod. Off they went. I waited a bit more and then I went round the back of the house. I tapped on the window of the door at the side on my way but there was no reply. The garden was well kept. There were some flowery type things in rows and a small greenhouse by the bottom fence.

I peered through the French windows. Nothing moved in the house. I looked it over mournfully. I couldn't understand why Mrs Wolffe wasn't in. Maybe it was just me but I couldn't think where else would she be. The plan was unravelling as I stood there. Smug wouldn't go through all this again. Actually, he couldn't do it again, could he. Not without some severe sort of disguise. The tall walls loomed above me. The sun gleamed gloomily over my head. The drizzle was getting under my collar.

Then I saw the open window. It was the top light of the kitchen window, about two foot by three foot and six foot off the ground. It wouldn't be easy but I was desperate. I looked round. This was madness, I thought. Then I imagined Stella's lips making those words again, her eyes, her thighs, her thighs! The hedges flanking the garden were quite high. I couldn't see over to the neighbours' houses so I reasoned they couldn't see me. I had to do it. It took a few goes to get purchase on the slippery woodwork but then I hauled myself quite easily up to the window's level. I pulled myself up to the armpits into the window frame and walked my feet up the stonework round the main window.

Pushing up the window's supporting arm I wriggled and tugged my knee through the gap. I was oblivious now to the noise I was making. I just had to get in. I was lowering my left leg down into the kitchen when I felt something very gently tug at it. I froze. From the angle of my head all I could see was the outside world reflected in the glass. Nothing happened. I lowered my leg away, getting to that point of commitment when I had to go down on the inside. I took a final breath.

Something pulled hard on my trouser leg. I pulled back

instinctively. It pulled. I pulled. Alarm poured through my heart and out through my sweat glands. My hands began to slip on the frame. I twisted my shoulders round violently and managed a glimpse into the kitchen. My breath froze in me.

A huge, grizzled dog with the face of a dinosaur had its teeth in the bottom of my jeans. The second its eyes caught mine it drew back its black lips and snarled unpleasantly. The hackles rose on its neck like harpoons and it rocked its head from side to side and rolled its eyes in their red sockets. I stared at it in horror.

Then it twisted its head and the jaws opened slightly as it tried to get a better grip. I wrenched the leg up and it came free with a jolt. I found myself wedged in the window. I seemed to have grown bigger with fear because I couldn't get out. I was jammed. And the dog, with its jaws free, was now barking crazily and was up on its hind legs snapping at me. Its claws screeched on the glass and the air rang with its barking bellows.

I was the only thing in its world right then. And I had to be bitten. Its head was getting closer each time it lunged. Sooner or later it would get those teeth into me and then the weight of it would drag me down to dinner. What a way to go. Caught like a common thief and chewed to shit by the creature that time forgot. All was lost. I grew dizzy with despair. I thought small. I thought nimble. I thought of many nasty things as well. But I was stuck. I panicked then and flailed round like a fish on a slab.

The dog sat down and watched. It put its head to one side and lolled its dripping tongue. Its eyes mocked my efforts. I took a breath and shifted my weight until I thought I could detect a faint movement in the right direction.

Then the beast went for me again and this time it jumped from a crouch and flung the whole of its massive head, jaws arched, at my thigh. It misjudged the distance by about four inches and instead of getting the teeth into me its nose hit my knee with the force of a train and I was propelled backwards and outwards in a tearing of wood as the window hinges gave way. I was pitched out into the world again.

Landing nimbly would have been a good idea but I was out of good ideas. I hit the ground hard in a shower of splinters. It was wet. I scrambled to my feet as the dog, robbed of its repast, pressed its teeth against the window and drooled, its eyes swirling in their sockets. As whimpers of anger bubbled on its lips I heard at a distance, in another world, a car brake aggressively in the street.

My left leg was numb. It was a wooden leg with iron rivets in and an iron boot on its end but I managed to drag it with me, clinging to the side of the house with trembling fingers. The pulse swelled and sank in my head. But I was out. I blundered as fast as I could through the saturated growths down the house side and out onto the gravel path. A car door slammed.

I leapt down to the gate and burst through like a madman. The woman who was about to come through the gate from the street met me with unfortunate intimacy. I clutched at her drunkenly to stop us both going down. Her shopping bags whirled, her umbrella swirled and her heels clicked crazily over the pavement as we waltzed among the screams leaping from her throat. We spun and clung, my hands in the fur of her coat, her face in the fur of my chest until I managed to balance us shakily and let her go. She looked familiar. And she looked angry. She stared at me in silent horror and I had the feeling that she knew who I was. I turned to run and the force of her shopping bag shot me into the gutter as it hit me in the back. I skidded on the palms of my hands and landed over a storm drain. She was shrieking something like, Get gone! Or was it, Get a gun! and I was off down the street on all fours.

I sat on the bus and nursed my wounds. All I wanted was the book and look at me now. I kept peering out of the window as if I might see Wolffe racing down the dual carriageway waving a great gun at the top deck where he could see my face staring back at him. I would almost have welcomed the annihilation of his twelve bore at that moment as fitting tribute to the greatness of my plan. Smug had been right. And that in itself was quite disturbing. I'd lost everything. It was becoming a familiar story. My whole body hurt and my mind was a black smudge like a dung beetle's mind under a big pile. It had not been a good day.

10

"Our survey, conducted amongst medical students in
Baltimore, revealed that the more hirsute were more likely to be
more intelligent."
(Dr Jimmy 'The Bear' Delgano)

Smug was at his TV when I got back but as soon as he saw me
walk through the door he threw the remote at my head. Missed,
of course, but worrying all the same. It was early evening and the
TV was gibbering with American adolescents with the hots for
each other's partners. Truly a depressing idea.

—What's up with you? I asked of his livid face.

—What's up What's up? You've got a bloody cheek standing
there and asking what's up without a care in the world. You can
be right brass-faced, you can sometimes, Monkey.

—You mean...I began but then decided to leave it... Look,
can't you see that I'm near the door of death himself, Smug.

—You will be if you stand there much longer looking like
you're not sorry or anything.

—What? Just a minute.

I staggered over to the sofa and sat down heavily. My leg was
hurting badly by now and the whack in the back from the
demented Mrs Wolffe had displaced about a dozen vertebrae.
That bag must have been full of tins. God knows what the pair of
them fed on but whatever it was it was heavy with sharp edges.

—That's right, sit down as if you own the place. You're mad,
you are. He picked a cigarette out of the ash tray, knocked off
the inch of ash and drew deeply on its smoky innards. His eyes
were angry with the sheen of hurt about them that reminded me
of the time Junior Planxy had realised I was cheating at

Monopoly. I eased myself backwards hoping that Smug would pick up on the fact that I was well and truly knackered and fit for nothing but a tin of beer and a six month sleep. But he wouldn't have any of it. He rolled his eyes to the ceiling and exhaled in a sort of contemptuous snort.

—Smug, I know you're not happy, but I've had a hell of a morning. I've been savaged by a giant dog-like beast with bloody tent pegs for teeth. I've been attacked by a mad...

—Monkey! Shut up. Just shut up. He turned his face away as he said this last shut up but I'd seen something twitching at his mouth, something very ugly indeed. It was a smirk. The swine was smirking. My various injuries coalesced into one serious attack on my nervous system and joined up with the mental bits of me that could experience pain. I was racked. Knackered and racked.

Smug turned back to me with a grin on his face he seemed to be trying to rub out with the back of a hand. He couldn't look me in the eye but there was a sense of triumph about him and I hated it.

—Got you there, Monkey. I got you for a change, eh. Didn't I? Eh?

—You need trussing up in jellyfish tentacles, you do, you manky bloater.

—Oh, come on, Monkey. Take it like a man.

There was an air of hysteria about the man as if he'd taken part in some daring scheme and survived. Which he probably thought he had.

—Get me a beer, Smug, and stop smirking.

—Sup this, he said, throwing a can at my head, you look as if you need it. Well, let me tell you, Monkey, it went like a dream. Doddle. Really was. I was really nervous after what you told me about Wolffe and that I had to keep him talking and all that. I mean, you know me. Never think of anything to say, hardly. But when I got there and he was there waiting and I saw him I thought I was dead meat. Thought he was bound to have seen us together or something and suss that I was part of a daring plan. But he didn't suss it at all. He was really, whatdoyoucallit? Polite. Like he really cared about letting me have the room, like...

—Like he really cared about your money.

—Whatever...well I had to keep him talking, right. Doddle. Couldn't shut him up, could I. He just went on and on. Couldn't get away. Did in the end, of course, otherwise I wouldn't be here now, would I? And what he said about you...

—He said what?

—He went on about you, Monkey, the former tenant who he had had to chuck out on account of his filthy habits and his never cleaning the bath and stuff like that. And that you owed him money and if ever I saw a low life creeping about the place looking like a man all covered in hair or a primate, whatever that is, he said I was to let him know straight away and he'd be round like a shot and sort him out good and proper. Said you were an ape. Then said, no...no that would be insulting to apes. You were more like a...

—Smug. Shut up.

—OK. But he did say that, Monkey and I mean, be fair, look at yourself. You are a bit on the hairy side.

—All right, don't get carried away. I can't help being very...masculine.

—OK, as you say. So how was your day?

—I got by.

—So the plan worked? You got the book?

—Look, I'm shattered. The plan didn't work. OK, I've got the book but I've also got a busted back, a knackered knee and enough depression to bring gloom to a weatherman. So I'm not exactly over the moon at the moment and would appreciate some bloody sympathy.

—You've got the book. Great. So the plan worked. I knew it

would. Here's to success, he whooped, stabbing his can at the air.

—Smug, the plan didn't work. In fact it nearly killed me. I've been attacked by a dog with the head of a T Rex, assaulted by some sort of ninja shopper from hell and suffered appalling injuries from…

—Yeh, OK. OK. But the book. How did you get it if the plan didn't work? He looked sobered by the fact that the plan hadn't worked. Like being successful was important to him.

—It's too painful for me to even think about at the moment. I'll tell you later. But Smug?

—What?

—Thanks for your help, mate. You did great.

He hid his smile behind his beer can and supped for a while. As he was stubbing out his cigarette he looked as if he was about to say something.

—What?

—What is it then, seriously, Monkey, that makes you so…well, you know, so well-endowed in the hair department?

—Too much testosterone, I said.

—Ah. That's the trouble with them foreign beers, isn't it. You should stick to Tetley's.

Later, what seemed like much later, I lay down in the clutter on the cushions and pulled the sleeping bag over me. What a world we weave, I thought, what a world. I woke up in the night dreaming of fur.

11

"Now, I'd call that poetic justice."
"That's because you're not bleeding."
(K Lowry, *The Gunland Murders*, 1955)

There are some events that deserve a little chapter to themselves. I had the book. But how I came by it cost me dear. It cost me dear because I loved Ginny. No, I really did. Don't let them tell you love's got no place in a postmodern world.

No matter the hook that Stella had in my vitals, I still had memories of being curled up with Ginny under the army blankets with the ice crackling on the windows. That first Christmas when we'd managed to stay the whole time together over the eve and through the day itself, we dawdled in bed making sweet Christmassy love, got up late and gave each other presents. I gave her an omnibus of erotic verse. She gave me a space pen. It had a simple phallic elegance. It wrote in baking heat and freezing cold; it wrote in the vacuum of space and even underwater. Very useful, said Ginny raising her eyes to the skies, when you're writing underwater. On your waterproof paper.

But there're so many crap biros out there that look like they've been designed by delinquents with some strange other purpose in mind than writing that fudge and burr and fight your forcing them across the page, that run out before they're run in and end up left on the floor in betting shops or down the crack of sofas or being chewed ragged by rat-faced gorms on the back row of despotic classrooms. Bin the lot of them, I say, and buy a space pen. Get some style.

It was the idea of writing reminded me of that. It was a pretty good Christmas. For dinner we took some chicken pieces up into

Hyde Park and sat on a bench and ate them and looked out over the frozen pond and shivered in our coats and ate with freezing fingers and shared a bottle of Coke, passing it between us and drinking through the ice in the bottle's neck. I'd written this poem for her. Not my usual thing. I was more the street poet, the voice of the city and all that. But this was a sharp little love sonnet. The sonnet of the century.

We sat there on the bench. I fingered the poem in my pocket and wavered. Women can be odd about things like this, I thought. I went over it line by line in my head and I was impressed. But would Ginny be impressed?

She asked me what I was thinking about and I told her I was thinking about nothing. Same as usual, she answered. I nodded wisely.

—What are you playing with in your pocket? she asked, nodding at my trousers. I let go of the poem. Maybe some other time. Then we were ambushed by a regiment of Canada Geese hyped up on pond weed and the ale clouds from the brewery so we went home and made love in front of the gas fire until we were hot as dogs and afterwards we killed some serious wine.

The snow came down, padding lazily over the road and the cars and patiently balancing flake by flake on the branches of the trees till the weight of it hung them down, surrendered. I gave her the poem.

We got to bed and did the monkey dance of love some more with such frictive energy it melted the ice off the window. We woke the next morning with our hair woven together and the snow still there and everything still.

—I'll never let anyone else write me poetry, she said. Anyone else writes me poetry, they're dead in the water.

Danby Houghton? I didn't envy him his wealth. Or his car. But his girl? Poor old Monkey. Poor Monkey had the book but it had been like getting a stake through the heart.

After the Wolffe attack, I'd got off the bus in Headingley and gone for some KFC bits and bobs and sat eating them in pain staring grimly out of the window. When I'd finished the bucket I went to The Skyrack. The memory of the dog was still strong, I could still smell the Kennomeat in its teeth and feel the heat of its breath up my trouser leg. I had a pint which helped to soothe my shattered spirit but I couldn't come up with a further plan that would win me the book.

I was limping out when I noticed Danby Houghton sitting at a table. There was a whisky glass and a wine glass in front of him. For a brief spell of delight I hoped that he was with another woman so I lingered by the door. Then she came back to him. She was wearing a dress, for pity's sake, and was disturbingly beautiful.

She slid into the seat beside the dummy one and slipped an arm through his. She started to fiddle with some feminine plastic device. Don't get excited or alarmed, I thought, looking closer, it's only a pink Blackberry. If that's not a design oxymoron. Bet the Danby creature bought her that. And I bet she hates it. Coldly I went over. He looked at me down the twin barrels of his nose. She didn't look surprised to see me.

—Well, Monkey, you don't look well, you know, she said, stroking the flanks of her phone.

I fumed, internally.

—I just wanted to say thank you. Thank you very much. I have today been savaged by a brute dog and battered by your mother and I just wanted to let you know that I'm really happy that someone who could plummet me into such a situation has ended up with Mr Sheen here. I'm sure you'll make each other blissfully miserable.

—Oh, Monkey, you didn't go to father's house, did you? You didn't. You did. You did, didn't you? She trilled with delighted amazement.

—I went and I was lucky to return.

—Didn't Bobo like you?

—If you mean the beast your father passes off for a dog, then yes, he loved me. Couldn't wait to get his teeth into me. Broke my knee with his bloody head.

—Poor Bobo…he's so sweet, really.

—Poor…How can you call a predator like that 'Bobo', for god's sake? He's not sweet, he's a killer. You should have him put down. With an elephant gun.

—Don't say such horrible things about Bobo. You must have startled him, Monkey. Did you startle mother, too? She's got a serious left hook, you know.

—She'd done some serious shopping, I can tell you. Do you eat a lot of tinned food? And I didn't even get the book.

—Of course you didn't.

—What?

—It's here, isn't it. You might as well have it now. She smiled sweetly at me and picked up her hand bag from the floor and took out the book. She told me how sweet it had been to punish me for my inadequacy. She'd sent me into the wolf's den for my sins. A wild goose chase. And I'd fallen for it. She'd wanted to see how far I'd go for Stella, and now she knew. And now I had the book she considered that all traces of our embarrassing relationship were now absolutely at an end for ever and she hoped that if ever I saw her again I would have the common decency to pretend that I didn't know her.

How could she have done that to me? Someone she loved? OK, had loved. How could I love her after that? I don't know how I managed it but I did. Sometimes us men have just got to be strong. Though a stake through the heart can often hurt.

12

"In many factories, community singing was not unheard of."
(Len Talbot and Dennis Weaver, *Factory Life in the North of England*, 1907)

Hello blue and hello sky
I got the girl and the girl got I
Down was down
But up is high
My baby

Hello sky and hello blue
I got the girl and the girl is you
I was young
But my love grew
Oh, baby

Tell me what you're going to do to me
How you're going to be so true to me
You're my world
And you're my sky
Turn on me your bluesky eyes

Hello blue and hello sky
Love for you will never die
It was raining
Now it's fine
My lover

Hello blue and hello sky
I got the girl and the girl got I
Down was down
But up is high
My baby

Tell me how you're going to set me free
Baby I am down here on my knees
You're my world
And you're my sky
Turn on me your bluesky eyes

Hello sky and hello blue I got the girl and the girl is you! That wretched song was spinning in my head like a ghost on a roundabout. I was paralysed with inactivity for a while. Just me and that song going on and on in my imitation Toby Joby voice, a sort of nasal whine with echo. And wow-wow. If I thought that having the book was going to solve the puzzle of existence, give me the answers I wanted, get me the girl, the fame and the fortune I felt I could do with, then I was much mistaken. I waited for Stella to appear and take the book from me with a touching display of gratitude involving a lot of...well...touching but it seemed that such was the stuff of dreams.

Nothing happened. No one came to see me. It was awful. I spent a long time looking at the book. I spent a long time fiddling with the lock, exploring the tiny cavern of its chamber with cocktail sticks, the tip of blades, a letter opener. Nothing worked. The book was a challenge I couldn't meet. I kept it in a drawer and looked at it from time to time. I thought of flogging it to a second-hand dealer but something held me back. Once I got as far as the counter of Ringworth's Purveyors of Quality Secondhands – *read and return our speciality* - but when I brushed up against the dusty lumberjack shirt of a tattooed heavy who was offloading a pile of vintage porn – collectible, no doubt, but wholly unwantable – into the quaking talons of Ringworth whose ravaged moustache was bent into a grimace of lugubrious delight, I turned tail.

By squeezing the leather covers as much into a tube as I could – admittedly not much of tube – and pressing the pages against the back cover, I'd managed to get a sliver of sight into the thing. But it was useless. All I could see were white pages covered in very oblique handwritten script. I couldn't make out any words that made sense. There were the edges of some crap sketches of figures or something.

It didn't even look to be an old book, more like someone's notebook that he'd taken on holiday and filled with the bits and bobs of whimsy that he'd found in his head while staring vacantly at a watery horizon. I knew I could break it open but I was still thinking of its potential. A broken book's got to lose some of its value.

Time passed. I got a job in a little factory packing display stands. They'd had a big order for the things and were stamping them out like biscuits. The job centre thought I'd be ideal, which worried me. I mean, what was it about me that gave them that idea. Not just suitable but ideal. I spent sleepless minutes worrying about that phrase. Is that what I'd become? An ideal packer of display stands? Anyway, back on the social ladder I got a little bedsit and life trundled along merrily. The bedsit was quite large for what it was, a downstairs room with a sink under the window and a bed in the far corner behind the door. There was a big rug that served as a carpet and a gas oven and table-top fridge. I made a bookshelf for the few books I had by stacking half a dozen paperbacks at each end of a plank. The bed was a pine-framed thing with a tired mattress. I got some new sheets and a quilt cover to cover the sins of my quilt. The window faced east and the sun would wake me at the weekend.

I used to meet Smug in the pub now and then and we'd have a laugh over the Wolffe business.

I'd to turn up to work at seven in the morning which is not really a human time to do anything except sleep. The nights were drawing in and the mornings were dark. The factory was a squat little concrete and corrugated iron affair built as a place of barbarous labour. It was pockmarked with amusing graffiti. The windows were covered with wire and the paint lolled off the frames. I had to walk the last half mile through the estate to get there. The houses looked much like the factory. There was always the smell of vinegar and blistered cooking fat in the air no matter which way the wind blew.

By the time I got in, Grafti would have the hot air blowers on and the frost would be melting from the stacks of sheet metal and the iron of the presses. The factory was small and cluttered. Round the walls were ranged the massive apparatus they used for shaping the steel sheets into component parts. At the back was the welding room where Bastard Two and his crew of torchmen sizzled and cracked over their joints all day. The whole place was filthy with sweat and oil and the smell in the air was always of burnt metal and the degraded odour of heavy work.

Grafti probably lived in the place. I never saw him leave. He was a short, squalid little man with a face like an earthworm. He chain-smoked double Rizlas thinly packed with the turnouts of ashtrays, broken-up butts and, when there was nothing else, Serious Service rolling stock. His grey mouth sometimes formed the shapes of words but I never got to understand them. I think there was only Bastard One who understood anything he said. He'd translate now and then into his flat earth Yorkshire speech. And then you'd wonder why he bothered.

Grafti used to scurry around the place, creeping over the concrete floor in his rubber shoes, sweeping, carrying off-cuts or bundles of rubbish, muttering to himself and spitting out smoke.

He wore a faded rope-knit jumper and oily corduroys tucked into battered cowboy boots.

There were a number of jobs I had to do. Gordon Bennett was the foreman and he'd give me my task for the day when I arrived and clocked in. Mostly I had to pack display stands. This meant rolling the component struts in cardboard and taping them up and then fitting them into their boxes. Then I'd stack the boxes against the wall and maybe Grafti or Bastard One would carry them down to the loading bay.

I hated it all but it was work and work meant money and money meant things like food and a hovel to hang one's head in. I got to saw off the screws sometimes, which was worse. The struts of the stands were box sections of steel and were held together with plastic screws. But they'd ordered the wrong size of screw. There were boxes of them. Big boxes. So the screws had to be cut down to size which meant you had to put them one at a time into a vice and go at them with a hacksaw. I hated all that. Fiddly sawing away like that. They were tough screws and only about two inches long. They never stuck in the vice for long without starting to slip and then you had to hold them with your fingertips as well because if you just tightened the vice it squashed them. And you couldn't have display stands with squashed up screws could you? Actually, you could. Loads of mine got squashed. Well, it was either that or slice your fingers to bits.

The days were long, the hours were long, the minutes were stretches of time you could disappear into. Verse swirled round my head like water down a plughole.

The clock's face is sick with time.
Grafti spills out smoke,
And sweats invective,
Padding round in his rubber shoes

With armfuls of scrap,
Talking to girders
In a language without vowels.

The radio doesn't stop.
The presses bend their sheets,
Shape us, too.
We're all screwed here
In this house of swarf.
Each of us
A punch-drunk time card.

We did ten hour shifts Monday to Thursday and then eight hours on Friday at time and a half. That way they reckoned to earn enough to fund the drinking and the dogs. Fair enough. In idle moments I used to saw the screws into little sculptures. Mostly the faces of people in the factory. Grafti was easy. Bastard One was hard. He had a long nose like the knocked-off corner of a flagstone and eyes about the size of match heads. He always wore a dusty woollen hat pulled down to his eyebrows. There was too much little detail in his face. I tried to do Gordy Bennett but I opened his mouth up too far with the saw and his head fell off his jaw.

After a few weeks of all this I was going mad. Everywhere I looked there was swarf and oil and cheap pornography. Amongst the hissing and the clashing and the metal thumping of the presses and the clang and scrape of moving metal and the hyena laughs of the cutters and the groans of tortured sheet, Teddy Wobegan's voice blared down at us from industrial-sized loud speakers like Big Brother's crazy brother. And the syrup of his lilt was rotting the sense out of my brain.

I decided to leave but there was nowhere to go. I daren't go back to the job centre in case they found I was the ideal candidate for the position of stoat groomer or pigeon fancier or they found out that my profile exactly matched the work of cat spaying or egg sizing. I couldn't bear it.

I used to sit for hours in the pub almost too weak to lift the glass to my mouth. Saved a fortune but it was doing my head in. Doing it in very cruel ways. I used to dream about plastic screws, armies of them out for me, or Gordy Bennett building a huge skeletal structure out of display stands and me being locked up in it like in the Wicker Man. And they were all dancing round. And once I dreamed that Bastard One put swarf in my sandwich and then laughed. No, just a minute, that really happened. It took my gums apart like a cheese grater.

Then they took on another lad to help with the packing. They called him Tim Summer. He was a skinny twenty-odd year old with untidy hair and a brown jumper. He said he was only doing the job to fill in time before he took up a career in publishing. A likely story, I thought, though there was a certain brightness in his eyes that might lead one to believe that he had not been described by the job centre as ideal for the work and that one day soon he might disappear into a more worthy pursuit. He smiled a lot in a sort of grinning way.

He set off working at a rate of knots at the packing. Fair dancing round with the work. He worked out this ultra-efficient system that no one else had bothered to think of and really went for it. He allotted locations for each component so that when the screws had been put in part three, or parts one and two had been fixed together, each piece, assembled or unassembled, was to be put in a particular place next to his work bench. All he had to do was pick them up in a specific order, making them all slot together neatly, slide them into the box and secure it with sellotape from the dispenser which he had moved to a place within reach.

He worked like a well-oiled machine which was somewhat faster and more efficient than some of the other machines who were often well oiled.

The two Bastards and Gordy along with a rag tag of other labourers used to tank over to The Swan with Two Necks for lunch. There they'd sprawl, wiping their stained fingers on the seats, and swill John Smith's by the bucketful, swapping dirty jokes and pigeon updates or betting tips and new recipes for corned beef while Gordy would stand at the bar with an expression of aloof disdain and read the Sun over a tuna sandwich and a glass of sweet Martini.

I used to sit in the canteen with the remnants of the work force. They'd give you a free mug of tea, even with real milk on some days.

So there I was one day, tucking into the bacon sandwich I'd picked up from the corner shop when Tim came over and sat down on the other side of the bench. The sandwich was slightly warm and smelled of grease. Just what you need on a cold day. He pulled out his lunch – a pork pie and an apple – and started munching away. I nodded to him and he nodded back. We'd not really spoken or anything up to then apart from the odd comment about the weather. And Teddy Wobegon.

Then he pulled out from an indoor pocket one of those miniature chess sets. It was about four inches square, a board in a little cardboard box and the pieces were red and white and fit with tiny pegs into holes in the squares. The box was scuffed and the colour had worn off the corners which had been reinforced with sellotape. He sipped at his white mug of tea and lowered his head over the board.

He sat like that for a long time. The pieces on the board were in the middle of a game. I swallowed some of my sandwich, sipped my tea and tried to work out what was happening between the red and the white. Tim chewed slowly on his pie and dribbled crust over the bench and into his tea. After about five minutes he made a move thus: Nd2. Then he went at his thoughts again. I couldn't stand it. The six benches in the canteen were half full of men in check shirts munching stolidly on sandwiches of various species and occasionally mumbling short words to each other. Feet scraped across the concrete floor and big mugs clashed against teeth. And here he was, oblivious to it all with his head stuck in the game of kings.

—Who's winning? I asked suddenly.

—What?

—I said, who's winning, then?

—Oh.... He looked up at me and grinned one of those smiles of his and shook his head vaguely.

—I am, I suppose.

—Are you Red or White?

—Well, both, I suppose.

—Ah. So who exactly is winning, Red or White?

—Well, Red has a better position but White has more material.

—I see...

—Do you play?

—I've played. I mean I know how to move the pieces and that. But I wouldn't say I was an expert or anything.

—Would you like to play? You could take up White if you like. See how it goes.

—I think I'll just watch, if you don't mind. I don't want to get in the way of you beating yourself, if you see what I mean.

—We could maybe start a new game tomorrow lunchtime?

—Sure.

He went back to the thinking again with his head bowed and the tails of his hair drooping dangerously close to his tea. So next day we played chess. It took him about five minutes to humiliate me but I resolved that being beaten at chess passed the time in a more agreeable way than sitting eating your lunch watching other people at food.

And I didn't think I'd done that badly seeing that I'd never played since I was a kid. I decided to learn from Tim and improve my game.

Spring came on as usual and warmed things up a bit. The order for the display stands was complete and I'd been put to the task of fetching and carrying with Bastard One. He talked less than Tim and was always looking for ways to dodge work. Sometimes he'd just disappear. I could be walking along with him, one of us at each end of a sheet of steel and he'd turn a corner and by the time I got round there'd just be his end on the floor. What can you do? I'd leave it and find something else to do and then he'd find me later and say —Are you going to shift this steel, or what? When I saw Tim sweeping up I got the impression that his days at the factory were numbered. Then Gordy came up to one day. I was untangling a pile of ribbon steel before I took some plate down to the welding room. He told me that he was going to put me on Press Four for the day. This was one of the smaller machines, used for making small bent pieces of metal. I had to stand round for about four hours while he set it up from the blueprint using steel rule and callipers, umming and erring and peering from the abstract to the machine with fastidious care.

When it was set he showed me what to do. I had to take cut shapes of sheeting from a pile to be delivered by Bastard One and insert them into the press the right way round, lower the guard, press the button, wait for the machine to do its thing, lift up the guard, take out the folded sheet, turn it the right way round, put it back in and press it as before.

Each sheet need four folds. By the time they were finished they looked like open tapered boxes. I've no idea what they were for.

Still, it passed the time. I'd no more pressing business. So the templates were stacked and I bent them into shape and they were taken away. A bit like life, really, I thought, into the fifth numb hour. There was purpose in the narrow task I was performing, I was changing things, making them different according to pre-specified instructions handed down to me by the great Gordy Bennett.

There was routine and repetition. I could take an interest in what I was doing, the way the metal slotted exactly into its place, the manner of the guard, the precision of the descending pressing edge, the beauty of the changed shape of the sheet. Or I could be bored. But where the templates came from and where the shaped sheet ended up and what the ultimate purpose of the operation was remained a mystery it was not my place to know or to seek to know. The hours passed.

I was at it one day when there was suddenly a great smash of sound and a whoop that sank into a snarl. I looked over to where the noise came from and saw Bastard One and Grafti having a go at each other with steel poles. Sparks littered their heads as they clashed the long steel together, whirling and wielding and slashing.

They advanced and retreated over a bed of silver swarf, their oversized boots scraping up sounds like ruptured pigs or calves with their heads in buckets. Tom was sweeping up quite close but as the blows got more violent he moved off with his brush and took up in the far corner round Press One.

Gordy must have been off in the welding shop or somewhere otherwise he'd have stopped it. Some of the others were gathering round now, Bastard Two had appeared from behind one of the lathes and was wiping his knuckles over his blackened forehead and grinning with his broken teeth.

They were shouting at them as the poles dipped and swung and the snap of steel on steel echoed amongst the big machines. I turned back to my work but a loud crack of steel on concrete brought me back in time to see the sparks chipped from the floor dancing around their feet.

People were moving across my field of vision. Eric the Elk came and stood right between me and the dynamic duo, his matted hair rising into the air and his sloping shoulders rolling with an eagerness to join in. Lured by the curiosity that violence brings to us all, I found myself sidling away from my press and over to where I could see the action. It was the first time I'd seen Grafti without a cigarette in his mouth. His earthworm face was pinched into a snarl and gouts of smoky breath were phutting from his lungs. Bastard One had lost his woolly hat and his greasy hair shone in the downlight like something living. He was taller than Grafti and had a longer reach but he was slower, like his brain was operating some robotic machine and there was a time delay between his thought and its execution. I pushed through a gap close to the fight as Bastard One swung down his rod at Grafti's head.

It was a powerful stroke but Grafti was up to it, blocking it with his own pole like a cross bar. There was a sickening clang, dust jumped off Grafti's sleeves and I heard the teeth snap in his jaw.

It suddenly dawned on me that they were serious, that this was not a play fight whilst Gordy was out of sight. Something was working itself out here. Grafti slid both hands to one end of the rod and swung it low, catching Bastard One on the top of his boot.

He went down and Grafti was over the top of him faster than a mongoose and pointing the rod at his head like he was going to spear him with it. For a moment I thought that was it, murder would be done, but just before the blow came Bastard One rolled heavily to one side and swept round the rod he was still holding in his right hand and the end of it whistled through the air and sliced across Grafti's jumper, scoring its way over his stomach.

This distracted him for long enough to let Bastard One twist away and scramble to his feet. He lurched against the crowd and someone pushed him back towards Grafti who, realising his moment had passed, was hissing and jabbing the air in front of him like a maniac spearman. Bastard One swung again at the point of his opponent's rod and caught it hard on and it seemed as if the two rods were welded together with the two men struggling at each end to separate a single piece of metal. They circled each other jerkily. Grafti's face was writhing and pulsing like a concertina and Bastard One's great triangle of a nose was dripping an obscene lather into the swirling dust.

Their boots scraped and groped for purchase on the concrete. Still they circled as the crowd jeered and waved encouraging gestures at them. It was difficult to tell who they wanted to win. It was like Godzingo versus the Worm Man. I noticed that their knuckles were bloody and there was a white piece of skin hanging from Grafti's right hand where he'd been smacked.

There was a sudden zing of metal on metal and Bastard One twisted round his rod and flung Grafti away in an arc. The point of his rod caught him on the ear as he went. The crowd parted sharpish as he shot through and landed against Lathe Two where he stood for a moment heaving on his breath and leaning on the rod. Blood welled down over his collar from the burst ear. He looked over to where Bastard One leaned on his rod, hatred bubbled in his eyes. He dabbed at his ear with the cuff of his jersey. The fight had gone out of him. The fight had gone out of both of them.

The crowd drifted away back to their work. There was a clang of dropped rods and Gordy appeared from the toilet block with the Sun under his arm. I was standing next to Bonzo who was ferreting in the corner of an eye with a loop of wire. He was supposed to have this glass eye only I could never tell whether he had or not. They used to say that he'd swap round the real eye and the glass one at times just to fool you.

—What was all that about, then? I asked, moving with him back towards the lathes.

134

—Must have nicked t'other's fags, he said. Or maybe he's went with his wife again, he added, and shuddered. I shuddered, too. He caught my eye with one of his and nodded conspiratorially. Better hope it was the fags, y'know, he said, or there'll be more pole dancing between them two. Women, he added, and spat on the floor and shuffled off into the lair of his work.

Next day, over the chess board, Tim told me he was leaving. I was disappointed. No more chess. I'd have to sit and stare at the gross mastication of bristling faces I'd been able to ignore over the last weeks. After the business the day before there was a subdued atmosphere in the canteen. Men bit dully into their sandwiches with the same mouths that had shrieked with excitement at the fight. Violence is the spice of life, I thought, so long as you're not tasting it. I asked Tim what he thought about it.

—Just a fight, I suppose.
—Bit nasty, though.
—What do you expect, he answered, staring at the board before making a vicious move: Bn5, pinning my Knight against my Queen and threatening Re3…Rg3 followed by the advance of his h pawn and his Queen landing on h7. I was learning fast but I was still losing.
—What do you mean, what do I expect?
—They're just not in touch with their profitable minds, Monkey, are they? He said sarcastically.
—Oh, right.
—Your move.
—Right. I pulled up the smooth little knight and repositioned it on d4. I was going to carve a chess set once, I said.
—Yeah?
—Yeah. Out of wood. Couldn't get the hang of it though.
—So what happened?

—Well, basically I was crap at carving. Doing them like these – I nodded at the tiny set between us – would have been all right. These look dead easy. I started with a proper set, though, and they were dead hard.

—A proper set?

—You know, like chess sets look normally.

—Staunton pattern?

—I don't know, you tell me. Is that like normal chess pieces?

—They're the most common. Used in all the tournaments and that.

—Must be them, then.

—There's some really weird ones out there, you know. Greeks and Romans, Alice in Wonderland, Lord of the Blings, Star Trek...

—You're kidding. Star Trek?

—Yeah. You can get a 3D set as well.

—3D?

—Murder to play. But that's what it's all about, isn't it, war. Beating your opponent. It's a war game. But all these novelty sets, they're too literal. They're OK for Christmas but you can't really play with them.

—And a chess set's not just for Christmas...

—Absolutely. A chess set's for life. And the Staunton set's the best there is. You get a good Staunton and you can't go wrong.

—Odd though, if you think about it. I get the knight and the castle...

—Rook, we call them rooks.

—Whatever...and the king's crown and all that. But the pawns are sort of featureless and why have the bishops got like big mouths? I mean, why did he design them like that?

—It's the bishop's mitre. You know, his hat. It's not his mouth. And anyway, Staunton didn't design them.

—But you said he did.

—No, Monkey. They're called Staunton pattern because

they're named after Howard Staunton. But they were designed by a guy called…what's his name?

—I don't know, do I.

—Cooke. Nathaniel Cooke. That's it.

—So who was he, then? Staunton.

—Clever bloke. Sort of Victorian England's unofficial world champion. Beat some French guy. You won't guess what he turned to when he got slow at chess.

—I don't know.

—Shakespeare. He took up studying Shakespeare.

—What, voluntarily?

—I presume so.

—'To play or not to play, that is the question'.

—Something like that.

—Think I'll stick to chess for the moment.

—Sure. You're not doing badly.

—For a beginner.

—For beginner.

He moved his bishop to e7 and it stood there laughing at me with its big mouth. I played my move: h6, which I thought was a pretty neat defence but it only saved me for another eight moves.

—What about Isle of thingy, then?

—Lewis? Isle of Lewis is all right. Historical, you see. Historical's OK, I think. Just about.

—Right.

—Long as they're not made out of resin.

His Queen broke through supported by a Knight and the laughing Bishop and when I saw Mate was inevitable, I gave up.

About an hour before the end of the day's work I thought that I hadn't asked Tim where he was going to. When the hands of the clock had crawled reluctantly round to six o-clock I looked out for him. For the last twenty minutes or so of the day the energy sank out of the factory and the workers slowed down to a dragging pace and the talk perked up beyond a grunt to exchanged monosyllables and figures slouched against the machines or leant on pieces of stacked metal or against the crumbling walls.

The clock, a large white-faced piece, suspended above the factory workings on the top wall near the stairs to the manager's office, was gauzed in a fine steel dust and in the sloping rays of the afternoon sun it sparkled like a jewel. Now, it pointed to both its zenith and nadir. Time. People went over and stamped themselves out, keen to get their cards punched before 6.01pm showed on the face not wanting to be seen to have worked a minute more than they were obliged to work. I caught up with Tim as he stepped out of the door.

—Where're you going, mate?

—Why? he asked, turning round to and fastening the zip on his jacket up to his chin, you fancy a pint or something?

I said OK and we soon found ourselves cooped up in the lounge of the The Swan with Two Necks. The bar man slid two pints over without a word and we sat down at a sticky little table near the far wall. The room was about as big as someone's sitting room and decorated with horse brasses and a faded print of some Victorian racer haring down the track with the tiny yellowing jockey suspended in mid-air and hanging on to the reins like a wild-eyed puppet dragged towards some frantic fate. Apart from us the room was empty. Tim started to reach into his inner pocket for the chess board but I stopped him.

—So, have you got another job, then? I asked. I was interested in this but there was something else in my mind at that moment, something he had said earlier. His eyes were laughing and he sipped at his pint and then set it down.

—I'll find something. It's not a problem.

—So they just sacked you then? A bit rough.

—I was only temporary. I knew I had to go some time. Now

is as good as any.

—Still a bit rough, though.

—Don't worry about it. It wasn't exactly my idea of the perfect career.

I took a drag of the beer. We sat in silence for a minute or two. I had to ask him now, I thought. It was beginning to go round and round my head and roundabouts always made me sick when I was a kid.

—So, are you really going into publishing, then?

—I thought I was going to for a while. But I'm not sure now.

—What else, then?

—Something will turn up.

—You know when Bastard One and Grafti were at it the other day with those poles?

—Yes.

—Did you say something then about their profitable minds or something? I asked him.

—I don't think so.

—You did, I'm sure you did.

—No. About their what? He looked puzzled.

—Profitable minds. Their profitable minds.

—Oh, right.

—You did?

—No. I'm sure I didn't.

He seemed adamant. I hadn't expected him to say that he hadn't said it. I didn't know what to say next so I had another mouthful of the tepid John Smiths. Tim had a drink as well and he took the level down to that place that would enable him to finish the drink in a single gulp and leave at a moment's notice. I was sure he was evading me.

—Have you ever heard of The Doorway Foundation? I asked, putting down my glass.

—The Doorway Foundation? He repeated cautiously, narrowing his eyes.

—Yeh. The Doorway Foundation.

He thought for a while, swirling the dregs round in his glass. I said I'd get another and went to the bar. Whilst I was there a couple of strangers came in and leant on the bar, scraping the mud off their boots on the brass foot rail. I took back the drinks and he looked at me, finished off the first, picked up the second pint and drew deeply on its foam. Then he took in a great swirl of breath and told me about The Doorway Foundation.

I couldn't help laughing.

13

"Everywhere is hunger, even Orion's tightening his belt."
(Jim Walder, *Lightfall, Nightfall*, 1978)

On my way back to bedsit land I weaved round a bit and ended up in the back room of The Skyrack. Tim had long since shuffled off to wherever and the long dark and lonely road had brought me to a squat, dim and noisy room. I'd only had about two and a half pints but I'm not a big drinker and the stuff tends to go straight to my head. I wanted a final drink of the night before I curled up in the horse blankets on the stripy mattress and sought the elusive lady sleep.

Smoke hung in the room. It was like a Victorian séance with great tendrils of ectoplasm shifting about like there was no tomorrow, lurking in the gleam of the pool table lights and drifting with sinister intent over the baize. Various voices called out in greeting and I recognised some of the few faces and called a general reply which came out a bit slurred. The smoke ran into my eyes and nose and I clawed its dry fingers away from my face.

Smallwit was there with his hand in a family-size bag of crisps, ferreting around for the crumbs, and Benny Bingo and Goldfish. They were in the middle of a game of pool. I'd beaten Benny a couple of times in the past but more by good luck, more by the run of the balls than skill. He was laid over the table now, his leather jacketed forearm adjusting to the line of his shot, the steady bridge shining with silver rings. I'd noticed his Harley outside. I picked up a pint and turned, leaning on the bar to watch the game. Benny put the twelve ball in the top corner pocket and the cue ball screwed obediently back towards him and rested for an easy shot on the next stripe into the middle right. He chalked his cue absently. Smallwit nodded approval and wiped his fingers with his flaky lips. Goldfish propped his cue on the edge of the bar and turned to drink.

Benny took out a steel comb and swept it through his blond hair with a calculated indifference, pocketed the comb and then the nine ball. The white ran on through the shot, came off the rail and headed at speed towards the left middle bag. Goldfish fumbled for his cue and took a step towards the table; Smallwit stopped rummaging in his crisp bag. I wasn't impressed. This was just Benny showing off.

I watched the white nick the edge of the pocket and use this to propel itself across the table, coming off the opposite rail just far enough to leave him the perfect angle on the thirteen into the bottom right hand corner. Pocketing this, the white squeezed through the clutter of the unpotted spots and nudged the black over the top left corner. An easy finish. Goldfish put down his cue on the table and went for his drink.

—How much, I asked him. He grinned sheepishly into his glass.

—Only two quid, Monkey, honest. Two quid, that's all.

—You never learn.

—I never learn, he repeated. It was just a bad habit with him, betting on certain losers. Benny rolled the remaining six balls and the white into a pocket and picked up the coins from the edge of the table.

—Yo, Monkey, he greeted me, casting the money into his jeans' pocket. How's the ladies, then? Any action on the horizon, so to speak?

—Not a kind question at the moment, Benny. If I were to say to you there were no ships on the sea, no sails teasing the horizon, nothing, no action at all, of any kind, would that communicate to you the depths to which the hope in my life has sunk?

—Nah, wake up, Monkey, he said.

142

—What?

—Sharpen up, ale-brain. The ladies, mate, they're out there. Just got to learn to find them, haven't you? Know what I mean? You've got to see them. They're there all right but you've got your head full of what's her name, haven't you? Old Wolffe's lass. Nice looker and all that but I hear she's left you. You leave her poor memory alone, mate and get looking out there.

—Look, *I* left *her*.

I had a quick look over my shoulder to the door at the mention of Wolffe. Shadows were passing out in the corridors like trolls on the late shift and I heard the crunch of glass under hard-shod boots. But no Wolffe.

—Yeh, I believe you, Monkey. As if. I heard she'd gone with some prat in a car. Money and all that. Let her go. If that's what she wants, let her have it. Get yourself out there, mate, you can't compete with money and that, find someone who's into... someone who's into *fur*.

—Thanks. Mate.

—Come on, Monkey, you know what I mean. Get yourself shorn, then. I mean, have you got a face under all that, or what?

—Look, this beard's distinguished.

—Amongst the ape-people, you mean, added Goldfish, going at his cheeks with beard-stroking gestures.

—Thanks a lot.

—Come on, laughed Benny, let yourself go. Here, I'll get you a pint. The Taylors is on form.

He dragged me into a game of pool, though not for money, and I was thinking as I potted the odd ball that I should get out there and find someone. But I was also thinking of what I now knew about The Doorway Foundation and thinking of seeing Stella again. I was sure I was going to see her again with what I knew now. In my distracted state I did well to get a couple of balls potted before Benny was on the black. But I'd snookered him tight behind the three ball.

The black was hanging over the left middle but I thought I was all right. Benny took a long look at it whilst he chalked up. He tweaked a sideburn and gave a little smirk. I looked at the white. It was tight up, tighter than Wolffie's coffers. If he potted it, that smirk told me he meant to do it the way it happened and if he missed it told me the shot had been impossible. Win, win. He got down to it. I blinked at the wrong moment, a weary, beery blink and my eyes just caught the white as it banked off the rail and clipped the black into the pocket.

—Nice one, he said and winked.

Goldfish sidled over to the table.

—Orion's belt, he said, looking at the remaining balls on the table.

—Eh?

—It's Orion's Belt, those balls there, they're like Orion's Belt.

—Oh. Right, said Benny and nodded at us. He went and sat by the solitary helmet propped on the bar. Wanda wasn't with him. She was working late tonight at the hospital, being a nurse. He's right, y'know. Voice of authority here. 'Nother pint, anyone?

He wanted another game but I declined, saying that I'd only humiliate him in front of his admirers. So he unscrewed his four-piece cue, put it in its box and stowed the box in his backpack. We bought more drinks and Goldfish bought Smallwit a packet of crisps and we sat down in the corner of the bar under the exploded bristles of the dart board and chewed over the bits of our lives we could bear to make public.

Smallwit worked in retail. Selling things, mostly. Sometimes just hanging around looking like he should be selling things. He was addicted to cheese and onion crisps and said he only drank lager to wash the detritus from his teeth. Getting smashed, he said, was an acceptable side effect of crisp-eating. He knew more jokes about pieces of string and talking horses than anyone I'd

144

ever met. More's the pity. Goldfish was quiet. His little mouth rounded on his glass every now and then, making sipping noises. He was a thin tough kid. We all called him Goldfish. I don't even know what his real name was. I don't know how he got to be called Goldfish. I asked him once but he said he couldn't remember. Smallwit had laughed at this but I thought it was pretty sad. But there you go again, jokes and all that.

He'd had a rough old childhood, I knew that. Brought up on Maltings Road in Hunslet where the air was sweet with the stink from Tetley's brewery and thick with the floating swarf from the machining factory. He'd been in a family of eight till his mother ran off with the insurance guy who might have been a bit decrepit but at least had a suit. The rest of them, from what Goldfish told us, used to survive on pinching from the local shops and eating baked bean sandwiches and digestive biscuits.

I went out into the main bar and went to the toilet and came back and had another pint. I propped my elbow on the bar and looked out over the room. The décor was faded and maroon stripes of wallpaper peeled in corners and washed-out prints were dotted around. The curtains were all big swagging drapes crookedly frozen round the window frames, their pachydermic folds like bowlfuls of dust.

Through the grainy grimness I noticed a familiar figure over in a far corner of the room. He looked more thinly-drawn than ever. Big shadows sloped under his eyes, his hair sprawled in spindly threads over his ears and the tweed suit, even from this distance, looked gravy-stained and world-weary. He was reading a paperback and beside him on the seat was the nasty briefcase like some sick side-dog or morbid trophy. Around him were vacant seats though the bar was quite full. A pall of intellectual gloom hung over him.

Sad old git, I thought, can't be much fun sitting around all day reading books, wandering around in the park with a satchel of smuggled whisky spouting the English language like she was never spouted before. I could understand Mr Wolffe - fumious beast that he was - prowling the grass with an eye on the ladies in their summer wear, but to sit all day worrying about whether the paint on the lion was just paint or represented painting, that was beyond the comprehension of hope. He looked up and saw me looking at him and picked up the glass and raised it to me and sipped his spirit and buried his nose in his book again.

—Sad old fool.

—Pardon?

—Sad fool, he is, repeated the voice to my left.

—Who?

—Him with the book. D'you know him or something? Standing there staring at him. Freak show.

—We met once, I said, turning to face the speaker of the hard word. She stared back at my gaze with a belligerent defiance as if challenging me to disagree with her verdict so she could do me some damage.

—Lucky you, she answered, taking a mouthful of froth from the lager glass in her fist.

—He's all right, I said, coming to his defence instinctively as if it were in my genes to speak for the underdog because it was also in my genes to be the underdog. She looked me up and down briefly as if only half interested in what she saw and drank some more. She was cute, her brown hair tucked behind her ears. She was wearing dark blue, a silky shirt and jeans. There was a sexy little smile hiding somewhere in her face, I was sure.

—Bastard.

—What? I asked. Who? Why? That smile was looking pretty well hidden.

—OK, she said, turning her white-blue eyes on me and nodding towards the teacher guy, where shall we begin? He's old. I mean, he *is* old. Isn't he? Old.

—Older than me, true. Older than you. But that...

—And he's a man. OK?

—What?

—I said, he's a man.

—Yes. So?

—So he's a bastard.

—He's a bastard because he's a man?

—That's it. You got it, she said.

—All men are bastards? How original.

—Of course it's not original; it's not original because it's true.

—Not sure I follow that.

—You wouldn't, would you?

—Because… I get it, I'm catching on, I said.

—Don't get too excited, Einstein.

—How d'you know my name? I asked, cynically.

—Oh, Einstein the Comic. Genius.

—Not keen on men, then, are you? I said.

—You know the trouble with people like you? You think you're so clever but what you can't see is that everyone's just laughing at you. Being men. I mean, if you weren't standing here talking crap you'd likely as not be out somewhere with a bloody gun, shooting people.

—I haven't got a gun, I said. Look, not all men are bastards or psychopaths or idiots or something.

—But all psychos are men, aren't they? See what I mean. See this, just think about this, will you: all men have got a big hang-up. And that's the problem, isn't it? That's their bloody downfall. Just look at it. Men just want to shoot off all the time and because they're physically incapable they have to invent substitutes. Guns, knives, bloody bows and arrows, they're all phallic.

—I see. Not exactly a new…

—You're at it again, aren't you. Course it's not new, is it? Because it's true. You stupid, or what?

—Probably.

—Problem is, men have the control, haven't they. It's a phallocentric world, see?

—That's a big word.

—For a small thing. Don't try to patronise me, you pillock. Phallocentric for now but not for long. You lot are finished. One day we're going to keep men on stud farms. We're going to milk you like snakes. Some of you, that is, she added.

—Take me to that farm and milk me now!

She looked me up and down again with cursory contempt.

—What are you, some sort of throwback or what? Look at you. You're weirdly hairy. Like some sort of monkey.

—Actually… I began but changed my mind. I frowned at her. No need to get personal.

—Everything's personal, weirdo. That's the truth. Anyway, Genesis, you know, in the bible, where some man-faced god makes that man-creature first, means nothing. Rubbish, it is. Don't talk to me about Adam, she said, peering at my beard as she gulped at her lager, not bloody primal, more like primate.

—Bishops are called primates, I said, wondering how I knew that, and thinking of the little bishops in Tim's chess set.

—Don't get clever, she retorted, putting down her glass firmly. Anyway, bishops have phallic hats. Pricks.

—OK, I shrugged. But you can't hold everything wrong with the world against men.

—Listen, I don't hold anything against men. Ever. And she turned away as if I suddenly bored her.

He looked up as I sat down next to him and put my pint on the table, frowned a bit as if he wasn't sure whether or not he recognised me, unsure of whether or not he wanted me sitting down anyway and then carried on reading his book.

—You into all that? I asked, seeing the title, Mother God's Children.

—What? He asked blearily, wearily putting the book to his lap and turning vaguely towards me. He was a bit grey about the gills.

—I thought you'd have been reading about art and all that, I ventured. I was sort of feeling sorry for him after what the feminista at the bar had been saying. There were a few shouts from the tap room and I recognised Smallwit's voice raised above its peers and caught a few words about balls.

—What? He repeated.

—Art. I said. Last time we met you were talking about art or something. In the park. The lion and the snake, remember?

—The lion and the snake? Don't know what you're talking about.

—The lion and the snake in the park. The painted ones; you were explaining to me...well, something about them. It doesn't matter.

There was a long silence and he looked greedily at the book. We drank on like that for a while and watched the light seeping out of the air. The toil of people at the bar swirled and eddied and I dollied the beer in my glass wondering whether I should get another while I still had a shilling to my name.

—You used to be a teacher, didn't you? I said to break the emptiness. I thought about the girl at the bar and speculated on her being an ex-student with bad memories. He seemed to brighten at this.

—The shoes, he said. It was the shoes gave it away, wasn't it? He looked accusingly at his semi-shined brogues.

—No, you told me last time we met. In the park.

—What? What was that?

—Yes, it was the shoes, mate, I said.

—Saw you talking to her, you know.

—Who? The girl at the bar?

—Beth, he said slowly.

—That's her name, then?

—Well, we christened her Doreen but she never liked it.

Never liked it at all.

—She's your daughter?

—She's our treasure. Grown up now, of course. Well, you can see. She makes me so proud.

—Oh, good, I said. His eyes were blearing over with unbearably beautiful memories and he dabbed at them with the tweed sleeve of his jacket and got a thread in the corner of his eye and ended up blinking and scratching at it and mopping up the tears with the back of his hand.

—In the park, did you say? I meet a lot of people in the park. You asked about the book? Beth gave it to me. Says I should read it to get things in perspective.

—Right. Is it any good.

—Oh, I'm no great judge of these things. But no. It is not any good. All this about god being an alien, I remember all that from the seventies.

—But that's like a new book, isn't it? I saw an advert or something for it. Hasn't it just come out?

—That's right. Quite recently, I think. Oh, all this stuff's still popular, you know.

—It must be.

—This one reckons god was like an alien queen who spawned the human species by interbreeding with apes. It's a sort of woman as god and man as muppet take on everything. Women and men as essentially different species. Like they're from different planets. And I don't just mean Venus and Uranus, we're talking the planet Choushoo. Oh, and earth, of course. Where the spacequeen found her little apemen. Reckons that half of America believes in alien abduction because it's really happening. You know, chips in the neck, people disappeared, minds controlled by telepathy. I bet it's another sort of tele does the 'controlling', if you know what I mean. As if anything fifty percent of Americans believe in could be true!

—Lovely.

—Well, I simplify, but not a lot. Clumsily written. Few grainy photographs of prehistoric stone mother figures – you know the sort of thing, all big curves and power breasts – and spindly artefacts of men with the heads of monkeys.

—Was it written by a woman, I asked, squinting to see the author's name.

—How do you tell, these days? he answered conspiratorially. But it sells.

—OK, but why?

—People need to think they're important.

—Yeah, I suppose.

—I mean, here we are, a species of sullen ape scratching about on a lump of rock somewhere in a tiny solar system in the oxter of an average galaxy in the middle of exactly nowhere. So we have god and everything's cosy. Gets bloody at times, but at least you know where you stand. Then god goes and dies. Then science explains how everything works. More or less.

The latest, by the way, is that we didn't crawl from the primeval soup but crept off the primeval pizza – apparently they think now that things first got started as a sort of pizza topping. Why all the food imagery? I don't know. Maybe those scientist chaps do a lot of thinking when they're eating. Or just a lot of eating. So we get to be sophisticated apes moping about our little rock world cursed with consciousness of the fact that that's all there is and it doesn't last long. And it drives us mad.

What was it Nietzsche said? 'Everything is possible because nothing is true'? Something like that. Food for thought, eh? He became quiet for a second.

—It's enough to drive you bananas. Hence books like these, I said.

—Hence books like these. Poverty of reason.

—Well, I don't know. All this clever stuff. You've just got to get on with things, haven't you. I mean, look at me. If I've got beer in my belly and a bird in my bed, I'm a happy creature.

—Is that what happiness is?

—Works for me.

—People need to think they're important, he mused. Well, maybe it's an anthropic universe, you know. That's one way of looking at things that makes us all seem important. Even us men.

—Whatever. Probably is an anthropoidic thing, I said, the beer making a Sunday afternoon out of my mind.

Time was being bellowed at the bar and a bell was rung. Drinking quickened and people pushed up for more. The teacher guy finished his whisky and nodded at my glass. I nodded back and he went to get refills. He was a drunk but one of those coherent drunks, if you knew what he was talking about. I sort of liked him. I went off to the gents. When I got back the drinks were there and he was smirking over something in his book.

—Cheers.

—Cheers.

—I got us an extra one, he said, putting two pints down in front of me. Don't want to be caught out in the final scrum, do we?

—Cheers again.

—Are you interested in this? He asked, putting the book down in a pool of overflowed beer froth.

—I suppose I've got a bit of an interest. Where we came from. Where we're going and all that. How to make the best of your life. Talking of which, have you ever heard of The Doorway Foundation?

—The Doorway Foundation? What's that?

—It's that place up in Hogswood. You know, up at the top of Brownberrie Lane. Used to be a college, I think. They've turned it into a sort of institution.

—Never heard of it.

—Have you not seen the adverts and that? And they've got people on the streets with leaflets. 'You know the truth, you just don't know it', that sort of thing.

—Adverts? Never pay any attention.

—You must have seen them in the street. Cream chinos, shiny shoes and right earnest expressions. Big collars. Stopping people in the street. Shop dummy meets dumb shopper sort of thing.

—Oh, them. I've seen *them*. Bunch of tossers, all of them. Nothing better to do than hang around bothering people. Bloody clipboards and leaflets and a system that will solve all your bloody problems. Oh, I've seen them all right. Bloody systems. All the same. I've met their sort before. A box for everything and everything in its box. Nearly put me in my box, I tell you. Bastards. All of them. They claim to have all the answers but all they really have is a need to control or a want for your money. Or both. You meet people like that, you've got to...

He went on, dabbing at his mouth with the whisky glass, becoming less coherent and more angry. It was as if all he had drunk through the night had suddenly caught him up and sandbagged him. He flailed his arms and knocked the book off the table. I drank away at the two pints as quickly as I could but he'd got me Jerkel's, a gassy thin tipple with a lizardish afterbite, and I was struggling.

—Wouldn't surprise me...wouldn't, you know, surprise me at all if all those bruro... bureaucret... bureaucretins didn't have a bloody little chip in the back of their necks. Pillocks. With their crapboards and their efficiency gains... and their bloody little chips in their necks. Pains in the bloody arse!

—Sure.

I gulped down the last of the brew.

—Not like me, he guffawed suddenly, not like me. Just a bloody chip on the shoulder, me. And he swept the last of the whisky down his throat and lurched out of his seat. I picked up the book and gave it to him and he pushed it, damply submissive, into his briefcase which he squashed under his arm and was away with a dismissive wave of the hand and a mumbled word of goodbye. I went back through to the tap room and caught Benny potting the black. We hung around for a bit until the barsqueak came through with his quiff of gelled hair and icepick eyes to tell us we were no longer welcome and would we mind just shooting off home.

As we got up to go Goldfish mumbled something.

—You what? asked Benny.

—All gonna go out.

—What?

—The stars.

—What are you talking about, ale-face?

—It's true. All gonna go out and then there'll be just like bits of stuff but after a bit longer all them atoms will fade away too.

—Snap out of it, said Smallwit and punched him on the arm.

—Not yet, elaborated Goldfish, rubbing the side of his arm, millions of years yet.

—That's all right then, said Benny.

—Probably billions, I added to the rigmarole.

—Hope so.

—What's an atom, then? asked Smallwit, winking at Benny.

—Not sure, said Goldfish, but they're bloody good little things.

We bundled out under the clear dark sky.

14

"Only the dealer deals."
(Harvey Golman, *Meantown*, 1958)

A few weeks passed before I made a move towards The Doorway Foundation. I was disappointed that Stella had not been to see me. I'd waited for her even though I'd no clear idea about how she might find me. Now I had to take the initiative. The bus dragged itself snorting up Brownberrie Lane with me inside staring out of the window and listening to the exhaust gagging on diesel. All would be well, I smiled to myself.

Spring was exploding mildly around me. Green was kicking in again and the light was getting harder at the edges. The ultramarine sky was ringed with fat cumulus dappled with grey. There were only two other passengers on the bus, an octogenarian in a plaid jacket with a tiny dog on the end on a piece of binder twine and a middle aged woman with straw-coloured hair and violent lipstick. Ahead, the driver whistled some spooky nonsense and then before I could stop myself I was whistling along too and realising with a pang of horror that it was Toby Joby, the hit from months ago, the wretched tune I'd just managed to clear from memory. The tune had sprung up like a demon and got its twisted nails into my head again. The bus driver was now tapping out the rhythm on the rim of the steering wheel and using the gas pedal as a wow-wow pedal as we lurched up the road, whistling.

The bus rattled and coughed along, rising above the city and entering a semi-rural area where the fields stretched around us and the long zippers of the dry stone walls wandered aimlessly between gangs of grazing animals. I was looking out now for The

Doorway Foundation. I wasn't sure exactly where it was but when I saw a white spire poke out above the trees and then the windows of the stubby blocks blinking in the morning sunlight, I guessed I'd found it. I stood up and lurched to the front of the bus and jumped off as it slowed to a halt.

The air was cool and I pulled the jacket zipper up to chest level and pushed my hands into the pockets. The bus pulled over the hill in a cloud of poisonous vapour and I looked over the place that was The Doorway Foundation. There didn't seem to be anyone around so I walked up close to the wall. There was a central block with glass doors about two hundred yards away and to the right of it was a round building with a tall aerial and a collection of satellite dishes. Around the perimeter were five squat blocks of what looked like flats. They had a rained-on scrubbed concrete look about them.

The air had become damp. I went through the gateway and started walking down the tarmac path, through the small car park and up to the glass door. This was The Doorway Foundation. My reflection walked towards me and I thought, as I advanced, of what Tim had said about the place and I thought of the book and I thought of whether there was anything in it.

The doors slid open with a shush and I went in. By the desk there were some big lily displays and on the wall behind it there was a huge oil painting of two faces in the shape of gearwheels on a course of imminent engagement. The foyer was large and subtly lit with lilac-tinted halogen bulbs. The carpet was deep and lilac and clean. There was some money in the place despite the drab appearance of the exterior. A girl was sitting behind the desk and she looked up at me as I approached. She was about twenty with long blonde hair tied back in a knot; her lipstick was icy and her eyes stared at me blank and blue.

—Hi, I began, offering her a smile.

—Do you have an appointment?

—I knew you were going to say that.

—And did you know how you were going to reply when I said that?

—Ah…

—You haven't got an appointment, have you?

—Not exactly.

Outside, by the door, on the grass had been a sign: The Doorway Foundation. Underneath was an indication to the effect that you wouldn't be seen without an appointment. Well, I had no appointment, but I did know where the missing book was and that I thought should be enough to grant me access to the place and to meet…

—Then I'm afraid that no one will be able to see you this morning. If you would like to leave your name and address and fill out one of our starter forms, The Doorway Foundation would be pleased to contact you with regard to arranging a meeting between you and one of our Initiation Trainers. The Doorway Foundation will be pleased to offer you the finest SHAFT training available.

—Well, I was hoping to see someone now.

—I'm afraid that's impossible. If you would like to fill out one of our starter forms…

—Well, no, I don't fancy all that formality. I don't really go in for the form-filling things in life, if you know what I mean. But if you would like to tell your Mr Damon that I know where his book is… Mr Damon is it? I think someone will see me.

She gave me one of those looks that receptionists give when they wish you'd just disappear or dissolve or die. But inside that look, swimming about there in her deadly eyes, was a little fish of doubt. I'd said something that she didn't understand. I fished for that doubt with the hook of a knowing smile and the nod of a head. And I waited while the little puzzling thought swam through her mind. She didn't want to do the wrong thing, did she?

—Well, Mr…

—Monkey. Call me Monkey. She looked at me briefly and blankly.

—Would you like to take a seat for a moment, she smiled, indicating with the flat of a hand the leather chairs around the glass-topped table to my right. A faint metallic scent of flowers wafted from her as she turned to the phone on the desk to her right and picked up the curved triangular handset. I went and sat down. On the table were a number of flyers. There was the 'My World' thing and the one about being there and the other one featuring the startling blonde above the words, 'You know the truth. You just don't know it'.

A door opened on the far side of the foyer and two figures passed through. They were both young and appeared lost in conversation. They didn't notice me as I flicked idly through the interesting reading on the table, fanning out the flyers like a gambler's deck. I'd been trying to hear what the receptionist was saying but her words were masked by the couple's voices. I stretched out my legs. I yawned. The girl put down the phone and began shuffling papers around on her desk. She looked neither interested nor bored. I leaned back in the chair and began to think of what I was going to say. I had to be careful not to give too much away nor to appear greedy. A suitable reward, that was all I wanted.

I went over one or two sentences in my head. I thought the clever bit was that I was going to demand that Stella, that woman of a thousand silky hushes, act as the go between in the little deal I wanted to set up. Nice one, I thought, and rummaged in my beard to kill an itch. I stretched my legs again. I waited for a few minutes more and then began to get restless.

What did I know about The Doorway Foundation? Tim had told me quite a bit. According to him, the whole place was a con. They offered you the true meaning of life, as if it had one, and claimed they were able to show you how to access the secrets of your mind and unleash its power to tune into the profitability of the universe.

The thing with Tim was that he was Danby Houghton's cousin and Danby was a big guy here at The Doorway Foundation. So poor old Ginny was not only engaging herself to money she was also tying herself up with lunacy. It wasn't good. What must she be missing in her life that she had joined up with such a bunch of sads? She was missing me, wasn't she? Tim said Danby did the publicity for the place and was really into it all. Like he believed that you could make millions if you followed the route of SHAFT at The Foundation, that if you opened yourself up to your inner universe you could see through the shadow play of our 'reality' and bathe in the glow of profitability for ever.

Oh, and he believed that humankind would come to fruition in 2020 when man's vision of himself would be made perfect and the shades of his mortality would fall from his eyes. And all this would be achieved through training by The Doorway Foundation. And why did he believe all this? Because he had been told so by the founder of The Doorway Foundation, Damon somebody. And how did he know? Because he had been told by, get this, an alien called Eeve he had met on a moor one evening when he was out for a stroll with the dog. Oh, yes. The full works. She had a silver jump suit and a nifty little saucer-styled spaceship and those big innocent wrap-around eyes. Oh, and, of course, the secret of eternal success.

That's why I'd laughed. Come on, I'd said to Tim, people don't really fall for that, do they? Oh, yes, he'd said. Not only fall for it but jump at it. Well, I'd said, there must be some money in it, looking at the motor Danby cuts around in. Money, he'd replied, like you wouldn't believe. So here I was, in the heart of cuckoo land with a deal that I hoped would make me a rich man.

After a while I noticed that the light was subtly changing

colour. It had started as lilac but now it was vaporous pink and on the way to becoming a very light blood red. I had also detected a background noise. White noise muzak. Very low but now I'd noticed it, very irritating. The girl was still working at her papers, unconcerned. The main door slid open and a man in a suit strode in and disappeared through the door to the left. Very purposeful. Distant laughter trickled over my head. I stared out of the glass front, looking for Danby Houghton's car but all I saw were the posh dark motors I'd seen on the way in. Quite a racket, all this. I got up and strode around the foyer a bit. The girl didn't seem to notice. I went over to the desk.

—Hi.

—Can I help?

—What do they do here, then? Is it like business school or is it more like church?

—Someone will be with you soon, sir, if you would like to take a seat.

I took a seat. No one came. I waited again. Then I went back to the girl at the desk. She looked up, her blue eyes focusing blandly on mine. Her wily receptionist's brain was doing its business, working on plausible strategies to keep me at arms' length.

—Will they be long? I asked.

—I couldn't say, really.

—Been here long?

—If you would like to take a seat...

—I've heard a lot about this place. I've got a mate, I lied, who reckons they brainwash you here. Is that right?

Her eyes focussed about a foot above my head. She looked bored now. Poor girl, stuck with all these losers. On the other hand, I wouldn't mind being bored and stuck here with losers if it was going to put a pretty penny in the bank. I smiled at her. She stared over my head and asked me if I would like a form to fill in. I wondered if she was homing in on the old monkey brain and sucking out thought waves like a hoover. I leaned over the desk and smiled again. Under the white dress she had a good figure. She looked completely unconcerned. A proper little Stepford receptionist.

—Hey, how's your profitable mind? I asked. For a split second a smirk moved over her lips wanting to come out to play. Then she gave a brisk shake of her head and picked up the phone again. She didn't speak into it, she just pressed a button on the handset. Then she replaced it on its cradle and pushed a form over the desk towards me.

—Why don't you fill this in whilst you're waiting? she asked. The form was followed by a silver torpedo-shaped pen. This time I shook my head.

—I'll give it a miss, thanks. I'll just sit down over here and wait for whoever, eh?

I know my watch ran slow but at least it ran. This was my Saturday ticking away. It had better be worth it. I started to make a house of cards from the flyers but they were too floppy to balance and the whole thing collapsed before I'd even got one storey built.

I was about to begin another tour of the foyer when the door opened and a young woman came out. She was dark-haired and wore a black trouser suit. She looked lithe and sort of athletic.

—Mr Monk, she greeted me with a porcelain smile, holding out a hand, welcome to The Doorway Foundation. Please follow me.

—Thank you.

She took me through the door and down a corridor. There were some expensive-looking pictures hanging on the wall in gold frames and a slight sense of incense nosed around the air.

She walked briskly and I followed. The office we ended up in was wide and long with an inch thick carpet and big plate glass windows overlooking a lawn. She asked me to sit down and then went and stood by the door as a tall man came into the room and went to sit at the desk. He leaned his elbows on the blotter and looked over at me. He was neat and muscular and wore a ruby pin in his tie. The plaque on his desk said 'Mr Damon Damon'.

—Mr Monk, we've been expecting you.

—How did I know you were going to say that? I replied for want of anything witty.

—Have you brought it with you?

—Do you think that would have been a good idea, Mr...eh, Damon?

—For us, yes; for you, Mr Monk, no. Therefore I'll presume that you have not brought it with you and thus flatter your obvious intelligence. But dare I suggest that you are also a man who has come to us with a proposal and one which you hope will make you a comfortable man?

—I've got a proposal, yes.

—Would you like to tell me what it is and then I can pursue the business of the day. I'm a busy man, Mr Monk and would be about my business.

—Right. Well...

His manner was brisk and, though not unfriendly, gave the impression that behind the mask of efficiency there was something just a little weird. Which would be about right for a place like this, wouldn't it. Two figures dressed in silver passed by across the lawn deep in conversation. The light dulled and grey clouds began to sweat a thin mist of rain.

—I think I've got something that belongs to you. Something that you want... I think you know what I'm talking about.

—I think so too. You want what? Some manner of reward for this object?

—Yes.

—All right, Mr Monk, we shall pay you for the book. We shall pay what we consider to be a generous amount for its safe return. It is safe, yes?

—Oh, yes. I'll return it. But not here.

—Do you not trust us?

—Trust? Oh, yes, of course I trust you. It's just that there are ways of dealing with business such as ours and I think that bringing the…eh, book here wouldn't be the way that these things should be done. If you see what I mean.

—I see exactly what you mean. I see more than you mean. And of course, I mean more than you see, Mr Monk. The book is of value to us, do not doubt that, but we shall only pay what we think is reasonable.

—Just a minute, you said 'generous' a moment ago.

—Of course. Is not generosity reasonable?

—Oh, yeh, OK.

—So, you have everything under control, do you not? What is to be the means by which the exchange might be expedited?

—How will we go about it? I've thought about that and what I thought was this. I want to deal with a particular person. Someone from here that I say. She can come to a pre-arranged meeting place and I'll give her it and she can give me my reward. I've looked after it, you know.

—You have not accessed it by any chance?

—Nah, I couldn't get it… no, I haven't *accessed* it.

—I see. Good. That is good. We would know if you had, Mr Monk, and that would change things. That would definitely change things. And now, tell me, who do you wish to deal with in this little affair?

—Right. Well, the awkward thing is that I don't know if you know her. But I'm pretty sure she's one of you lot. I could point her out if you like.

—Mr Monk…

—Why're you laughing? Did I say something funny at all?

—Mr Monk, forgive my humour. Do you have any idea how many people work for us here? How many people have joined our select People here? How many Initiates, Sub-Initiates, Post-Initiates and Advanced Becomings are here with us at The Doorway Foundation?

—Well, no. Don't suppose I have and from what you say there're probably quite a few. But I want to deal with Stella and no-one else. She's the one who came to see me and tried to get the book back.

—Go on.

—Well, she's tallish, got black hair and these amazing eyes. She's got a red coat and well, she's all woman, if you know what I mean.

—So...

He tapped the tips of his fingers together like Sherlock bloody Holmes and stared at the ceiling for a moment. Then he looked down at me and rested his hands on the blotter again. A spasm of fantasy shook me for a moment as past encounters with Stella ran their fingers through my hair.

—Ask Stella to come in now, please, he said to the woman by the door.

—Ah, you recognise her?

—No, Mr Monk. She recognised you. When you arrived this morning I asked her to confirm that you were, in fact, who you are.

—So you were watching me.

—Of course we were watching you. What else should we do?

There was a noise behind me and the woman returned followed by... well, by Stella. It was her, though she didn't look quite the same dressed in a black trouser suit with her hair tied back and a pair of titanium framed glasses balanced on her exquisite nose.

—Mr Monk, she began. We meet again.

—You've changed.

—So have you. Nice jacket.

—Better mood?

—Stella has ascended to Level Two since you last met her, interrupted Damon Damon, waving away the girl in the doorway and indicating that Stella should sit down in one of the remaining chairs. She looked a little disconcerted at my comment and sat down looking at Damon though she addressed me.

—Level Two, Mr Monk. You see, you still having the book has not held me back. You will not prevent my ascendancy. Mr Damon says that I will soon be a candidate for Level Three.

—Well, congratulations, Stella.

Damon was doing his Sherlock fingers again, looking from me to her and back. Then he smiled and turned to me.

—The book, Mr Monk. The book. I will tell you what is to happen.

—Well, you seem a reasonable man. I don't think that what I'm asking is beyond your pocket, having seen this place. The book is obviously worth a lot to you or Stella here wouldn't have been so keen to get her hands on it. By the way, why didn't you come back for it? I asked her. I did intend to trade it then.

—Mr Monk, cut in Damon, once the bait is in the water the fisherman has only to wait for the bite. Then he can reel in the prize. My beautiful Stella was such exquisite bait, do you not think? And here you are, on my hook. Our business, Mr Monk is now simple. You will hand over the book and we will pay you what I consider to be a generous amount of money. You will determine the location of the trade and the time of the trade. Stella will bring the money and you will bring the book.

—And what is this generous amount of money? I had in mind...

—No matter really what you had in mind. The sum of money we are prepared to offer is...one thousand pounds. I trust that will be satisfactory.

I heard the hairs of my beard and the back of my neck bristle in unison. The feet I had landed on wanted suddenly to dance. I closed my mouth and then opened it again.

—A thousand pounds... my voice sounded faint, an echo of a voice from a long way away. Could I trust my ears? I'd been hoping to get a hundred or so. But now the stars were truly singing in my sky.

—Mr Monk...?

—Fine. That'll be fine. Just what I had in mind. A fair price.

Bloody hell, I was thinking, are these people mad. Or do they just have too much money? Is there a difference? Stella stood up and smoothed down the front of her suit and I thought then that the other reason for giving the book back had been her. Either to save her from the dogs – was that what she'd said? – or to give me time to tempt her into my life in a more physical way than I had yet managed. For a minute the money had put those things out of my mind. I looked at her. She was still magnificent. Sex on a stick. I cleared my throat.

—...will we meet? she was saying.

—Pardon?

—Where do you have it in mind for us to meet?

—The Hyde Park. I'd thought The Hyde Park. Big and busy. I thought a public place would be best then there could be no funny tricks or anything. Sound reasonable?

—The Hyde Park it will be, said Damon Damon.

—What about tonight? Nine o-clockish? I asked.

—Very reasonable, said Damon.

I smiled and stood up and walked over to the door. A drink with Stella, I was thinking, and some cash to spoil her with. From The Hyde Park we could go to... I began to hear Damon calling me back. Damn. I knew it had all been too easy. There had to be a catch. Now he was going to tell me something I didn't want to hear. He smiled at me and rose behind his desk. He shook out his cuffs and came round to where I was standing and put an arm round my back.

—Before you go, I would like you to see something of our work here. It is important to us that we tell everyone about our work here. Our mission is of such importance that you must not ignore it.

—Well...

—Do you not think that the future of mankind is of importance?

—Well, yes. Yes, the future is important, I suppose.

—Good. You would like to see a more profitable and efficient world, would you not, Mr Monk?

—Sounds a bit far-fetched to me.

—This world is our world, Mr Monk, and we are responsible for it. And we can change it by changing ourselves. And we can change ourselves by learning what we are and what we might become.

—As long as we do it your way?

—We can make it happen, Mr Monk. We really can. By the year 2020. That is our work here. We are learning to be guided and we are teaching others how to learn.

—I see.

—How does that sound to you, as someone from Leeds?

—Pretty crazy, if you want me to be honest.

—That is how we all start. Pretty crazy. What we learn here is our true sanity. We learn to strip away the shadows from our eyes and see truly for the first time.

As he was talking to me we had moved back out into the corridor. Still his hand on my back kept up a gentle pressure and I found that we were walking through a pastel corridor in the opposite direction to the main entrance. I started to drag my feet a bit and he sensed this and continued.

—I would like you to sit in on one of our little sessions. Nothing too strenuous or taxing, you understand. Just a little something for the early initiates. Just to show you something of what we do. There will be no charge. And you will not have to fill out our introductory forms. I know how you so hate filling in forms, Mr Monk. An understandable aversion.

—I don't think I will, today. I've a lot to do. Like you, I'm a busy man. Got a bus to catch and that...

—It will take only an hour of your so precious time.

—No. No, thanks. I'll give it a miss.

—Let me put it another way, Mr Monk. No session, no deal. We have to be sure that you are serious about returning our book. Call this a demonstration of good faith. This way, please.

And he moved quickly round the corner and through a set of double door into a small lecture theatre. The room was whispering in hushed tones. About a dozen or so people were scattered in small clumps around the seats. Some were hunched over papers, others stared into space and one or two looked round absently as we came through the door.

—Well, I said, It's a pity I won't be able to stop, I haven't reserved a seat.

—Sit down, Mr Monk. Anywhere, he replied acidly, and waved an arm round to indicate where anywhere might be. Then he turned and left without another word.

I shrugged, resigned to the nonsense if it was going to get me my hands on the money. I took a seat near the back, well away from the weirdos, and folded my arms. It had been a long morning, maybe I could have a little snooze before Damon Damon came back and let me out. Behind me the door hissed to a close.

And so I waited again. There were some quiet mutterings and shufflings, the usual stuff. The light wasn't good and it seemed to be getting dimmer. Down at the front there was something familiar about the back of the head of one of the weirdos. I was peering through narrow eyes at this head, trying to make out who it was, when the door at the front of the lecture theatre opened and...just a minute, I thought, why am I sitting here in this room with a bunch of geeks waiting to hear some midget-brained instructionist unload a garbled list of must-do's for creating wealth and happiness? A thousand, said my brain. There was a faint hum from the loudspeakers. Loads of money. Just stick it out. But there was something else lurking around in my mind, and that was the fact that I was curious. Well, wouldn't anyone be? Here I was on the outskirts of Leeds in a place where apparently large numbers of seriously-minded people were claiming that they knew how to get more out of life than they otherwise might by just following a few weird but simple instructions. I was curious. Just a bit curious. Maybe there was something I could learn. I mean, my life had hardly been a barrel of belly laughs so far.

The hum grew louder. Hum harmonised with hum until I realised that what I was listening to wasn't a bit of feedback but was being passed off as music. The light fluttered through a variety of shades of purple and then settled down into a pastel twilight somewhere in the vicinity of lilac. A figure stood at the front on the dais and as she raised her head I saw with a start that it was Stella. This should be interesting. I sat back and laced my fingers over my belly. At least I was going to have something to look at. The music faded and died. Silence hung around for a while like a lonely guest at a party and then she began speaking.

—Welcome…to The Doorway Foundation. What you are about to hear, what you are about to see will change your lives for ever. And that change will reflect the change that is coming over the whole of mankind, a change that is moving us towards the glorious year of 2020 when those who know will stand above those who seek and those who seek will stand above those who do not. And in that world, that changed world, you will stand with us for we have the knowledge that you now seek and you will have that knowledge because you sought.

I was impressed. Stella could certainly weave a bit of a spell. There was some more like this before the music-type hum returned and behind Stella images were projected onto a large screen. Clouds sprang across brilliant skies, flowers opened, babies sang.

The hum faded a little, became a slither of syrupy glissando before somehow resolving itself into synthesised violins trilling Elgar. Then we were away on an cosmic journey, pulling away from earth, a cosy meld of blue and green, back past the planets hanging big and solemn and beautiful, back through the light-pricked darkness, swooping now through light years of emptiness splashed with the filigree jewellery of galaxies and tall spouts of interstellar gasses thrown about like candyfloss.

And then back again, sweeping now at speed homeward until we lurched finally up in front of good planet earth whose watery blues looked a little tearful to see us return. It was a bit like that opening scene from the film Contact but with more pretension. 'This is our world,' intoned what sounded like the guy from the Carlsberg ad. 'It is small yet it is infinite.' Stars swam across the screen. 'It is fragile and yet eternal.'

Clouds of interstellar gas lit purple and orange by starlight swung towards us and then away and we were looking at darkness. Blackness. And then a tiny point of light appeared in the centre of the screen and grew.

'Everything we do is for ever.' The light grew till it was a brilliant sun in the darkness. 'Everything we are is for ever.' The sun moved towards the top left of the screen and we moved closer. 'We live in a world more complex than we dare admit, more beautiful than we dare imagine.' Through the dark of the lower screen, lit by the sunlight, shapes were coming into focus. Were they planets? Two of them. Dark orbs haloed with gossamer white. 'We are of the world....'

We moved closer and then I saw that we were looking at two eyes. '...and the world is of us.' Milky light bathed the screen and we were looking at the blonde girl from the flyers staring back at us and revealing, as the camera pulled back, that she was wearing little more than a touch of shadow and her smile. Very tastefully presented, I thought. Which was a pity. And then the poor girl morphed into a star. It was very Greek. 'Be guided by us to the world within you,' intoned the voice. This was probably the best nonsense in the world. I would have laughed except there was something about it all that held me, something ineffable that kept me from toppling over the brink into hysteria.

Then the screen faded and we were back to Stella. She looked down to the lectern in front of her, a pale block in the dimness. Everything about this place was clean. Every line was clear. Each subtle shade of colour silkily complemented its neighbours. Even in the twilight of the lecture hall the tones of the shadows blent in nonchalant harmony. The receptionist's voice, Damon Damon's voice, the voice of Stella all were one voice. And at the heart of it all was...

—The Doorway, Stella was saying, can reveal to us what we might become and how we might become. We will teach you to understand how profitable your mind might become.

There was a zinging of the synthesiser again, this time a bit of ersatz Wagner and the light flamed through various blushing shades till it arrived at a lurid scarlet mist. The air was suddenly stiff with incense and the screen began throbbing with light. The Wagner-type blare faded and a deep bass beat began pulsing, pulsing, pulsing. There was a background hiss and the beat got almost imperceptibly faster.

There was an air of expectation. There was a sense of quickening. The white light of the screen was becoming something. Something was emerging from the whiteness. A shape. The focus hardened and soon you could see that it was a face. It was Little Miss Poster. Those large black eyes stared out from the screen at us with a calculated impassivity. Her mouth was not smiling. The face of salvation was serious. The air was thick with anticipation.

What on earth was she going to say?

I yawned. And as I yawned I realised with a disturbing twinge that I wasn't actually bored. The girl stared out at us for a while as the music flared around us. There was something odd about her face. It was too heart-shaped, too wide around the temples, too narrow at the chin. And the eyes were as big as sunglasses. She said nothing. Just looked out at us, unmoving.

The bass beat had been getting faster because I noticed now that it was slowing down, slowing to a throb that beat in my temples, that I could feel echo in my chest. It got slower but it also got louder. Slowly, she began to smile. For some reason I felt happy. I got the distinct illusion that I was in the right place at the right time. I felt my mouth smiling. I could feel everyone in the theatre staring at this unearthly face on the screen and as we stared the face began to fade. Almost imperceptibly, the face was dissolving in front of us, retreating into white light, into nothing. I felt a sense of unease: we were going to lose her.

The pang of loss was mixed with the sensation of happiness as if I had touched something inside myself that I had known was there but had never reached, a childlike sense of dependence, a sense of wonder, a sense of belonging. The theatre was silent. The screen was blank. The light came up gradually to reach a milky opalescence. Stella was speaking again, her melodious voice sliding round the room like thighs in silk.

—Have you ever felt that you're different from those around you? Have you ever felt that you're special? You might feel that there is something in your life that is missing. That you have a need to belong but you don't know how to belong. This is your mind wanting to know itself. Only you are stopping it from knowing itself. We can show you how to achieve your desires. Everything is within your grasp. Everyone here can be successful. Anyone here could be standing up here instead of me, presenting this, successful, ascended to the second level of attainment.

We can show you what you really are, a profitable mind in a profitable world. What you can imagine having, you can have. Think about that. That is a fundamental truth. What you can imagine having, you can have. Think about that tonight, think about that tomorrow.

What The Doorway Foundation can show you is how to make that happen. There is no limit to what you can achieve. Look around you at all these people who have come here in search of their dreams. They are all like you. They, too, are looking for fulfilment and hope and success. They, too, will find their dreams fulfilled, their hopes realised and their success achieved because they believe in The Doorway. They believe in the principles of SHAFT which will bring them to true fulfilment. They are just like you. You are just like them. And you are all on the first step of a journey, a glorious journey from which there is no turning back, a journey that will lead you to wherever you desire. We are all part of the same system. This bountiful earth, this rich world, our home.

As she said the word 'home' I felt the air move with that deep sound again and I felt in myself a quickening towards something. There was more in the same vein that I don't remember. She talked a bit about releasing the power of the individual to work with the many. She went on and on about how business needed to recognise that people were profitable and that a quick SHAFT course could help boost sales figures and keep the workforce happy into the bargain. What was SHAFT all about, I wondered. No doubt we all wondered. She elaborated, not very illuminatingly: S, it transpired, stood for self-determination. Anyone can be successful in any way they choose. I thought about this for a second. Anyone can be successful, I thought, like anyone can become the president of the McStates. Anyone, but not everyone. H was for Harmonisation. A was for Accumulation. F was Focus. T = Trust.

Then she threw up a load of graphs and charts onto the screen and seemed to prove by some jiggery-pokery that if you tapped into the SHAFT way of doing things then fortunes were within your reach. All for a modest fee. Just change the way you saw yourself. See yourself The Doorway way, join all those who have joined and release the potential in yourself to make a fortune. It looked a doddle. A quick SHAFT was all it took. SHAFT me! SHAFT me now!

As if.

At the end the lights came on. Some of the people went down to the front and started talking with Stella and there was a general exchange of paperwork and scratching of biros. Hands were shaken and smiles matched smiles. I got out before one of the guys in cream came for me. I was sure that Damon Damon was watching everything.

The bus bucked and dragged its way back down the hill towards the city centre. It was early evening and the traffic was making snake lights and dusk was powdering the trees. Could mankind really grow up and get 'perfect vision', whatever that was? Did life have a purpose, did the journey we travelled have a real destination? Could my life be made more profitable? We ground round a steep twist and I looked down over the city below, where a multi-coloured fluorescence of lights glimmered. I imagined, amongst the lights, the dark figures of men and women moving about their lives like dolphins dreaming in a sea of fairy lights. Purpose or porpoise, we are all at sea. No little star children are going to zoom down and make us holy. We have to do that all by ourselves.

Once again the bus whined to a halt and people got on. A small grey guy limped down the aisle past me. His cap was down over his eyes and his tweed jacket was twisted round his shoulders. He sat down, wheezing, behind me. I heard the dog scratching at the back of the seat before it stilled.

I was thinking. The figure at the front of the lecture theatre I thought had looked familiar was Ginny. At the end I caught sight of her going out of one of the doors at the front. Danby Houghton was no doubt waiting for her there. Creepy git. The bus wound down to the illuminated city streets, grinding its way through the traffic to its terminus. Where was I going? I was going to KFC for a bucket of bits.

15

"Sweet lady won't you stay awhile,
Have a little drink and make me smile."
(*Sweet Lady*, popular song, 1952)

I put the book in a pocket and turned up at The Hyde Park in what I thought was good time, to find Stella sitting at a table just inside the door. She was sitting very straight in her chair and she smiled coyly when she saw me, a sort of conspiratorial smile like we had some big secret to share. I smiled at her. The old feelings were coming back, which wasn't really a surprise when you looked at her and imagined her licking banana milkshake off your belly. She was wearing the red coat again and I couldn't help wondering if that was all she was wearing.

On the table in front of her were two bottles of *Clepo* lager and two half pint glasses. I sat down opposite her. I could see no one else I recognised in the pub. It wasn't busy. Only four or five locals mumbling over their usuals. It was too early for the long drinkers, the droolers and the ale-brains.

I was a bit jumpy. It's not every day you come into the money. It was all buzzing in my head like it wasn't really real. I seemed to have stepped back a distance from the real world and started to float in a quasi-real place where everything was going to be all right. I could almost smell the money in the room. Stella poured the lager into the glasses.

—Look, I said, I'm going to get a pint. I can't drink lager. I need a couple of pints of bitter.

—OK, she answered brightly. But I'm sure I saw a little twinge of concern trouble her eyes. When I got back she was sipping gingerly at her glass. She seemed to be making an effort to look me in the eye. Such is life, I suppose. The seductress had turned into the delivery girl. But, god, she was still beautiful. She became business-like, drawing up her shoulders and, placing on the table a brown envelope, rested her hand for a minute on it and then withdrew. My brain was on a roundabout of lust and greed. I watched her slim red-nailed fingers creep over the wallet again, caressing

—Is that…I began, nodding at the wallet.

—Don't be so vulgar, she said. Keep your voice down and stop nodding like a dog.

—Yes, but is that the money? I asked in a whisper. A couple of the mumblers turned round and looked us over but then went back to the usual.

—Please, she said, if you can be discreet, count it.

Discreet? We're talking a thousand quid here. I was just about to rip open the packet and bury my beard in its beauty. But then we're different, aren't we, men and women. Our brains are all wired up differently. I mean there she was supping that pissy lager when she have had a decent pint and telling me to be discreet about latching onto the most cash I'd ever seen in one place in my life. Different.

I slid the envelope across the table and opened it on my knee. OK, so in the end I did do it discretely: we were in a pub and flashing around such a crucial amount of cash would have been a bit like opening a vein in a shark pool. There were a lot of notes inside. Twenties, so many of them, and each so crisp, so new. The weight was comforting. I frilled the edges and counted up to a hundred. I had to start again twice. The hundred was a sliver of the whole bundle. It all looked to be there. I put the envelope back on the table. I looked at her. She drew a cigarette from the packet of Clouds on the table and lit it with a gold lighter. She was cool.

—I didn't know you smoked, I said.

—There's a lot of things you don't know.

—So fill me in. Anything interesting? Like where you'd like to eat with me tomorrow night.

—Let's stick to business, shall we? she said. Is all the money there?

—Yes, I said. Thank you.

—No, Mr Monk, thank *you*. And she held out a hand.

I drew out the book from my pocket. Should I hold back and raise the price? If they were so willing to pay a thousand, how much might I be able to persuade them to pay? My hand hovered. I looked at her again. Her eyes were fixed on the book. She looked as if she was holding herself back from jumping at it. I could feel the sweat leaking from my fingers over the book, could feel the plastic getting slippery. I put it down in front of me. She took another sip from her glass and made a face of distaste.

—I think you may be right about the lager, Mr Monk. I need to check over the article. Then we can conclude this business in the right spirit. Not that we don't trust you. But one must be careful, mustn't one. Sometime things might not be that which they appear to be. Do you think I might try a little of your beer?

—What? Oh, yeh, see what you mean. Sure. Go ahead.

She picked up my pint and slopped a generous amount into the empty half glass. The foamy head crawled towards the rim. She put down the glass in front of her and drew on the cigarette. I watched the tip glow happily.

—May I see?

—Sure. Go ahead.

I pushed the book over to her and she took it and checked it over. She didn't try to open it but she did make a point of looking closely at the catch, probably to see if it had been scratched or forced. She seemed satisfied at last and appeared to make up her mind about something. She tucked the book into a bag and sucked in another helping of smoke. She moved her cigarette over towards the ashtray but before it got there the leaning tower of ash fell off into my pint.

—Oh dear, I'm so sorry. Let me get you another pint. We must drink to our exchange. She slipped to her feet.

—It's all right. Well, go on then, if you insist. It's Bodger's. Don't get the Jerkel's, it's like diluted water.

—Bodger's. Right. But look, I'll get myself a fresh drink, you finish this – and she pushed the half pint glass of beer over to me – there's a bit of a queue.

She was right. About five minutes before a number of whiteshirts had come in from the offices and were milling around the bar hee-hawing to each other about the market price of shires or shares or shoes or something. Throughout the city offices would be disgorging numb whitefaces like these into the evening to soak up Lambrusco and micro fodder in front of brittle gameshows or the fearsome hyper-reality of soaps or to wander through the streets in search of love or lost dogs or death. I thought about going to the bar for her but then thought not. I wanted to keep an eye on what was happening, I didn't want to let the book or the money or the woman out of my sight.

Part of me wanted to get out now with the money and run somewhere very fast and count it note by note and then count it again but I felt that I should leave it on the table until we'd sealed the deal with an ale. It seemed the right thing to do. And, of course, I wanted this to be the start of the evening with Stella. I knew that if she went now I would never see her again and my loins would never forgive me. I could hardly keep my hands off the wallet. Its black skin gleamed seductively in the grainy light. I moved round onto the bench seat, picked up the half glass and swigged off its contents.

Stella was still waiting while a lad of about sixteen in an Persil shirt and power tie was served a clear drink in a tiny glass. Maybe the Bodger's isn't as good as it might be, I thought, licking my lips, this beer smells distinctly like wax. Or candles. Snuffed-out candles. And then something odd happened to my eyes....

Someone had screwed an iron spike through the base of my skull and was trying to tighten it. My head had been chopped off and put back on sidewards. Big fat fish faces were swimming up to me and away and bubbles as heavy as cricket balls were belching painfully up through my throat. Oh, shit. Oh, shit. My eyes wouldn't open more than a knife-cut. And the faces out there were swimming around like bloaters. What had happened to me?

Things pulled into painful focus. The faces slowed down and gained edges. I was still sitting on the seat but my hands were draped like dead things in my lap and my head was fallen over to my right and resting on the shoulder of someone smelling of onions. I pulled myself upright and slid a bit to my left. Pain rattled its chains in my head. The onion man barked and reached for his whisky, missed the glass, tried to fit the ashtray to his lips, failed and snorted up a cloud of grey ash.

He went for the glass again, caught it up and suckled it for a while before exhaling a stream of fricatives. The onion smell clung to his skin like a rind. Reality floated up through the pain. The book and the wallet were gone. Stella was gone. The pub was darkened and full of sweat and noise. Some appalling dance number thumped out of the speakers, flooding over the bodies which were pressed together and moving jerkily around like waltzing syphilitics. I closed my eyes. Maybe death would be merciful and take away poor Monkey somewhere quiet and cold for ever. My sight sank back into the darkness of my head for a second or two.

And when I opened my eyes. When I opened my eyes...oh what sick fancy Fortune favours. Sitting opposite me and nursing a near transparent pint of Jerkel's was Mr Wolffe, his face slashed with a smile and his eyes fixed on my poor eyes. When he saw me looking at him the smile gaped towards me and I smelt the beer ripple off his breath.

—Well, well, if it isn't young Monkey. You don't look well, you know. You pillock.

—Well, I'm not.

—But I thinks you look well enough to pay Mr Wolffe his money. So come on, Fur Boy, cough up the cash.

—I'm not well.

—I can see that, he answered and slurped up a bit of the Jerkel's. I can see that, indeed. But that doesn't mean you can't give me what's my due, now does it? Where are you lurking these days, then anyway? Not that I care. Not at all. What I want is you out of my life, Fur Boy, out good and proper. But not till you've coughed up the readies. Or things could get a bit unpleasant, know what I mean? In fact, maybe they'll get unpleasant anyway.

He wiped off the beer from his lips and coughed.

—What've you been doing to yourself, anyway. You look nasty, d'you know that? And that's saying something. Been snorting up the whatdoyoucallit, the powdery stuff, the hokey cokey? What's the matter? Been pipping the poppers or something? Been doing it with the dough-heads? Don't look at me like that. You look right nasty, Monkey. Look, will you stop your eyes doing that, it's putting me off my beer.

I tried to keep my eyes still but they had a life of their own and were bobbing up and down on their strings like yo-yos. Two or three Wolffes were gurning at me, weaving backwards and forwards in and out of focus.

—I need a drink.

—That looks like the last thing you need.

—I had a thousand quid. Honest. I could've given you the money. Really. Could've. But you're too late. Should have been here…

It suddenly occurred to me that I didn't know how long I'd been snoozing with Oscar the Onion. What time was it? I stared at my watch. It was quarter past ten.

—A thousand? Don't make me laugh. Look. It's simple. You give me the money or you'll be crawling home with your legs on your back.

—Couldn't get worse. Look, Mr Wolffe, just get it over with. Do what you're going to do, tear me in parts, drown me face down in the gutter but just do it quickly, will you?

—A grand...! You've never had more than ten quid, and that probably deviously found. Face it, Fur Boy, you're a lost one. It's what I said to Virginia. He's a lost one, I said. I was going to kill you when I found out about you and her. I really was, I swear. But I'm better now. Virginia put me right. Said you were past history. She's got a human boyfriend now. He's got money, he has. And a nice little car as well. And he treats her proper.

—Ah, I said, about old Danby...there's something you might...

—Shut it, Monkey. Mind your nonsense or I'll be getting mad again. All that's between us now is the money. So cough up.

I leaned over the table. The cricket balls were back. I opened my mouth to say I had no money at all and threw up a gobbet of grey sludge into the empty glass in front of me. Wolffe went pale.

—That's disgusting, that is. Stop it. What have you been drinking?

—Jerkel's.

—You what?

—Jerkel's. Only had two and a bit. Then it came over me. Don't know what it is. What're you drinking there? I gasped.

—What? Me? This is ... look you'd better get that money. I'm looking for you. You'd better... Look, stop it! he said as I rolled my stomach again, acting it up. My head was clearing a bit now and I could see Wolffie wasn't going to sit there and watch me hawk up more of the same. Didn't realise he had a weak stomach for the sight of a bit of sick.

—You hear what I say? I'm looking for you. You bring that

money down here…stop it…tomorrow if you know what's good for you.

He stood up leaving his half-drunk pint on the table, backing off and feeling his forehead and his stomach. As he pushed the chair back Benny came up by his side. There was Goldfish with him.

—Hey, Monkey! God, you look awful.

—Just what I said, said Wolffe, backing away. Don't go near him! There was all this grey stuff…disgusting. Take him home or something.

—Who are you?

—Never you mind. Just bring him back here tomorrow with his pockets full, know what I mean?

Wolffe shouldered his way through the crowd towards the door. I tried to explain to Benny and Goldfish what had happened but as I wasn't really sure how it had come about and it was sort of a long story anyway, it all came out a bit confused. I got the main points over but they did look sceptical about the thousand. Not just that such an amount had been involved but that it had actually sat there on the table at which they were now sitting.

Goldfish did a thorough search and ended up stroking the table where he imagined the cash had rested. I still couldn't work out how it had all happened. How had she done that to me? Poisoned me like that. I didn't drink the lager she'd got me. The beer had come straight from the bar. I hadn't taken my eyes off her. Or the beer. Not even when I was watching the money. I was sure of that. Benny bought me a pint of Bodger's and a large whisky. I sipped at the whisky.

—I know how she did it, said Goldfish suddenly.

—Did it?

—Slipped you a Mickey Thing.

—What? I mean how?

—It was the glass. Like in that film.

183

—The glass?

—You said you drank that half that was in that glass that she had when you came in when she went to the bar 'cause she ashed your pint, right?

—Yeah, something like that.

—She must have put the Mickey in the glass. Smeared it on the rim. Saw it in that film with Charles Brodson.

—Charles Bronson?

—Could've been, I suppose. You were lucky, Monkey. He got done in like that in the end. Poisoned to death, like.

So that was that. Even Goldfish saw through what I'd been too stupid or greedy to notice. Might be safer to do the Lottery. Sooner trust the odds on that than a woman in a red coat. She was sure to end up with your heart on the point of a stiletto and all your hopes in her pocket. So I'd lost the book. There was nothing I could do about it. Except learn from yet another error in a life that seemed to be a comic book of errors. But Stella gone, gone for ever. And a thousand. A thousand lost pounds. The pity of it, Monkey, oh, the pity.

On a cold morning two weeks after my visit to The Doorway Foundation hail snickered against the window as I stared out into the world from the comfort of my little room. A cup of coffee was going cold on the table and the half-eaten toast congealed slowly on its saucer. I was half-clutching half a poem. There had to be some reason, I reasoned, for reason; unless consciousness and all its attendants is just the cruellest of jokes in a cruel universe. But what had happened to my powers of reason? My primitive brain was writhing in the tentacles of loss, pinched by the suckers of folly. I had *failure* running through me like a stick of cheap rock. Sweet.

Cold rain runs down the roofs,
Cold rain falls in the street,
Dogs stumble down the sidewalk

Past my weary feet.

I walk on by a church
That tolls a lonely bell,
Down this one-way street,
A street called farewell.

The sweetness of it all had turned to dust in my mouth. I'd lost the book. I should have seen that one coming, shouldn't I. Yes, I'd trusted Damon bloody Damon. More fool me. And fool of fools, I'd trusted Stella.

So now what? I stared at the hail playing ping-pong in the street. The last thing I wanted to do was go to work. When you've had your hands on real money, grubbing about in a concrete snake pit for a shilling a day was not a rewarding experience.

I finally got it together telling myself that it was the last day I was going to work and that I was going to tell Gordy I was leaving. Coming down through the estate I called in at the local shop, D.P Prents, Newsagent, and bought chocolate and chewing gum. I was served by Mr Prents himself. His wire glasses twitched nervously and his bald head looked heavy as a pebble. His fingers shook with the weight of the change he heaved over the counter to me. I pocketed the coins. I'd called in a few times before and he never smiled. He hardly spoke and if it wasn't for the greed of his grasp on your money you might have felt sorry for him. Day in, day out. Eight till late, peddling bubble gum and tooth decay and cigarettes and soap and plasters and toothpaste and balls of string, magazines top shelf and bottom shelf, tissues and tablets. Newspaper carbon had turned his hands grey and the greyness was getting into his whole body, spreading its dullness under his skin and over his eyes. I'd never been so depressed buying chocolate.

But when I got to work, despite my decision to leave, the

grotesque familiarity seduced me into the habit of it all and I fell to with the brush and then the press. Teddy Wobegon went waffling on and the smell of the steel and oil and the dirt got into me again. It began to take my mind off things.

So I fell back in with the noise of the tortured steel and the grim residue of swarf in the creases of my collar and the dull work talk and the frightening bellows of Bastard One as he stalked the concrete in his seven league boots. I was hollowed out. But even there in that theatre of the lost I thought of Ginny and when I thought of her I thought of that beer-blessed tee shirt and our first meeting in happier times. But I also thought of Stella. Despite what she'd done, part of me still wanted to clutch her knees and gasp, take me you beauty, take me, burn me on the altar of your body.

16

"She was on the street, a beauty with fire in her eyes, seared with the memory of a man she couldn't forget. A man called Ronson."

(Dalworth Slade, *Never Say Goodbye*, 1953)

And then I met Ginny for the first time in a long time. It was one of those evenings when the weariness of the day hung in the air and the grey clouds couldn't be bothered to rain but just lolled there waiting for the darkness to put them out of their misery. As soon as work had finished I was dodging out of the door and down the estate, weaving through the streets until I got to the bus stop. When I got off, I picked a course through the little shops till I came to the first big slabs of plate glass where the department stores rose in their mastery over the streets. Some of them still sported stone mullions around which the stainless steel and tinted glass were arranged like punk embellishments of historical figures.

I was still wary of being seen by Mr Wolffe. I'd managed to keep out of his way but I was never confident that he wouldn't find me. The Headrow was steaming with traffic, restless steel trembling through its own bad gasses in a daze of mechanical fury. A herd of taxis appeared and swaggered over the tarmac, their metallic bonnets glinting and the stooped sages at their wheels giving everyone the hard stare. Two yellow JCBs wedged into the flow and began shouldering their way up at ten mph and the whole scene cranked down into second gear and began to sweat frustration like pearls of bile or the bitter beads of madmen curled into hoops in the corners of locked rooms.

I kicked at the grey pavement under which the arteries of the city snaked: cables and pipes of monstrous length pumping life to us, fuel and nourishment and vital elixirs and game shows. Half the population are addicted to game shows. It could be worse, I suppose, the things might have some quality and then we'd all be at them. The noise of the traffic ground up inside my head and the acrid fumes boiled in the gutters.

I kept going.

I'd passed the Law Society and got to Albion Street when I saw Ginny. She was with Danby Houghton standing next to a No Entry sign. They were handing out leaflets to the passing public. When I got closer I saw that it wasn't Danby Houghton but someone who was suited like him and of similar appearance. Curiosity led me nearer.

Closer, I stopped by an adshel brandishing another wretched Doorway poster, this one featuring the usual blonde with the usual smile. I gritted a fair sized grimace and peered out at them both. Ginny was looking happy. But to me she wasn't happy. Take my word for it. I know the girl better than anyone. And what in the name of Stepford was she wearing? I watched for a while without her seeing me.

The Houghton clone was prancing up and down the pavement handing out leaflets to anyone who was fool enough not to blister past with a withering look of contempt. Ginny didn't seem to be as enthusiastic. She seemed to be a bit slower off the mark, a little less eager to spread the word. Ghostly visions of us together swam over my sight. My eyebrows began creeping down to meet my upcreeping beard. The clone kept offering Ginny significant glances and from the distance I was at I was trying to work out whether they were looks of encouragement or intimidation. A girl of about seventeen, dressed in a pink jacket and jeans, stopped briefly and took a leaflet from Ginny then walked away looking over it. She didn't look impressed.

Some students went by and ignored them standing there. Then a middle-aged man in a mac stopped and seemed to be talking to

Ginny. The Houghton clone watched. I watched. I felt a rising feeling of anger. Why was she doing this? Standing in the middle of the street accosting strangers and letting them leer at her like this. The man smoothed a hand over his balding head and took a leaflet and stood there and appeared to be reading it. Like he was reading it right there in front of her. He kept nodding and looking up at her and grinning vacantly.

The clone moved in a bit and I could sense, even from where I was, that he thought they'd caught one. As if. The dirty old git was just leering at Ginny. The clone got in close, then closer still till the three of them were standing together like Musketeers. I was relieved a bit when the clone took the man away and walked a few paces over towards the door of Boots. They parted, with the man waving a hand and shaking his head like he was disagreeing with something that the Houghton clone had said to him or maybe just offering a general rejection of his nonsense.

Ginny meanwhile was talking to a young guy with an earring and denim jacket and jeans. I'd had enough. When he moved off clutching his leaflet I moved out from my adshel and advanced on them.

I was closer to her when I stood in the puddle and felt the scum of the water come up through the hole in my right shoe. I'd tried to repair it by putting cardboard wrapped in a piece cut from a plastic bag inside the shoe. I thought it had worked but the wet foot now mocked my efforts. I thought of Danby Houghton's cream chinos and the shine of his shoes and the glossy coat of his BMW. His vacuous gawp rose in my memory like some hideous fish and I wanted to tear Ginny from his side and take her to some distant place. Maybe even outside Leeds. Damn you, Houghton, I spoke through bared teeth. Leave mine to me.

As I walked, the drizzle drifted in from the east and the breeze grew up and blew the damp air against the shop windows and the statues and blew a cold skein of wet across my face and the heat of my anger made it hiss and steam and I wiped it out of my eyes and I looked for her to find her again and for a moment I couldn't see her and then there she was in front of me holding out a leaflet to me. I looked down at the thing in her hands and I was reaching out for her when I thought, what am I doing? I looked at her eyes. She didn't know me. She didn't. She was just sort of staring at me with a blank smile on her face like it had been left there by someone else. The clone was looking over like he could see something was not right. I wanted to say something.

—Ginny, I said.

—Pardon? She stared at me blankly.

—Ginny? It's me. Look I know you said...

—What do you want?

—Ginny, what are you talking about? What are you doing here? I looked at her quizzically.

—What am I doing here? Isn't it obvious, Monkey you cretin? I'm working. So, actually, no, it wouldn't be obvious to you, would it? Work, I mean.

—Ginny, for pity's sake girl, snap out of it. At least tell me to sod off or something, you're worrying me.

—Sod off, Monkey.

—You don't mean it.

—Sod off, Monkey. I do. She stared at me. Out of the corner of my eye I saw the Houghton clone gurning at some hapless buffoon in a puce dress and pigtails. She was nodding furiously at him and clutching at the leaflet in her hands with a sad desperation. Ginny just went on staring at me.

—Ginny, you don't mean it. Come on, talk to me.

—Take a leaflet. You might learn something.

—No, I don't want a leaflet. Look at me, Ginny, what's happened to you?

—And stop calling me Ginny; I'm Virginia.

—You'll always be Ginny to me, Ginny.

—Oh, for pity's sake, Monkey, give it a rest. Either take a

leaflet or sod off.

—OK, give me a leaflet.

—Sod off, you don't really want one, you're just taking the piss.

—Look, Ginny, I began but as I said this I noticed the Houghton clone talking into a mobile phone and walking with some sense of purpose towards us.

—Ginny, I shouted as if she were deaf to me, stop all this. What's the matter with you? What have they done to you?

—Danby says you're a bad person and I agree with him, she said wearily.

—Talk sense, woman, I snapped. The whole thing was beginning to bug me something serious. Your father thought that and it didn't stop you from seeing my good side. Talking of which, he's still after me, isn't he? Wants his rent. Tell him I'll pay him when I've got the cash together. Like when hell freezes over. He can wait.

—He's not happy, Monkey. I don't want... She looked down and I thought the clever Monkey eye caught a flicker of concern in her eye.

—What? Don't want what?

—Nothing. Look, just go away, will you?

—Ginny, we've got to talk. There's a lot we've got to talk about. Don't throw it all away.

—If it comes to throwing, Monkey, I think it was you who chucked it all away.

—Fair enough. You're right. It was a big mistake. But how have you got involved with all this nonsense? Danby Houghton? The Doorway? I mean, what's that all about? You're not really going to tell me that you've signed up to all this rubbish? And Eeve, for pity's sake? Been off to any distant planets or anything recently? Got your focus on 2020? What's going to happen then? You and all your little cronies get whisked off to the planet Eden where success is not just round the corner, it's round the bend?

Or does success mean you just stay up there in that place up Brownberrie Lane in your weird outfits staring very clearly at each other? Or what? You all pop up suddenly as happy little millionaires? It's mad!

—You don't understand, she said. But her eyes were looking shifty and her hands fidgeted with the nasty little leaflets.

—Of course I don't understand. It's all complete bollocks. Look at me and tell me I'm wrong. Look at me and tell me you really believe in Damon Damon's bloody fictional alien.

—Don't talk like that. We don't need to talk, Monkey. You're just not listening, are you? I've moved on. Just go away and leave me alone.

—I don't buy it. I don't think you believe any of this crap. I think you just like driving round in that sodding car and hanging on whatsisface's tweedy arm like he's some sort of sugar daddy. I think you're just trying to make me jealous.

—Don't be absurd, Monkey. Just go away and screw your old girlfriend.

—Ginny, *you're* my old girlfriend.

But she backed away. There were a number of people in the street all dressed like Danby Houghton. They stood there, arms folded, the blade creases in their trousers making their legs look like cream mechanisms. One of them wore mirror shades despite the gloom and the gauze of rain over the lenses turned his eyes into bug's eyes. I stared at them and they stared back. Other people in the street didn't seem to notice the strangeness of it all and milled in and out of the shops, parading about as usual with their plastic bags and damp faces. The Foundation people closed in on Ginny and when they moved off, she was with them.

I watched her go. The rain in my hair and beard made my head heavy. I wanted to call out to her. I wanted to run after her. But all I did was stand in the street outside Boots and look at the rain trembling over the shop windows and the people moving through their wet world like a silent movie running in an abandoned cinema.

I lay that night under the peeling ceiling of my room and counted the things I'd done wrong to lose Ginny. There must have been something I'd done. Must have been something. It had probably been a combination of things, really. If I'd had a bit more cash I'd probably have taken her to better places and probably had a decent place to bring her back to. But then, surely she'd fallen in love with me despite the size of my income. It can't have been just that. Admittedly, I'd sort of got distracted by Stella. Well, she had a certain feminine charm. Not that Ginny didn't. Just that Stella – good God let me wipe the memory of her body from the tatters of my mind - Stella, before she revealed herself – well, afterwards as well, to be honest – was the sort of woman you'd crawl over broken glass to get to.

Not that she'd be too impressed if some lacerated dog-like creature started pawing at her hem but you get the idea. I wanted to kneel at her feet and…oh, never mind, there no chance of any of it so I might as well cut her from my mind with the scalpel of reason and sing a different song.

Got no hat and I got no shoes
Oh my baby got nothing to lose
I want to take you somewhere
Make you someone tonight

I got so lost I got no clues
I want you baby but I just can't choose
I want to take you baby
Just can't work out how

Love comes free if it comes at all
You climb that mountain but you gotta fall
I want to walk you down

My lonely road tonight

I walk the streets till I hear you call
When I reach you, lover, I can only crawl
So take my hand
And tell me it's all right

I got up and had another beer. The kitchen end of the room was a bit of a disgrace, though I say it myself. The sink was stuffed with KFC detritus and the splashback from my kettle-filling had congealed the fat white. I kept washing up, I know I did, but someone just kept using the plates and things and leaving them unwashed all over the place. I'd found half a plate of fish and chips abandoned under the bed when I was looking for a shoe. It was ages ago when I last had fish and chips so I don't know whose this was. I had another beer. Soon be dawn.

Already a pink gleam was creeping under the blinds and trailing over the white edges of plates. The kitchen clock wasn't straight but it still told me the time was getting on. I leaned against the edge of the steel sink and sipped the beer. The clock ticked on. Each second took her further away from me into the mad world of The Doorway Foundation. I had to have a plan. I had to get her away from those people. But what could I do?

The next day I phoned Mr Wolffe. I was going to tell him the truth about Danby Houghton and what Ginny had got herself involved in. But he just kept yelling down the phone. He still had this obsession about money. I got in a bit about Houghton but he just raged about my unsuitability to be on the same planet as his daughter. The next few days passed with me preoccupied with the problem. Work went on but my mind was not on it and my heart was not in it.

When Gordy came round one day looking for layabouts to lay

off I wouldn't have cared if he'd pointed out me. But he didn't. I hoped that Bastard One would get the push but he was apparently the hero of the day having saved Gordy's cat from a flat fate in Press Four by piking it out with a pole. The smothering grubby dinginess hung around our heads and the radio juddered on and on and the morning turned to afternoon slowly.

When the next week started and the little guy called Snibble from the back of Workshop Two was missing, everyone assumed that it was he who'd been given the layoff but as it turned out he'd just disappeared and Hamster, who we all thought had flu or something, was given the elbow for taking his mistress to Skegness instead of coming to work. A week or so later they took him back on. He was all right at his job and Snibble really had disappeared. Apparently October's the most popular month for men to do that, to just go off to the shop or something and never come back. Too cold for me, October. I'd take off in June or July. Have a holiday. Doss down on some beach among the bikinis and tequila and grow a new identity and live a life of peace and sun, hard drink and soft women till the Grim Reaper turned up like a beachcomber after half an eternity and picked the husk of my grinning body from the sand.

I couldn't think of work. I had more pressing things on my mind. I had the plan. And I also had the feeling that I was being watched. Maybe it was just that there were more than a few people around who looked like The Doorway guys but those days I seemed to be tripping over them. They were in the street ambling past the arcade shops without a care in the world; they were sitting in the pub like Gilbert and George pretending not to be aware of their statement of the personal as art; they were talking seriously to woe-faced students on corners where the smoke from the dust of leaves palled over them like some miasmic emanation of significance.

It was getting creepy. They were watching me and I didn't know why. Didn't Damon Damon believe me when I'd said I hadn't opened the book. What had he said? Accessed it. Wasn't it obvious it hadn't been forced and wasn't it obvious I was too bloody stupid to find a way to open it, me who was making a habit of being duped and eluded and half-seduced? I tried to ignore them. But it was creepy.

I'd not spent much time cooking or cleaning and I'd not been eating well. What I had been doing was saving money. I did a bit of bar work at The Hyde Park. I'd see Smug and Goldfish and Benny and Smallwit of an evening and I kept them pretty much up with what had been going on. I told them all about Ginny's present state of mind and we swapped ideas about what to do without coming up with anything very practical.

The more I talked about her the more I wanted her and the more I wanted her the more I hoped to save her. One night, after a particularly vicious bout of drinking, I hit on what we all thought was the real thing to do. Excellent scheme. White knight stuff. I kept going to work and after two months I'd saved a reasonable amount of paper money. I kept it sellotaped to the bottom of a drawer. I didn't want Mr Wolffe finding out where I lived and turning the place over. Don't suppose the ruse would have worked really with a man of Wolffe's calibre when it came to debt but it was a gesture. When I'd got what I thought was enough I went to see Smug.

I found him sitting on the steps at the back of The Metropole where first I had met him again all that time ago. He was smoking a Lambert and the tip glowed as he inhaled. He dusted a few specks of ash off his knee and crossed his legs. When he saw me he grinned and scrubbed out the fag under his trainer.

—Yo, Monkey. You been hiding in a tree?

—Good to see you, Smug. Still working?

—Still doing whatever it is I always seemed to be doing,

Monkey. Look at these hands, they're like rubber gloves.

—How's Chef?

—Chef's OK.

—Still preserving himself for posterity?

—You what?

—You know, still sucking on the sauce, popping the pickle, still at the booze.

—Oh, yeah. Still shouting as well.

—Chefs do that, don't they?

—Why's that then?

—Only an angry man could spend all day in the kitchen.

Smug looked over his shoulder. Steam was bucketing out of the ventilator in the wall behind him. There was the sound of something sharp hitting something dull repeatedly. I could smell the grease floating on the air.

—What are you up to, then?

—Still at the factory.

He took another cigarette out of the packet in his pocket, struck up a flame on a match and lit the tip. He flicked the spent match towards the bin.

—What's it like, then, any better?

—It's grimmer than a witch's oxter. But it gets me by. And that leads neatly on to why I'm here, Smug.

—OK.

—Listen, mate, you did a grand job with the Two Little Pigs plan. Grand job. I'll always be grateful to you for that. But I need your help again. I've been thinking. All this with Ginny, I mean, what's a man to do? Do I just say, well, she's grown up and can make up her mind about things and if she wants to hang out with a bunch of geeks...

—Rich geeks.

—OK, rich geeks. Should just say, well that's all right then and leave her alone. Or should I go up there and drag her screaming back into the real world?

—Tough one, Monkey.

—I know. What do you think, Smug.

—We've been through all this. You know what I think. I think you were bloody mad to bin her in the first place and chase that bloody tart.

—I didn't dump her, she dumped me.

—Look, Monkey, Chase the Tart's a dangerous game at the best of times, isn't it. That's what binned whatever was between you and Ginny.

—Yeah, right, my fault. I know that now, Smug. But what am I going to do about it?

—She doesn't want you. Face it, she doesn't want you.

—OK. But what if I want her?

—Too late for that now, isn't it?

—Do you really think so?

—Isn't that what she said?

—Well, yes, but you know what women are like; she might not have meant it.

—Like you didn't mean to get the tart horizontal, mate?

—Don't remind me. OK you might be right. She might not want me but she might want saving anyway.

—Not your job, mate.

—It is.

—Nah. Tell her dad. He'll sort it out. Not your job.

—I've tried that.

—No good?

—Git just wanted his money.

—Well, you do owe him, Monkey.

—Look, don't get on to all that. What I want is for you to help me get her out of that place.

—Not me, mate. From what you've said, they're all blood weirdos and creeps.

—Come on, Smug.

—Not a chance mate.

—Please, Smug.

—No.

His face was set against me. He bent down to fasten a loose lace in his trainer and tied it up slowly. I thought he was kidding, that when he looked up he'd be grinning but he wasn't. Chef's voice rose above the hiss and sizzle behind him like a monstrous belch. I felt awkward. I went over and sat down beside him on the steps. Smoke moved slowly through his moustache and melted into the air. How could I persuade him?

—You've got to help me. I need you.

—Very touching, Monkey, but no. I must decline. He rolled his shoulders and stared off into the distance. I followed his gaze and we sat like that for a while, each of us watching the gates swing minutely on their hinges and the dust fluttering and the dusty hedge swaying its long head over the wall.

—I need a car, I said at length.

—Oh, yeah, he snorted, don't we all?

—And someone to drive it.

—A bloody chauffeur? You've lost it, Monkey.

—More of a getaway driver.

—Thought you could drive.

—I can. Haven't for a while but I can drive.

—Just got no car? Join the club. If I had a car you'd be welcome to borrow it but do you think I'd be stuck in a job like this if I had a car?

—Well I don't know. But I need a car and someone to drive it. I'm going to kidnap Ginny. I've just decided. With or without you.

—When did you think of that? You really have boarded the bullshit express, haven't you.

—Just now whilst I was thinking.

—Thinking! He snorted. You can't do that. That's kidnapping!

—I know what it is, Smug. But it's for her own good.

—You're mad, Monkey. You're stark monkey mad. You can't do that.

—Look, it's not *really* kidnapping, is it? I mean I'll be saving her from that lot, who are, as you so rightly say, weirdos. She needs help.

—Still kidnapping.

—No, it's not. I mean I'm not going to be holding her to ransom or anything, am I?

—I don't know.

—You don't... what do you think I am? It's me, Smug. It's me. And I want to rescue Ginny before they turn her brain to blancmange with all that mumbo jumbo. I've got to do it.

—But look, she doesn't want you. Just face it, Monkey, she doesn't want you. If you go and kidnap her you're going to end up nicked. You are. Seriously nicked. And what about Mr Wolffe? Have you thought what he might think of you kidnapping his lovely daughter? Have you thought of that? Because I think you should. What with owing him money and all. And him not liking you anyway. And him being so...

—All right, Smug, I get the picture. Stop jabbering on.

—I'm not keen on this whole thing, Monkey.

He stood up and began pacing up and down alternately dragging on the cigarette and rubbing the back of his hand over his moustache. I could see he wasn't keen. I leaned forward and rested my elbows on my knees. For a while the noises from the kitchen and the crowded sounds from the main road made their music uninterrupted by either of our voices. I felt a calm settling over me as I sat there. The breeze flicked dust at my eyes. Smug did his pacing. I sat and thought of myself as hero. I had no definite idea of how I was going to snatch her but at least now I had purpose. I had destiny. I had somewhere to go. I was smiling. And as I smiled the plan began to form itself in my head. Smug would drive. Everything was falling into place. But I still I needed a car. Smug stopped suddenly in front of me and repeated:

—You're mad.

—I know.

—Stop grinning like that. It makes you look mad as well as being mad.

—OK. But I'm going to do it. You've got to help me find a car.

—Where are you going to find a car?

—That's what I need help with.

—And why do you want someone to drive it?

—Just to begin with, to get us off to a flying start from The Doorway place with Ginny. Like a getaway driver. Then once we're out of the way I can take over and drive the two of us off somewhere.

—Somewhere?

—Away from Leeds.

—Away from...? Have you thought about this at all?

—Course I have.

—You haven't. You can't have.

—All right, I haven't. But I'm going to do it anyway.

—I don't know where you're get a car.

—Do you think Benny would lend me his bike?

—You're mad.

—Will you stop saying that. Even to a madman it can get a bit boring.

—Sorry Monkey. But you are.

—You're right; Benny and that bike are like two halves of the same animal.

—Goldfish has got a car.

—He hasn't.

—He has.

—He's got a push bike.

—He's got a car as well.

—I've seen him on the bike covered in mud and stuff coming

down from the woods. I've seen him in his flash racing snake outfit and that yellow helmet. But a car? Never seen him anywhere near a car. Are you sure?

—A Fiesta. Think it's a Fiesta he's got.

—Amazing. Do you think he'd know where it was if we asked him?

—What do you mean 'we'?

—Oh, come on, Smug. If you'd seen her in that state on the street spouting garbage, you'd be straining at the leash to help me save her.

—Are you sure you're not just going to bin her again when some other tarty piece blows you a kiss?

—Of course not. How could you think that?

—Oh, who knows, Monkey, who knows?

—No, come on, Smug. I feel terrible about her. If I hadn't fallen for Wonder Woman she wouldn't have got caught up with that Danby Houghton and she wouldn't be wandering round the Leeds like a bloody zombie saying profit is love, baby, to every passing mug. When I think of what I threw away…and for what?

—Don't get excited, Monkey. It was better when you were grinning. All right. Look, I'll help you find a car, all right. I'll help you get a car but that's all. OK?

—Thanks, Smug. You're a mate.

—But if you do this, Monkey, if you do this and then you bin her I hope you get ate to death by Wolffe's bloody dog.

—If I throw her over after this, I'll go and sit in its dog bowl.

—So I'll see you, then. Tonight?

—Thanks, Smug.

Without a word of farewell he went back into the hotel. The door shut behind him and chef's voice rang round the big steel pans and tore out of the ventilator in a cloud of noxious steam. It was a hard life.

17

"You ain't done drivin' before, have you, son?"
"Well, mom always said I'd drove her round the bend."
(Ed Bale and Tommy Krueger, *Stooge Loose*, 1946)

That evening Smug met me in The Hyde Park and Benny was there and Smallwit and they listened to my plan. The future was looking rosy. All I needed now was a car. I was going to start a new life. We'd go somewhere new, Ginny and I. We'd...

—Monkey. Monkey!

—What?

—Are you with us?

—What? Sorry, I was just thinking.

—I was saying, how are you going to get her out of that place?

—What? Oh, I'm going to park outside and then wait till she comes out and then get her into the car and put my foot down.

—Like tell her what's what? asked Smallwit, grinning.

—More like put the pedal to the metal, said Benny. But that's not going to be easy, mate. How do you know when she's going to come out? How do you know she's going to be alone? What are you going to do if she doesn't want to get into the car, cause like what Smug says, she's blown you out good and proper.

—And, chipped in Smug, what happens if they see you waiting and keep her in, like keep her away from you?

—Minor details, I answered them, minor details. It's going to work out. I know it is.

They looked from each to each and drank off some beer. The table was crowded with empty glasses. They were all with me, I knew that, despite their doubts.

—So where are you going to get a car, Monkey? asked

Smallwit, leaning over the table.

—Goldfish has got a car.

—Has he?

— Smug says he has. Said a Fiesta, didn't you, Smug?

—I said a Fiesta or something.

—I didn't know that, said Smallwit. How come I've never seen him drive anywhere?

—Likes walking, doesn't he.

—Goldfish's got a car? You mean he can drive and all that? Is it a bubble car, you know, like a goldfish bowl?

—Droll, mate, very droll.

—Must have hidden talents.

—How does he remember all the pedals and that?

—I don't know.

—Maybe he just takes pot luck.

—Do you think he'll let me borrow it, then?

—Don't know about that, Monkey. He's a shy beast is Goldfish. Keeps his cards close to his chest.

—I'll have to ask him, though.

—Should be in later.

We carried on drinking and I carried on thinking about the rescue. It's what my life needed. You can muddle on for so long but there comes a time in a man's life when he has to do something for the future, take a grip on things and get things sorted out. Otherwise there's just that lonely road to go down on a dark night alone.

Goldfish arrived and not only said that I could borrow his car, not only said that I could have a practice in it on account, as he said, of my driving skills maybe being in need of refreshment seeing as I'd not driven anything larger than a trolley for years, but also that he thought the whole plan was a great piece of tactical machinery the gods themselves would be envious of. Or Goldfish words to that sort of effect. Great.

The next day we went in search of the car. We stood, Smug and Goldfish and me, in the road outside Goldfish's flat and looked around. There was a red Astra with a handwritten for sale notice taped crookedly to the rear window, a yellow MG Midget with rusty trim and a scooter propped against the wall. Of Goldfish's blue Fiesta there was no sight. Goldfish looked bemused by this and insisted that he'd left it there though he couldn't be a hundred percent sure — who could be that sure about anything? Then he said he could have left it round at Smallwit's and walked back after a few tins. It wasn't at Smallwit's.

Smallwit was sipping oily coffee when we arrived and paused in this to suggest that Goldfish might have left the car at his mother's. He hadn't. His mother's house had a large number 14 painted on the side wall with a two inch brush and there was a clotted mess of roses dusty from the road and heavy with thorns thrown up against the garden wall. Goldfish went and rang the bell but it can't have worked because no one came to the door.

It took us two days to find the car. Goldfish himself chanced upon it. Benny had given him a lift in on the back of the bike to do some shopping and there it was, in the Arndale car park behind the shopping centre. He drove it round to the bedsit.

—Goldfish, I said, are you sure this is your car?

—Course I'm sure. I drove it here, didn't I?

—But it's not a Fiesta, it's an Escort.

—Did I say it was a Fiesta?

—Well someone did.

—They must have meant Escort. Cause it's an Escort. You can see that.

—I can see that. Yes I can. And it's not blue.

—Yes it is.

—It's not blue, Goldfish. It's green.

—It's bluey.

—Green.

—It's called Tropical.

—It's called rusty.

I took it for a test run round the Ring Road with the evening sun slanting through the windshield and the spring drizzle sluiced about by the haphazard wipers with Goldfish sitting next to me chewing the ends of his fingers and looking pleased with himself every time I changed gear right. I found I remembered how to do it all but the traffic was stiffer than I recalled, more swirling and bulky. A taxi cut me up on the big roundabout heading for Armley and blared curses at me. Incredible.

It was Thursday and I was driving again. I told Goldfish how grateful I was for his lending me the car and assured him that I'd look after it. —Sure, he said. He pulled out from the back seat well from under a litter of Tizer bottles and sweet wrappers a yellow krooklock and told me to use it.

—It's busted, he said, but if you hang it over the wheel it puts thieves off this car and onto another.

—Some hope.

—Yeh, I don't want to lose it.

—And don't forget this, he said, lifting from the door pocket a plastic clipboard with various sheets of written-over paper attached and a biro wedged under the oval metal of the clip.

—What is that?

—Mileage, isn't it.

—I don't know, do I? You tell me.

—It's my mileage record so I can work out fuel consumption and all that 'cause if I don't keep it written down like this, I'd forget. Wouldn't I?

—Right. What do you want me to do with it?

—It's dead easy. Just write down when you put petrol in what the mileage is and how many litres you fill it up with.

—That's all?

—I think so. Let me have a look a minute. Yeah, that's all, look. Just put down the mileage and the litres.

—OK. But why would... I paused. Why was I quibbling? It was good of him to lend me the car.

—Why what, Monkey?

—Nothing.

He gave me the spare key I found in the glove box. Keys were about the only things Goldfish never lost, probably because he had them tied to his belt and he never went anywhere without his trousers. For the next two days I watched the rain drain from the sky through the bedsit window. Creepy Willards, the landlord, came and took away his rent, stuffing the notes into the back pocket of his jeans as if the money I'd worked so hard for was no more than a bit of change.

I watched him walk down the path to the road twisting to avoid the overgrown monster of a hedge that fell across the path in a sprawl of decayed leaves and trapped polystyrene trays. The gate whammed back on its spring, missed its post by a couple of inches and see-sawed till it met its rest dangling crookedly into the street. Creepy Willards spat onto the leaves in the gutter and bent his legs into walking down the road, adjusting his greasy trilby as he went.

The weekend came. Saturday, the rain slackened and clouds began to whiten over the drenched rooftops. People talked about sunshine and good weather. But they said it wouldn't last. Mrs Padgett in the corner shop held onto my change from the pound I'd given her for the morning paper till I'd listened to her theory about why the weather was so poor and would continue to be so for ever in this country. To paraphrase, she thought that the weather reflected the national temperament and reckoned the rain would fall, the cold winds blow and all the seasons dump on us their terrible lot because the temperament of the Englishman was one of pessimism and self-pity. Could it be, I suggested, finally getting my hands on the few coins of my due, that it was the other way round. She stared at the coins in my hand and then stared at my face and then stared at my eyes. I left her looking angry. But then she always looked angry. Probably on account of her husband being so nice a man.

And so it was that I looked at the long road ahead. It was pretty straightforward when you thought about it. All I had to do was drive up to The Doorway Foundation and park outside the gate and wait. It might be a long wait, I knew that. But I also knew that at some time Ginny would come out of or into the building and that was when I should be able to leap out and get her into the car. She'd just have to see sense. She'd just have to chuck out all this profitablility nonsense and face reality. And I was her reality. She just didn't know it yet. She didn't need plastic Danby, smooth as a lube. What she needed was something raw and real, something like me. Me.

The car stuttered and coughed and. I waited a minute and then tried it again. It stuttered and coughed again. My brain froze over and nothing happened for a while. I became aware of the low sun yellow and flat hanging in the mirror. It was seven twenty. It was early. Tufts of rubbish under the hedges jittered in the breeze. One or two cars nipped past, their engines hot and happy. I tried the key again and this time the thing fired up and rattled its oily throat and expectorated wads of black fume from its exhaust. I kept the pedal down and the engine whined and raced. This was it. Plan meets action.

When I thought it was ready I let off some of the revs and eased up the clutch. The seat pushed me irritably in the back, there was a loud clack and then silence. A seagull landed on the bonnet and winked at me. It was going to be a long day. I waited and then tried again.

As I pulled up Brownberrie Lane, my foot aching on the pedal and the car whingeing in second, I was full of anticipation and hope. I was going to make something of myself. I was going to look after Ginny and take her away from all the nonsense of the world to a place of serenity and good beer. She wanted someone with money? I would learn to earn that lucre. She wanted someone in cream pants? I could wear those chinos. She wanted wit. I had wit. She wanted smooth? Did she?

But even as I thought it, a whiff of an image taunted me, an intoxicating image of Stella unbuttoning the front of a tight-fitting coat. Who could forget something like that? I had to let it go, to focus on Ginny. It was Ginny I wanted. But each time I pulled up an image of her she was with the clown Danby and they were holding hands or smiling or something. I couldn't figure her out on her own. And Stella kept slinking across my mind's eye. And the thing was, I didn't want to let that image go. She was so much woman.

The engine whacked its little pistons. The Lane was passing by at about seventeen miles an hour and faces were mooning past of passers-by on the pavement lost in their fantasies. I tried to get my mind back to think about Ginny but something was pumping through my body that wanted Stella. I passed the oak the ash and the beech. The dry stone walls were draped to the shoulder with moss and lichen. I had to keep my mind on things. The plan the plan the plan. I settled down. The hill rounded off and the road turned east towards the turret of The Doorway Foundation.

I got it all sorted out in my head. After two hours sitting in the car waiting, chewing on chocolate and sipping tepid juice out of a box, I had it all back in perspective. Stella was the one who had poisoned me with dodgy champagne and Mickey Finn beer, ripped up my coat, robbed me of my reward and ruined my relationship with Ginny. Ginny was the woman I loved. Ginny was my muse. For Ginny I had deceived the beastman Wolffe and for her I had written the sonnet of the century. Now she had been seduced by the evil Danby Houghton into his world of nonsense. It was simple, really.

But, hell, I was bored. Bored and cold and nothing was happening to change either condition. I ate another bar of *Chocolube*. Smooth as a crooner's kiss and tasting slightly of toluene. I was having another go with the radio when things started to happen.

Maybe they got up late at The Doorway Foundation or maybe they all got together for one of those spooky little sessions before they came out to play. Whatever the reason, they were coming out now, all dressed in the same ways: the men in their suits and sunglasses, the women in dark skirts above the knee and jackets. And as they lined up in front of the building I noticed with a vague sense of unease that my plan was not perfect.

For a start, I couldn't see from the road whether or not Ginny was amongst them; all the suits were the same and the more I stared the more of the women began to look like her. And then I realised, as a mini bus came round the corner of the car park and stopped beside them, that even if she were there I wasn't going to be able to snatch her in front of everyone. I got out of the car and crossed the pavement and stood by the hedge. The mini bus swept past me and down the road. But I had a good look as it passed. All the women were sitting on one side of the bus, my side, and I saw that Ginny wasn't there.

Without really thinking about it, I was walking down the path towards the entrance. A second plan was getting its boots on inside my head as I walked. A desperate plan. One that was born of determination and a steel will and the refusal to give up. And desperation. I would go into the place and hunt her out and take her by the arm and we'd race out, out through the ranks of zombies trying to hold us back, pushing them aside like skittles, through the coloured corridors, past Damon Damon - snappy uppercut to the jaw, down goes Damon - out to the car and burn rubber to the very horizon of the world.

I stopped suddenly. There was a better way: subterfuge. I set off back up to the road. I'd get Goldfish's clipboard and pretend to be from somewhere with a delivery of something. Light bulbs. They must get through a load of those. Or leaflets. I'd pretend to have a truckful of leaflets and that I needed a signature from a Mr Damon Damon. 'That's a name to remember, remember,' I'd say to the girl, 'Do I go this way?' and I'd be in. I got up to the gateway and had started towards the car when I realised that it wasn't there. It had gone. I looked up and down the road. Nothing. A cow belched in the field opposite and hung its white face over the wire to stare at me. My stomach felt like a sock that had been pulled inside out.

To my right the road swept away down the hill. There was not a car in sight. To my left the road banked up and round a sharp bend about a hundred yards away. I was panting by the time I got there, my feet pounding the dirty flagstones, my blood pounding through its courses like some unloosed hectic. In the middle distance a car disappeared among the houses and the hung-over tree branches. It was red. I went back. What would I say to Goldfish? Lost your car, mate, and this time it looks real. For a moment the thought crossed my mind that he might not notice. He might not remember lending me the car.

No. I couldn't do that to a mate. I owed him a car. I owed him a car and a clipboard to boot. I ran a hand through my beard and tugged. It was all too real. The plan was done for. Everything was done for. I sat down on a flat stone on the top of a low wall. There was a grating sound and I slid slowly on the unmoored stone into the field behind me and lay there on my back in the damp grass staring up into the black silky nostrils of a cow. It chewed on. Ropy tendrils of spit wobbled over its lips. Then it slowly turned its back on me. There was a shuttering sound and loose wodges of shit pattered onto the grass and flecks of dark porridge danced over my beard. Life was strange.

It was some time before I found myself back at the gates of The Doorway Foundation. By now, anger had shouldered aside the weak figure of hopelessness. I was angry with myself for not locking the car or even draping the crippled krooklock over the steering wheel; I was angry with the whole Doorway thing for bringing me to all this and I was angry with Ginny for needing to be rescued. I bowled down the path.

The receptionist looked up at me with a bland smile. I was back in the lilac foyer just as it was changing to pink. The stink from the lilies hung in the air like cheap perfume. The receptionist was still looking at me, the wet-look lips poised on the brink of speech. I pointed my Monkey scowl at her and took it up close. When I was near enough to the desk to reach out and straighten the girl's lapel badge I veered sharply to my left and went quickly through the door leaving the girl calling feebly at me about an appointment.

—Not now, I snapped over my shoulder and went on, her voice trailing behind in its sorry echo. I knew they could see me. They'd told me that last time I was here. I looked around for the cameras but saw none. Maybe they had really tiny cameras. I'd gone through three sets of doors in the corridor before I heard voices. I turned into a room and shut the door behind me.

The room was empty so I went and sat behind the desk. The limed wood was really veneered chipboard and the swivel chair had an irritating wobble. There was nothing on the desk so I went through the drawers, hearing the footsteps go past. Two or three people. In a hurry. The drawers were full of pens, tacky biros with the gearwheel logo and The Doorway Foundation picked out in gold letters against the maroon barrels. There were some flyers and a half-empty half bottle of whisky. The desk of some minion.

I sat for a while and listened. When it seemed quiet I eased out of the door and went further down the corridor. I turned left at the bottom and continued past a number of potted plants. The place was big. Further on I heard voices making loud urgent whispers and the dull fall of feet on carpet. I dodged into an alcove and waited till they passed. I thought I recognised Stella's voice but it might have been the work of fancy. I squeezed myself against the wall. The arch cast a pink shadow over me and I found myself hugging the cheese plant. When it was quiet I slipped back into the corridor and set off again. I reckoned, now my anger had slackened and I was looking more at the world as it was than through a mist of fury, that my best bet was to try and circumnavigate the place and hope that somewhere on my voyage I would bump into Ginny. As you might.

I stopped for a breather by a picture of nine happy faces smirking in front of the Foundation place. Damon was one of them. The others just looked like ordinary people though a patina of joy shone on their mugs like sweat. There was a cloud in the sky I would have sworn was the shape of a pig.

I went on. For some time I moved through the corridors and rooms of the Doorway Foundation without meeting anyone. The place was quiet. And then, without any warning, the next door I opened precipitated me into a tasteful room of pink and beige where chairs were arranged in a number of rows before a podium from which a swarthy little man was addressing the assembled two dozen or so of his audience.

One or two heads turned and stared at me without interest and then turned back. Mostly they seemed to be couples and most of the men had notebooks and biros and one had what looked like a dictaphone, for the sake of all that's good and holy. The man glanced over at me and waved me towards a chair at the back and then turned to his big pad of paper which was balanced on an aluminium easel. He'd drawn various triangular diagrams on the big sheet of paper and he now swept up the sheet and folded it over the back of the pad to reveal the virgin territory on which his wisdom would next intrude. I looked round, noted the doors at each end of the room, one of which I'd come through, and then slunk into the seat and kept my head down.

I needed to orientate, I needed a little breather, I wanted to let the heat cool just a little. The guy carried on without pausing for breath, staring round the room to make eye-contact with everyone there. I stared at the backs of their heads. There were some real cheap haircuts and one so recent the clippings still clung to the guy's nape and the white moon of his collar. The guy on the podium wrote in straggling black letters down the left side of the pad:

S
H
A
F
 T

He stepped back.

—Any one of you, he said, could be standing up here like me. Every one of you has the potential to do what I am doing. You can all succeed. You can all be a success. The Doorway Foundation could open for you an opportunity to enter a world you have hardly dared to dream of. I want you to think about your dreams. Just think about them. I want you to imagine what you would buy if you had the money. What would be your dream house? What car have you always wished for? The Audi A6? The BMW Z4? I want you to imagine sitting in the driving seat of your dream car, I want you to imagine what it feels like to drive that car, to be the successful man behind the wheel of that Audi or that BMW or that Infiniti G35. Feel the power. Feel the power of the car. Feel the power it gives you. You could be that person.

—You may be sitting there thinking, 'I'll never have that car', or, 'I'll never have the money for that house, that dream house in that dream location.' Banish those thoughts. Negative thoughts are the demons of failure. Think positive. Just imagine walking up that drive and opening that door. Feel the key in your hand. What does it feel like? It feels like power. It feels like a dream come true, doesn't it? I want you to hold onto that feeling, hold onto that power, hold onto that dream. Because you can have it, you can have that dream, it can be real. If you have the dream you have the reality.

—And I'm going to show you how. I'm going to tell you my story. I wasn't always a success. Four years ago I was an operative for Benton and Bloford, the food processors. I had a steady job and a steady mortgage and I thought I was doing all right. But each month there was the little problem of balancing the budget, paying the bills.

You know what it is like to sit there trying to spread around that money just a little further. Just a little thinner. I paid the bills, balanced the figures. But it was getting harder. And I got to thinking. I got to looking out there at those people in their swanky cars and their big houses with their holidays out of the city and I thought, 'I can do better than this, I can be successful, I deserve more than this'. And I looked over at my wife – she was in the kitchen opening something for dinner – and I said to myself, 'A wife deserves a successful man'. I had that dream of success, you see, before I knew how to make it come true.

He stooped down into the crowd and urged a woman from her seat and led her up onto the podium from where she gave a nervous smile and patted her hair and blinked at him. He went on with her standing there just to one side of the easel looking meek and sort of proud at the same time. There was much about his lowly job and his lowly life and all that sort of crap, like he was over-strawing the barn ready for the big transformation into rich guy.

Then came the invitation to join the Doorway Foundation and the hard work that followed and lo! Before our eyes he turned into Captain Success, wonder of the world and wealthy man. All down to SHAFT and the Foundation. And it was so simple… just follow these easy rules and bingo: success.

He recounted his last day at work, telling the boss what he thought of him, champagne flowing like a fountain, the waiting white stretch limo and a hired chauffeur and the goggling distorted faces of his co-workers as they pressed their noses to the window and watched him motor into the sunset of success. No more holidays on the west coast for him. No more the toe-rag of the tinning business. He was jetting around the world now lecturing on success and how success was for everyone. Ha. Ha.

He took a breath into his taut little body and wiped a hand over his head to loosen the perspiration from its moorings and give the brow the sheen of affluence. He exhaled slowly, deliberately, purposefully. He smiled a rich smile and breathed in again. I felt the audience tense – this next exhalation would be it, would be the secret of how to transform yourself from the middling and mundane to the material world's best mate: a rich man. He pulled off the top from his magic marker and raised it in his hand towards the board where the letters S H A F T stretched down in damp anticipation of being transformed into something of sense.

I found my mind glazing over with a frost of boredom and soon my eyes were shutting out the marionette with his marker and his magic wife and I was sliding towards oblivion. My head jerked up suddenly and I became aware that I had hadn't been aware. I seemed to have been sitting there for an eternity but a glance at my watch told me that it had only been an eternity of minutes. From the podium the voice pressed on into my ears. He was telling us how following SHAFT would improve the efficiency of industry and transform the public sector into a nirvana where contented worker and smiling manager would stroll arm in arm down the road of success and the laurel leaves of SHAFT certification would be blazoned on the walls of every factory and shop and school and hospital in the city. Everyone would be SHAFTed.

And then he turned his attention back to us poor failures who sought significance in our sad little lives. The road to success was pretty straightforward, it seemed, all you needed was a guide to point out the right route for you. To open your eyes. The Foundation was that guide. All you wanted was the self-belief, the trust and the Starter Pack. Which came with the commitment to purchase just twenty four essential CDs in the first year of membership. He gurned at us and turned and wrote in looping letters down the flip chart.

The guy next to me was scraping the ball point of his pen along the margin of the page. Then he got to work copying down the SHAFT definitions, finished, and sat vacantly with pen poised over the paper waiting to inscribe the next pearls. The woman to his right stared straight ahead and when he nodded, she nodded. He nodded a lot. The synchronised acquiescence of noddy dogs in the rear windscreen of life.

I reasoned that by now the fuss might have died down in the building and it might be about time to pursue my objective when I noticed that the guy on the stand was giving me odd looks. This wasn't entirely a surprise, I suppose, I'd had odd looks in the past and at the present moment I was dishevelled beyond my usual dishevelment: my jacket was streaked with grass stains and flecks of dung, my eyes were in surveillance mode and my beard was angry.

Then I realised that he was talking about money and I thought maybe the bastard thinks I haven't got any. Which was about right but it was still a bastard thing to think. From what I could gather from the guff he was giving out, they were offering a plan that would change your life at a knock-down price. Everything in life has its cost, he was saying, and success is no exception. The guy next to me wrote down, *Success costs everything*, in his laborious hand and drew a little circle over the *i* instead of a dot,

over a couple more pages. More full of crap than the first. On one, a young woman sitting in a lotus position was shown with what looked like a door in its forehead. The writing this time was in English, though that didn't render it any more sensible. The title to the page was The Portal and radiating out of the door in the woman's head were streams of words and tiny pictures. It seemed to suggest that through the door, or portal! were many bountiful things of great beauty (though you wouldn't have guessed beauty from the execution of the drawings – they were scrawled like a hasty paranoid might sketch the figures that ransacked his mind).

On the facing page were a series of figures growing, left to right, from a baby into a child into a man into a man hovering in mid-air in the lotus position (actually looked like his legs had been tied in a reef knot by a crazy wrestler) with an idiot grin and a door half open in his head. In the background a woman, the mummy from the earlier page, was sending out beams of pencil strokes that linked her to the doorway. The title was *Opening the Portal* and there was a sub-title written small in wavering letters: *Opening the Third Organ of Ocular Perception*. If this female figure was Eeve, it seems the artist wanted to convey the idea that she could open up your head like a tin of beans and make you see dozens of bad drawings. I flipped on for a short minute and came across page after page of weirdness. But a calculated weirdness. And that calculation in execution cut against the strangeness, suggesting artifice. What it didn't suggest was revelation. What it suggested more was, as a cartoon once said: now for something spontaneous. Ho, ho.

Someone ran past the door and I stopped and listened. It went quiet again.

Then I turned to the laptop. I leaned forward to read the screen: there were six folders displayed: *Correspondence, Codes, Administration, Accounts, Real Accounts* – interesting...maybe why old Damon hadn't followed a more usual means of getting his book back - but the one that really drew my eye was called *Snake Oil*. I opened it. This led me to *Text*, *Blurb*, *Ads* and *Drafts*. Short of time, I clicked *Blurb*. Up popped a page:

It was not in the Nevada desert but on Ilkley Moor, a peaty expanse in the North of England, that Dave Darke encountered Eeve, a being from another world. Visiting our planet from star-dimension 96, Eeve, one of the Chosen Choosers, had chosen Dave Darke to be her emissary on earth. And on that summer evening she introduced him to The Portal, *a doorway into a true understanding of the universe. In this fascinating account of his journey from small business manager to guru, Darke explains the journey we must all make if we are going to see the world as it should be seen and achieve what Eeve revealed as a 'state of the personal universal'. Twenty years in the pet food business have given Darke a particular insight into success and a down-to-earth, no-nonsense approach to achieving it. This book shows how, by following the wisdom of star travellers like Eeve, we can all reach our personal goals and achieve the wealth and happiness we all deserve. With an introduction by Larry Tinkler ('Stardust in Your Eyes' and 'Telepathy: a Cure for Loneliness') and a step by step guide showing how to enter* The Portal, *this book is essential reading for anyone who wants to truly understand the true meaning of themselves. As Darke says, 'This book won't change your life if you don't buy it.'*

Well, well, it looked as if Mr Damon Damon was a bit of a dark horse. I opened another file and found word from Troubadour, Purvey and Waistcoat, Literary Agents, thanking Damon for the original and thought-provoking first chapters of The Portal, and squealing with delight over their vision of the book as a rampant best-seller.

What a guy. He was running the biggest con in Leeds since pre-peeled oranges. He'd written a book. And he had an agent drooling over it. Envy sparred with repulsion in my mind and envy had the bigger punch. I thought of Monkey's Typewriter lying out cold on the floor of Phibre and Phibre. Who would want to read my little work when they could have their lives transformed by a git like Damon sodding Damon. The credulous would always form an orderly queue for salvation. Clever bastard.

Silence hung in the room and there was no sound of pursuit outside. How long had I got? In answer, the phone on the desk suddenly bleeped. It went on for a while and then stopped. I didn't have long.

18

"Whereof one cannot think, thereof one cannot spill the beans."
(Art Sharpe, *Philosophy Again!*, 1989)

With a flash of my usual inspiration, I shuffled through the desk drawers. They were full of normal office junk, a nest of paperclips, nasty biros, that sort of thing. And a handful of pen drives adorned with the company logo. I hesitated... and then picked one and stuck it into a USB port on the laptop. I rummaged around with the little mouse and started to copy *Snake Oil* to the pen drive. I was going to get what I could out of this. Maybe Wolffie would like to know something of the people his dear daughter was mixing with. The laptop bumbled and burred and I was beginning to get a bit itchy when I heard distant voices and the sound of feet working their way purposefully over the carpet out in the corridor.

I looked from the laptop to the door. I looked from the door to the laptop. The copy was still doing its thing. I slid out of the chair and lowered myself closer to the floor, my eyes fixed on the screen and my ears picking up the approaching footstep and voice noises. I sank lower till only my eyes stared over the edge of the desk focussed like a maniac on the screen. I reached out a hand as the corridor people stopped right outside the door. My fingers rested on the little black pen drive. Two people had stopped outside the door and were talking. I let out my breath and refocused on my situation. It didn't look good. The copy finished. I paused. Somebody took the door handle and turned it but the talk edged up a notch at this point and the handle was dropped. It was Damon out there, I was sure of that, and I thought the other must be Stella from the dark vowels rolling in the dulcet purr. They seemed set for the moment. I pulled out the pen drive.

I looked round the walls for any chance of exit but the window had an obvious lock on it and there were no man-sized heating ducts for me to wriggle through. That was it then. I sat down in the chair again and twizzled round for a bit. I began to feel the potency of villainy.

I was facing the window when the door opened and Damon himself walked in behind me. I spun round in the chair thinking I could've done with Smug's tatty cat to stroke with sinister effect, and saw his eyes going in and out of their sockets like he was inflating them from the inside.

—So, Mr Damon...or may I call you Damon? This is a fine kettle of fish and no mistake, I said, slipping the pen drive into my jacket pocket and not caring whether or not he had seen it. Words wrestled on the front line of his lips and the dark suit undulated with curious spasms like Rolf Harris warming up a wobble board. I stared at him. He stared at me. I folded my arms and leant back in the chair, enjoying the moment.

—So here you are, he said rather pointlessly, his eyes shifting from my face to the laptop on his desk and back again.

He smoothed down the front of his serious suit and adjusted his stance. Cogs were obviously spinning in the cunning Damon brain. What next? He took a step back and closed the door behind him without turning, without taking his eyes from me or the laptop, and then he walked round the desk to where he could see the laptop's screen and looked down on me. He seemed to be thinking about what to do. I bet he was thinking about what I might have seen and whether or not he could buy me off. Maybe, I thought, I could barter some help to find Ginny.

Without taking his eyes off me, he darted out a hand and seized the book and slid it into one of the desk's drawers, took a key out of his pocket and locked the drawer. He drew a little breath of relief. Then he leaned over and closed down the laptop. I heard him draw in another breath and then he leaned very close to my ear and whispered savagely,

—Whatever you have seen does not exist, all right. How long have you been in here?

—Damon, you surprise me. You lie to me, lure me with Sirens, drug me and steal away my girlfriend into the clutches of one of your clones and then you stand there and tell me the thing that got me involved in the first place doesn't exist. You surprise me, you really do. Careless, leaving the door open, by the way.

—Well, well…have it your way then. Tell who you wish what you have seen. A bit of advance publicity never did any harm, did it?

—All I want is Ginny and I'll be out of your little world. It's all a bit alien to me, if you know what I mean.

—You may mock, he said.

—OK, I said. It looks crap to me. All that stuff about aliens is crap. So all this fuss was about a crappy book.

—That book is going to make me a lot of money.

—Yeah, right.

—You are a puzzle to me, Mr Monk. A puzzle. On the one hand, he said, suddenly all oily, you allow me to get back that which is mine and – let us not beat about the bush – I am truly relieved to have got it back. Our books are like children, don't you think, Mr Monk? We must look after them. And I was negligent. A negligent parent. I let my book get lost and you have helped me get it back. Believe it or not, he said and laughed a short, embarrassed cough of a laugh, it is unique, so you see what it means to me to have it returned.

—You were careless, Dave.

—On the other hand… He eased one leg into a sitting position on the desk beside me and tapped his fingers together, ignoring my use of his real name. There was a whiff of some après rasage coming off him like little flowers and between the cuffs of his suit and the back of his hands half an inch of bright white sleeve moved up and down in time with his tapping. His teeth were clenched. I could hear them grating. I looked at his face and saw the muscles under his jaw pulsating. The trimmed brows were inching over his eyes.

…Mr Monk, he said, turning aloof, you are an insignificant person, a nobody…

—Hey, man, everybody's somebody.

—A nobody who is pushing his nose into the business of an organisation he just does not understand the power of. It is a dangerous game you are playing, Mr Monk. Let me give you some advice. If I were you I would just disappear, just walk out of here and vanish. That should be quite easy for a nobody, now should it not?

—Damon, Dave, there's no need to get all het up, I began, leaning back in the chair again and offering him a grin. I've told you, I didn't come here for your wretched book.

—It's about time you left. Stay away from here and stay away from Virginia Wolffe. Just stay away.

—Ah, now there's a point. Where is Ginny?

—Obviously I'm not going to tell you that. She belongs here with us and here she will stay. Her future is very bright, you know. I have my very special eye on Virginia, you know. Your future could have been as well, if you'd been born more reasonable.

—You mean more gullible, I said trying to dislodge the idea of Damon's very special eye from my mind.

—I know what I mean. And now, if you would follow me I shall escort you from the premises. I have work to do. We are very busy here. Do I make myself clear?

—Clear as a cliché. But I want to see Ginny. Then I'll go.

—Maybe I should summon someone who will help you off the premises, he said.

His jaw was working at itself again and his eyebrows were

tilting at each other dangerously. I was thinking quickly. I couldn't run through the building looking for Ginny with Damon racing behind me like Godzilla. On the other hand I wasn't going to leave without her.

I needed a plan now like I never needed one before. Damon went for the phone on his desk but as his hand moved the phone bleeped. He pressed it to his ear and I heard the jabber squeak out of it in an alarmed torrent. Damon's brow deepened its descent over his darkening face. I became aware that out there where The Doorway meets the world something was happening. I could hear voices raised. The receptionist's voice sounding indignant. Someone else with a flat voice. In my exploration of the place I'd come almost full circle: reception must be just around the corner.

Damon put down the phone and hesitated, looking at me with a mixture of hatred and indecision, a comical combination. I was out of the chair by now and advancing on the door. I leapt out into the corridor and immediately leapt back again, jolting into Damon and sending his fumbling figure careening into the office. He stopped himself against the desk and turned but by this time I was peering out again to check what I'd seen.

It was Smug. He'd done a U-turn further down and was now coming back as I watched, steering his push bike and peddling at it with the strength of champions. Behind him, his Bad Mountain shirt billowed in his slipstream and the moustache whistled in the wind as his legs pumped the cranks round. As he came almost level with me he hit the back brake and swerved to a halt smoking a black arc into the carpet. From the reception end of the corridor two figures shot round the corner and stopped. One was the girl from the desk, the other was a security guard complete with epaulettes and clean shoes. His face was the shape of a cardboard box and he was not smiling.

—Yo, my old man Monkey. You doing all right there? shouted Smug.

—Smug. Smug, I repeated in some confusion. What's going on?

—All sorts of stuff. Come on, Monkey.

—Stop right there! yelled box-faced-boy, squaring his chest and pointing at us but not moving in our direction. He flexed his epaulettes and tucked one or two of his chins into the top of his collar.

—What the hell are you doing? squeaked Damon Damon, recovering his voice.

—Yo, a suit, let's get out of here, shouted Smug, jumping up into the pedals. Take a spin with the king.

—I'm not going without Ginny, I yelled at him.

—Not here, he gasped.

—What?

—Not.

—Where?

—Get on, he said grimly. Damon had got his brain in order and was looking like he wanted to do something. I swung over the saddle and as I clung on to his waist Smug bowled round the cranks with an energy I hadn't thought him capable of. I could smell the nylon in the carpet melting under the tyres; the air flew at me and Smug ran up the gears till we hummed with speed and shot down the corridor straight at the waiting figures. The receptionist went first, a flurry of skirt round the corner but epaulette man hung on to the last shouting for us to stop as if we had a choice. We went past him flattened to the wall in a rush of his froth with Smug driving us in some big gear and swinging round the corner on the back brake.

The automatic door at the front just got open in time and we were down the path and out towards the road before Smug seemed to suddenly tire and the bike lost speed. He racked down through the low gears, made some throttled noises and stopped. He was wheezing great sobs of breath and his shoulders had died. He rested his head on the handlebars and moaned. I got off the saddle and held the bike to try and support him in his hour of need. After a while his breath seemed to come back and he coughed for a few minutes and shuddered. I patted him on the back and he coughed again.

—Smug, what's going on?

—Trust me, Monkey, he gasped.

—OK, Smug. But what's going on?

We pushed the bike up out of The Doorway territory and out onto the pavement and over to the bus stop. Smug was getting his breath back by now and the moans were becoming less frequent. He wiped a shaky hand over his pale forehead and blotted the sweat off on his shirt.

—Never come up that hill before. Never again.

—Good move, Smug. Good move. Thanks and all.

—Bloody bike. Knew I should have binned it.

—I didn't know you were a cycling man.

—I'm not. I'm a dying man.

—So, go on then, what're you doing here?

—No bus fare, mate.

—You're going to have to leave those ponies alone.

—Tell me about it.

—Come on, Smug, tell *me* about it. What's going on?

—For one, he said, Ginny's not here, is she.

—How do you know?

—Because her and that guy...

—Houghton?

—If you say so. Anyway her and him passed me in that little yellow breezer as I came up the hill. Doing quite a speed, they were, engine whining like a girl. And I'll tell you something, Monkey, I did not like the look of that guy. He had this real look on his face.

—What sort of look?

—Like he was thinking on something nasty.

—Right. Thanks, Smug. Where do you think they were

going?

—Where…? How do I know, Monkey, I was killing my legs at the time and just like trying to breathe. I only saw them at all because I happened to be looking up because my neck was locked up with cramp.

—Cheers, mate. Good job about that cramp, then.

—What?

—Worth a pint, this is.

—A pint, Monkey, you tight git? He wheezed. I'll not walk after this.

—OK. I'll see you're right, mate.

As we went over to the bus stop he filled me in on the rest. When I'd left the car outside The Doorway and set off I'd obviously been unaware that Goldfish had taken it into his mind that morning to go for a jaunt on his trusty velocipede and had spent an hour or so pedalling his way up out of the city via the woodland tracks. His timing was perfect, if you want to look at it that way. Just as I'd been walking down the drive towards The Doorway, Goldfish had popped out of the wood a hundred yards further up Brownberrie Lane. He'd come down pounding the pedals and seen his car parked on the roadside. He had no idea why it was there. He had no recollection of lending it to me or of my mission. Though not a man of memory, Goldfish is a man of action so, swerving to a halt, he whipped off his front wheel and put it and the rest of his bike in the back of the car and drove away. I must have just missed him.

He'd parked up and, luckily, he'd bumped into Smug who, on hearing his tale, had reminded him that he'd lent the car to me. The problem was that by that time Goldfish couldn't remember where he'd left it. The usual story. Smug, the hero, had decided to get out his old bike and pedal up to update me on the way things were. He'd arranged for us to meet Goldfish at Bloaters later. What he hadn't done was to appreciate the size of the hill.

He left me at the bus stop and gingerly eased himself into the saddle and slid, wincing, over the brow of the hill. I waited. I kept looking over at the Doorway place but nothing was stirring. Time passed. Cars went by but no bus. I sat on a stone and leant against the trunk of an oak tree and stared out over the hills. I took the pen drive out of my pocket and gave its shiny blackness the once over. For the first time I felt that I had some control. I put it away.

A crow mooched over the tussocky roadside slapping its beak into the grass every now and then. Road dust specked its hard, aggressive feathers. Its actions were hard-wired into its midget brain and, as it wrenched some curling soft shape from the earth, I saw that even it was having more success than me. Another plan had bitten the dust. I was just settling down into an unaccustomed despondency when a streak of yellow lurched to a stop in front of me and the whitish figure of Danby Houghton scrambled out of the car waving his beak around in a state of childish agitation.

He slammed the car door and strutted over to me and came very close and started to hiss something at me. I stood up and hunted round in the hissing for the shape of words but all I found was a sort of syllabic hysteria. A diaphanous film of spittle wavered in the breeze between us. His face was too close and pinched with loathing so I smiled at him and he didn't like that. He bared the roots of his teeth and swung his arm at me with the fist on the end of it like a skittle ball. Now, I'm no kick-boxing son-of-a-bitch hard-case fighting man but I have learnt over the years to swerve and duck, both of which I achieved before Danby could make contact.

The force of his swing whirled him round and, off balance, his right foot caught in a clod and he twisted over on it and went to ground like a hero. He looked up at me, his eyebrows spiky with mud, his eyes dark with new sensations. He'd gone a deep shade of tortoiseshell. He got back to his feet staring in horror at his trousers which were doused in wet mud the colour of gravy. He went to dab at them with his hands, recoiled in horror at the thought of getting his hands dirty and then realised that they, too, were covered in mud and this set him pirouetting in hot fury with the grit grinding under his soiled brogues, waving his fists in my general direction and spewing oaths and saliva over his sleeves.

Whatever, our cream chino hero was not getting his filthy little hands on the pen drive, I thought, looking round for something heavy to put on top of him. He stared at me for a moment in mid dance and suddenly defeat filmed over his eyes and he opened his muddy mouth again.

—Don't forget, he expectorated, backing towards the car, that I have money.

He whipped out a white handkerchief and opened the door with it and then spread it over the seat.

—Money! he shouted over the car roof. Money, you sad pillock.

He got in delicately and took the steering wheel in his finger-tips, started things up and slunk up the road and through The Doorway gates.

19

"Don't talk it, do it."
(Jav Hanger, in *The Lightning Man*, 1993)

When I got to Bloaters, Smallwit and Goldfish were already halfway through logs of bacon and tomato. A girl with the legs of a ballerina was clearing dead coffee cups from the tables and mopping up spills with a brown dishcloth. Alf was behind the counter cleaning his nails with a knife and mopping the bark-like structure of his face intermittently with a tea towel. I joined the other two at the table. Benny arrived and while he unzipped various layers of leather Smallwit got me a coffee. Benny had a coke.

I told them what had happened. They nodded wisely. But there were still a number of questions in the whirling Monkey brain, two of which were uppermost. Where was Ginny, for instance? And where was Smug? The answer to this second question arrived even as I considered asking it. Smug soft-shouldered through the door and pushed his bike into the room. It was a weird sight, the bike seemed to be in charge, pulling him along, and was certainly holding him off the floor. His hair was standing up straight from his head and clumps of his moustache were wedged up his nostrils. His shirt was loosened and wet with sweat and the legs beneath him were bowed and shaky as he crossed the floor.

Goldfish rescued the bike and Smug collapsed into a seat and laid his head on the table. The breath was wheezing in and out of him, making little clouds rise from the ashtray and a tendril of gritty saliva manoeuvred its way over his lips and onto the table.

—Want a coffee, Smug? I asked helpfully.

—Wanna die, he murmured thickly before his eyes closed.

—You weed, Benny laughed, it's all downhill from up there.

I got about telling it all over again for the benefit of Smug, though I wasn't sure whether or not he heard a word I was saying. And as I spoke an idea came to me and suddenly I had Plan B: *Into the Lion's Den*. It was risky but it was a risk worth taking.

—I know what I've got to do. I'm going to see Wolffie.

—Hang on to your hosepipe just a minute, Smallwit said.

—Hang on to – listen buddy, I want to find Ginny, right. If she's had a row with Houghton, she might have gone back to Wolffie's. It's worth a try.

—You're mad, says Smallwit.

—Monkey, calm down, said Benny. Think about it. Are you really that keen to get over to Wolffie's place.

—Smallwit's right, put in Smug. He'd picked up his head from dangling it over the edge of the table and was in the business of bringing himself back to the world of the breathing.

—Look, it might all sound like you need to go rushing in like mad and get it all sorted out but really you don't, said Benny.

—Benny, I trust you when it comes to most things, especially most things mechanical or related to the playing of the game pool at which you are no doubt the best this side of Leeds when I'm not in the mood to beat you, but when it comes to things of the heart and especially when it comes to things of the heart involving Ginny, then I've got to go with the old heart. Know what I mean. So no offence, mate, but I've got to find her. Wolffe or no Wolffe.

—Do you think that's wise? adds in Smallwit. What about the business…

—I've got a plan; that should help.

—What are you going to do if Wolffe starts to separate you from your guts?

—He won't, will he? I said. He must like me really. I mean

I'm still alive, aren't I?

—Rather you than me finding that one out, mate.

—Wolffie? I mean he wouldn't really do anything.

—Monkey, did you know Wolffie was in the SAS? When he was younger, I mean.

—You're winding me up.

—He was.

—No, I know you're winding me up because Ginny once said about his stories of being in the SAS and she said they weren't true.

—She just didn't want to frighten you, Wolffie not approving of you and his daughter, like. He's a monster. Did you hear that story where he'd left some guy in the gutter with his own feet in his mouth because he got so far behind with the rent Wolffie was losing count.

—I don't believe a word of it. Wolffie never loses count. Look, there comes a time when you've just got to face your fear and do it anyway. I'm going to go to Wolffie's and get him to let me see Ginny.

—If she's there, wheezed Smug, his wheezing going through the café like a rattlesnake in a tin.

—I'll tell Wolffie that Ginny's in with a bad lot, tell him Danby Houghton's only after his money or something. I'll tell him he's a con artist. He'll hate that. He'll appreciate me warning him. I'll give him the pen drive. Then he'll see I'm telling him the truth.

—You live in hope, Monkey.

—Got to live somewhere.

20

"Chicken ain't nothing but a word."
(Hank Teller, *Love Me*, 1959)

I drove out to Meanwood in Goldfish's car. It had been parked outside Bloaters. I was hungry and thirsty and tired. The evening was closing in on me, wrapping me in its grey bandages, and all I kept thinking about was seeing Ginny again and knowing that she wanted to see me, as if imagining it could make it happen. Damon bloody Damon might still have his little fantasy book. And he might still make a packet on the whole publishing deal, the git. But he'd always know that out there in the real world there was someone who knew the score. Someone with digital proof of his nasty little con. I didn't really care about him anymore. Snakes like Damon would always find themselves slithering round in fields of cash. What did I care? I was an artist. And I was going to get what Damon could never have: Ginny.

I spent a long second or two staring at the blackness of Wolffie's door before I worked the knocker. I heard the dino-dog roar for its dinner. I wondered what I was doing. Was I up to this? I hesitated and as I hesitated the door rattled and locks were loosened.

—Well, well, if it isn't my young friend Mr Monk, said Wolffe when he opened the door and stood there chewing on the tail of his tea. The old dino dog was making muffled hellish noises in the hall and he pulled the door to behind him.

—Look, this may seem like odd, but I've got something you might find interesting. I put a hand into my pocket and took out the pen drive. He didn't look at it but stared at me with an expression of mock surprise.

—You're a cool one, he said. I thought I'd warned you. No matter what Virginia might think of you – and it beggars belief that anyone, never mind a respectable girl who's been brought up proper like Virginia, could find any interest in you – never mind what she might think of you, you are to keep well away from her if you value your fur, boy. Know what I mean?

—I get the idea. But look, this guy...

—Then vamoosh, before I'm tempted to do something you might regret. You're a no-hoper, Monkey, like 'em all. You live hopping from one thing to another, crawling back to your little pits at night. You've got no ambition and no money. Where are you going? Nowhere. That's where.

I could hear Bobo the dog trying to get through the tiny gap of the doorway. It sounded like someone chopping wood.

—I just want... I put in briefly, thinking those little pits were what kept Wolffie in his big pit, but he leaned closer to me and I felt the air part before the snarl of his teeth and the smell of his garlic sausage and ketchup came across the small divide between us and bemused my weary senses. His yellow eyes fixed on mine in judgement.

—You're going nowhere. That's where you're going.

Where was I going? Maybe this had been a mistake. I fidgeted with the pen drive. It reminded me of Stella and of course I wanted to forget her. But even forgetting her was like remembering her. I tasted the sweetness of her sweet flesh, I felt the flesh of her; the temptation of her was in me like an ache. She stimulated me to hell. What beauty. But what betrayal of beauty. That I dreamt of her was only testament to testosterone.

—You're going nowhere, he was saying again. Nowhere. And that's where you belong.

—Look, I said, about Ginny. She's in with the wrong crowd. I don't want to see her get hurt.

—Monkey, you cowboy, you keep your nose out of her affairs. Mr Houghton is just what Virginia needs. What she doesn't need is a grub like you with your idle layabout ways and your nasty little ideas. What is it you think you do? Poetry, is that it, is that what you do? Makes me want to wash just thinking about it. I'm going to have to sluice that step you're standing on. Virginia was muttering about bloody poetry this morning. Thought she had more sense in her head. I hope Danby's not been messing with the stuff. Nah, too much the successful man for that.

I was just saying to Mrs Wolffe this morning, I was just saying how pleased I was that Virginia had found herself someone who knew what's what, someone with ambition and drive and a good job who can make her happy and keep her in the style which she's accustomed to. I knew it as soon as I saw that BMW. Have you seen that car he's got? I shook his hand when I saw that car. We brought her up to want the best and I'm glad she's found it. So get, Monkey. Get off my drive and crawl back under your stone.

—She's not here, by any chance, then?

—Monkey, he said, sniffing at something in his nose and leaning back on the door jamb as if he owned the place, Monkey, why should I tell you if she's anywhere? But looking at your poor pathetic hairy face something in me wants to put you out of your misery, so, I'll tell you this...she's where you'll never find her.

There was a silence. The dog seemed to have given up. Maybe it was listening, biding its time.

—Right. Thanks for something less than nothing. Look, take this, you might find it interesting. He ignored my gesture.

—Any concern she might have about you is merely like you'd feel if a pet was sick. I put it down to the eternal mystery of the female, know what I mean?

—What? You mean she said something about me? You mean...

—I said nothing of the sort. That's a horrible suggestion, that is. Now sling your hook before I forget that Mrs Wolffe's indoors and do something that might raise the noise level of the neighbourhood. He leered over at me and rubbed the fist of one hand in the callused palm of the other like a mortar and pestle. You listen out for those wedding bells, Monkey, my little princess is going to get hitched to a bit of class. Now, get your filthy carcass off my drive.

I was eight or nine paces away when I turned and slung the pen drive, arcing it up the path, spinning like a tiny monolith from 2001. I almost waltzed. The sun glinted on its metallic finish as it shot towards Wolffie at head height and for a moment I thought he was going to get it in the face. But there was a sudden huge movement round the side of the house and Bobo, his teeth bared, gums trailing froth and splinters, sailed through the air, caught it almost without noticing and landed with a belly-sagging thump. There was a nasty sound of snapping and sobbing and choking. I legged it.

—Oi! shouted Wolffie. Don't feed the dog, you pillock!

21

"Love, like light, is called for most in darkness. So they say."
(Li Tzi, *Sayings*, 140 BC)

I was not down at heart. I'd not given up on Ginny. The road moved smoothly under the car. I took corners at speed. A squall of diesel fumed under the streetlights. I arced past a blur of torn hedges. The roadside was filled with staunch buildings, their windows gleaming in the falling light.

The wheel under my hands was hot, the gearstick taut in its socket. Rain came skidding out of the sky and slicked the windscreen and I turned on the wipers. I flicked on the lights and the dashboard lit up green for go, go, go! I pulled into Otley Road and stopped at Macrae's All-Nighter to pick up a sixpack of Badger's. Now I went faster.

The air was cooling. I started up again and ran up the gears. I was feeling power all around me: the ebb and flow of the city, the lights holding off the darkness, the car moving over the solid smooth track of the road. Right now I knew where I was going. Things were good. The lights over all the signs were coming on; they were crammed with white writing but one thing was written big: City Centre. I was counting down the miles. I was coming back to my city on the flood tide of the traffic with the sound of the road going through me and the lights around me. There was something burning in me. There was something that Wolffie had not said that puzzled me. He hadn't demanded his money. Now, why would he not do that? The man was mad for his money. Hope was dancing somewhere and I was dancing with her.

I took the car back to Goldfish's and locked it up and walked out into Hyde Park. The rain had lifted and the sun was on the edge of the city's horizon, a scarlet disk smouldering among pink clouds. I sat on the bench by the lion and cracked a can open and had a drink. The lion's fleece was gold and the snake around it was the colour of ash. Its eyes were dark where the sun made shadows. I sat a long time there sipping the beer as the cold began to move over me and hope shrank to the size of the sun in its setting, going over the edge, leaving shadows pale and ghostly to fumble through their short lives on the grass. The park was still. I moved in on the fifth can.

—Yo, Monkey, you alien! A shout rose through the evening and at its root was Smug shortcutting it through the park to the pub with Goldfish at his side. They came up quickly.

—Ta for the car, said Goldfish, nodding.

—Thanks, mate, I said.

—What are you doing, anyway, sitting up here?

—Just sitting.

—Why's she down there, then?

—What?

—You've not done it again, have you, said Smug. I meant what I said about that dog.

—Make sense, Smug. You've been at the ale before you've been at the pub.

—Monkey, you slow sot, why's she down there and you up here? Why's Ginny sitting on the bench by the bloomin' bandstand with you up here carting your brains off with ale?

—Just a minute. Ginny's where?

—You mean you didn't know?

—Course I didn't know, I said standing up and reaching for the last can. Down by the bandstand?

—Just passed her on the way through. Said hello and that. She was reading a comic.

—A comic? I said from ten paces.

—Looked like. You off then?

—I'm off. Cheers, mate.

I came down to her as the darkness was drinking up the last of the light and the clear stars stared down like random points picked in blackness. Love was cooking my heart on a fast flame. She was sitting alone by the bandstand staring up into the night sky. On her lap, I saw as I came close, she had a copy of *La Plume*, the issue that had featured a couple of my more esoteric little verses. That was good. I sat down next to her and opened the can and offered it to her. She took it without saying anything and took a swig and handed it back. She was dark and silvery, beauty set against the infinite openness of the universe.

—You all right? I asked.

—I'm all right.

—What's a nice girl like you doing in a dark park like this?

—Shut up, Monkey.

—OK.

—And don't smile at me like that.

—I'm smiling?

—Shut up.

—OK. Another drink?

We sat in silence for a while as the stars sharpened their edges in the oval darkness. She knocked back another mouthful. We sat there for a minute. I could feel she was building up to saying something so I waited. I reached for the can and she moved her arm away.

—Don't touch me, she said.

—OK.

—Yet, she added.

—OK.

The moon sprang up out of the clouds in a grainy aura. The stars showed for a moment over the rim of the city.

—Touch me now.

I turned to her and she looked more beautiful that I could ever have remembered. We kissed among the fat lights of the city floating on the edge of the park, while the traffic sank into the distance. The night was cooling.

—Where are you living now? I asked, wondering if I really wanted to know the answer to a question that made the leaves restless on the dark bushes.

—I've been staying with mum and dad for a few days.

—Ah. I went to see him, you know.

—I know. He said.

—So he knew you'd chucked deadbeat Danby when he was talking to me? When he was saying all those things about you and him. Weddings and everything. You mean he was winding me up?

—Monkey, he thinks you're low life.

—Well, so do you.

—I don't, she said quickly, patting my arm like I was a pet or something.

—At least he's forgotten about the rent, incredible though that might seem.

—He hasn't forgotten about it. It's paid.

—It's what?

—I paid it for you, Monkey. I earned some money working for the Doorway.

—You shouldn't have done that. I wasn't paying that on principle. Property is…is…theft, you know. You shouldn't have done that. I was holding out. For the principle.

—Monkey, you weren't paying it because you're a fool.

—Well I suppose I should say thank you.

—Don't sound as if you mean it or anything. It wasn't easy, you know. He didn't want to take it. He said he wanted to make you pay.

—OK. No, I mean it. Thank you. To be honest it's a weight off. I'll pay you back. I will. So what happened?

—I told him it was the only way he'd get his money.

—You told him I was a man of principle?

—I told him you'd never have any money.

—Money isn't everything, I said, feeling hurt at her lack of faith in the old Monkey potential.

—And no money isn't anything.

—Clever.

—Anyway, she said, why did you throw a pen drive thingy at him?

—*At* him?

—What he said. He said Bobo saved him from losing an eye and nearly choked on it. Dad thought it was a ninja star for a moment.

—I was just being playful, I said.

We got up and started the walk out of the park.

I took her back to the bedsit. We got through the door and made for the bedroom. Her coat went one way, her bag went another and something happened to my trousers. Later, we sat in bed for a long time over half a bottle of Don Stupendo. It was good. Everything was good.

—And don't start thinking that I fell for all that Doorway crap, she said suddenly. No woman in her right mind would be taken in by a bunch of geeks like that. All that bollocks.

Somewhere in the conversation Danby Houghton's name popped up like an idiot goblin.

—Can you believe this, Monkey?

—What?

—He wrote me a poem.

—What?

—The idiot wrote me a poem!

—That's bad? I asked, raising an eyebrow.

—Of course it's bad.

—Why did he do that then?

—Because he's a fool. Because he wanted to be romantic. Because he wanted to be like you, I suppose.

—Like me? How did he know about me? I asked.

—I suppose I must have said things sometimes.

—Like what?

—Oh, I don't know. Maybe I said something about you and writing poetry.

—I bet you never stopped talking about me, I said, raising the other eyebrow a couple of times.

—Shut up, Monkey. Don't push your luck.

—So you dumped him.

—Whatever.

—It was the chinos as well. Wasn't it?

—What can I say?

—And the conversation.

—OK. And the conversation.

—And…

—Monkey, shut up.

—He's got a smile like a shop dummy.

—All right, he was a complete disaster. And maybe I only started to see him because of you with that creature, Vampira. So I blame you. But he was civilized, Monkey, and he had money. Lots of money and that's something that has its attractions. Driving round in that car. But when he said he'd written me something — a 'little verse', for God's sake — something just went funny in my head and I couldn't look at him anymore. She curled up over my legs and rubbed her cheek against mine.

—But I wrote a poem for you.

—That's different.

—Because I'm so lovable?

—Because you're a poet, Monkey. You're *supposed* to write me poetry.

—But…

—Look, Monkey. Engage brain. You're a poet; write me

245

poetry. A girl can put up with a lot if she gets poetry. And flowers.

—OK. I can do flowers. But...what do you mean, 'put up with a lot'? I asked, suddenly suspicious that she thought I was less than adequate when in fact I'd begun to feel reasonably pleased with myself. Things were going well. All I had to do next was get some sort of better job that brought in the shekels, smarten up the place, that sort of thing. Life was looking good.

—Monkey, you're a man. What more does a girl have to put up with?

—I'm going for my pen.

—Not now, you're not. You can do that in the privacy of your own home.

—This is my own home.

—This? This isn't a home. I've seen tidier skips. I've seen more homely tips. You need someone to sort you out.

—Maybe I don't want sorting out.

—Maybe, you do, she said, resting her head in my lap.

—Maybe I do, I said.

—But this will have to go, she said, reaching up and tugging my luxuriant beard.

— What?

—This. This beard thing.

—Beard thing?

—It'll have to go. I mean, let's face it you look like you're peering through a toilet brush.

—I'll have you know this is a manly adornment.

—It's a bloody abomination, Monkey. It's like sleeping with a porcupine, or kissing a donkey.

—A donkey? Is that all bad?

—You know what I mean, you ass.

—I like this beard.

—Monkey, it's not a beard, it's a hedge.

—No, I can't do it. It's my beard.

—It's the devil's own, Monkey. Get rid.

She slid out of the bed and went for the kitchen drawer and came back with a pair of cooking shears slashing away nastily in her hand. I felt my legs crossing involuntarily. She stood at the bottom of the bed and pointed the shears at me.

—Whilst we're at it, we might as well have a go at waxing your back.

—You're mad.

—It's very fashionable. And I'm curious. I want to see if there's a man under that lot. And don't fold your arms at me like that.

—Ginny, this isn't a good idea.

—Come on.

—OK. OK. You can trim the beard a bit. OK?

I woke up the next day feeling peeled and confused. I got up to make some tea. I passed the mirror a few times before I dared to look in. The face that squinted back at me was the face of a younger and more devilishly handsome Monkey than I had thought possible. A smooth Monkey. I couldn't understand what had led me to grow the facial fur in the first place. Full frontal wasn't bad. Not bad at all. And in profile I was positively rugged. In shirt and boxers, new-born, I scalded the tea bags and squeezed them on the side of the cup. I put in the last of the milk and stood one cup on a little tray. I slipped on a shirt and made a dash for the garden and tore off a couple of roses from next door's overhanging rose monster and laid them next to the cup.

—Darling? Ginny?

—Umm, she slurred and rolled over.

—There's a cup of tea for you.

I sat on the edge of the bed and sipped my tea as she slithered into a sitting position and drank hers. She put the roses on the pillow beside her.

—Where are these from? I asked, picking up some letters that had fallen out of her bag where she'd thrown it the last night. They were addressed to me.

—Oh, she said, at tea, they were lying around at dad's. They must have come from your old flat. He likes to read people's mail if he gets the chance. Some of them have been opened. Sorry. She ran explorative fingers over the razed plains of my cheek.

—What do you think?

—You'll do.

—Is that it? All that hacking and soap and scraping and I just do?

—OK. You'll do fine. Which is more than can be said for you when you were an ape.

—Bloody cheek.

I leafed through the letters. There was the usual junk stuff, one proclaiming that I'd won a ticket to throw in the pot for grand draw winnings guaranteed; one offering a Bison Platinum credit card, for the discerning buyer; one addressed to Mr E Mink, offering me an insurance workover. But three real letters. One was a late Christmas card from Aunt Greenwich, one a rejection slip from the ingrates at La Plume de Ma Taunt, returning the five works of genius I had been kind enough to offer them. The third was from Phibre and Phibre. Earth and air and all bodies heavenly paused for a respectful moment as I unfolded the heavy manila and cast a glance over the script. I read fast.

—They want me. Ginny, they like me. Phibre and Phibre like Monkey's Typewriter.

—They're going to publish you?

—Looks like it.

—Phibre and Phibre?

—That's them.

—But they're big.

—They certainly are.

— Monkey's Typewriter?

—That's it.

—That's a terrible title, Monkey.

—It's a great title.

—It's an abomination.

—But a great abomination, eh?

—So you're going to be famous?

—You never know.

—So can I tell everyone? she asked.

—That's the idea.

—Monkey, that's brilliant.

—That's me. We're going to be scooping up flutes of champagne and dancing on candlelit tables. You're looking at Mr Monkey, Mr Success. Monkey magic.

—Monkey, stop gibbering.

— Monkey's Typewriter everywhere!

—Stop.

—What?

—You're gibbering!

—A man can gibber if he wants to. Anyway I wasn't gibbering, I said, going back to the letter. I was...

—What's the matter?

—But they say they like it. 'Raw and uncompromising', they say, 'a genuine voice', they say. 'Tough on poetry, tough on the causes of poetry.' But...

—But what?

—But current taste isn't in keeping with 'this kind of thing'. So blah, blah, blah, market forces, demand and supply, fol di diddle dol etc etc etc. It is with regret that...Phibre and Phibre...at this moment in time...suggest you try another publishing house such as Dawbert, Pangoon and Rustler. Tossers! Two-bit tossers.

Outside, a branch of the little sycamore tapped on the window. I looked up from the letter to Ginny's smirking phisog. I crunched the paper into a ball and threw it at her head and saw it ricochet off the wall, missing her tea by an inch. Which was lucky; she likes her tea. I moved closer and slid the tray and the teacup to the floor, feeling the heat of her against me before I straightened back and sat on the edge of the bed.

—Well, who cares. Books. Who wants to be reading them? Dodgy things, books. Books can make a mess of your life. Who needs them? Get out and live, that's what I say. What I'm going to do is I'm going to get a guitar and get out there on the street.

—Monkey, you can't play the guitar.

—I can learn. An image jumped into my mind of me standing on a street corner offering up imaginative interpretations of *Streets of London* for coppers chucked at a greasy cap. There must be worse ways to earn a living. Maybe. Fresh air, the smiling public, room for creative improvisation. Might get spotted by some passing record magnate with a fat cheque book and an ear for the unusual.

—You can't sing either.

—Of course I can sing.

—Monkey, that's not singing, that's howling with rhythm. You can forget busking right now. I'm not going out with a busker. Oh, no. I'm going to make damn sure you get famous. I'm going to chain you to a table and taunt you till you write. You're mine now. I've always wanted to sleep with someone famous. So I'm going to make it happen. You're going to do it for me, Monkey. You owe me. I've got some cash left and I'm going to buy you a little laptop and get you going. You're going to write if it...

—Right! It's going to happen, I said, suddenly certain of everything. I thought of Ginny lying before me draped in red silk as I fingered the keyboard to please her as a goddess, as a muse. Her moist lips pouted as I typed faster and faster. She rolled over onto her back and unsheathed herself from her night dress, offering me her hot breasts, sliding the silk down over her hips. I could feel it happening. I was typing and typing. And Ginny was

250

pouting and writhing in unusual passion. I was growing. Multiplying. I felt a thousand fingers, ten thousand flashing over the keyboard, over a million keyboards. I was expanding, filling the universe — an infinite number of monkeys at an infinite number of keyboards, typing, typing. I would write everything. I could write anything. I could...

—Monkey! Ginny was saying.

—What?

—You're not listening to a word, are you? I said what about a novel?

—That's a new idea. Not a bad idea at all.

—Is there a novel in you, Monkey?

—You never know...

—Monkey, you're going to write if I've got to pump books out of you by hand.

—OK.

—What are you thinking about, you've gone all shifty.

—Nothing, I said, going back to my vision of silk and lips.

—That's the problem, Monkey, you've got to concentrate.

—Right. I looked at her watching me. What was she saying? I pulled my thoughts back into the room. Right, I said, let's do it. The curtains shivered above the sill and the dawn chorus hit a barbershop harmony.

I looked at her, her hair spread wild over the pillows, the sheets embossed with the hot glory of her body, her naked arms warm in the morning light. Ah, what a world we live in. Ginny lowered her eyelids and lifted her arms to frame her face. Her breasts swelled towards me in a cocoon of taut cotton and her thighs shifted restlessly. Her eyes were full of sex and laughter. She slicked her tongue across the glazed lust of her lips and pushed at the covers, squirming towards me, wriggling free. Put the writing on hold, I thought, and let me get to grips with the muse. The world lay open before me. Things were looking up.

CPSIA information can be obtained at www.ICGtesting.com
Printed in the USA
BVOW07s2224151013

333865BV00001B/118/P

9 781449 542887